SOUL SURVIVOR

Visit us at www.boldstrokesbooks.com

By the Author

Sanctuary

The Rarest Rose

Salvation

Soul Survivor

SOUL SURVIVOR

by

I. Beacham

2017

SOUL SURVIVOR

ISBN 13: 978-1-62639-882-5

THIS TRADE PAPERBACK ORIGINAL IS PUBLISHED BY
BOLD STROKES BOOKS, INC.
P.O. BOX 249
VALLEY FALLS, NY 12185

FIRST EDITION: APRIL 2017

CREDITS
EDITOR: CINDY CRESAP
PRODUCTION DESIGN: SUSAN RAMUNDO
COVER DESIGN BY SHERI (GRAPHICARTIST2020@HOTMAIL.COM)

Acknowledgments

Huge thanks as always to Cindy Cresap, my editor. Her editorial brilliance improves my books tenfold.

Dedication

To RZ—Thank you for all your help and enthusiasm.
A friend indeed.

Chapter One

Northern Syria near the Iraq border

Josephine Barry tucked her long hair behind an ear, breathed deeply, and composed herself. She looked into the camera.

"I'm standing in the small town of Balshir on the disputed boundary between El Sharai and Kabali. Behind me in the distance, you can see smoke from what was once a thriving town where cotton was farmed and where for centuries, Muslim and Christian lived together in peace. The rebel forces moved in months ago, and that town is now in ruins. There are rumors of daily brutality where rebels go from home to home butchering those inside. Their bloodthirsty fighters show no mercy to those who resist their reign of terror. Options are limited. Die fighting, be forced into brutal slavery, or be radicalized.

"Here in Balshir, so far untouched by this regional devastation, its people are nervous. Many are fleeing, believing there's a high probability that the rebels will strike here next. This is a town where no one feels safe, and everyone is afraid. You can smell the fear. It's contagious. Those left are the ones who can't leave because they are ill or not strong enough." Joey paused. "And they wait."

Kurt Youngman waved a hand across his throat to signal cut.

"That's wrapped, Joey. Light's fading. I think we're done for today."

Joey, the chief news correspondent for RSB Broadcasts, relaxed.

"*I'm* done with this place, Kurt," she said. "Tomorrow can't come soon enough to get out of here."

The two of them walked off the balcony, back into the gray unattractive concrete block building.

Inside were a set of rooms that had been home for several days while Joey reported from this part of the war zone. It didn't give much privacy to the four of them—Kurt and Mitch Jacobson, her two-man production team; and then Mohammad al-Salit, "Mo," their guide and interpreter. But they coped.

"I hate this fucking heat," Mitch said, kneeling as he put away equipment.

Kurt agreed. "When we hit base, I'm heading straight for the showers."

It was the smell of the town that got to Joey. Its stench pervaded everywhere and locked onto the back of her throat making her cough. It was a sour odor that made her want to hold her nose and not breathe deeply. Totally the opposite of what she needed to do in this heat. Maybe a drink would help.

"You guys want tea? Whose turn to make it?"

"Yours," Kurt and Mitch answered in unison.

She smiled. She knew the answer anyway but always tried her luck. Kurt knew too.

"Listen, Warrior Queen. All you do is stand around and talk to the camera. Don't forget the real workers here. We make you look awesome for the American public. It isn't easy."

"No milk for me. I hate that powdered shit." Mitch looked up at her with his usual lopsided grin, his face encased in a mop of blond hair. He looked like a teenager, but wasn't. He had seven-year-old twin girls and a wife who doted on him.

Joey acquiesced and tipped her chin forward. "It's lucky I love you guys." As she turned to head for what was loosely termed the kitchen, Mo spoke.

"I go to the truck and get more water."

You couldn't drink the water here. It was contaminated. If you did, it gave you diarrhea, turned you dizzy, and made you sick.

Joey peered into the kitchen across the narrow passage that separated the room. There was still enough water in the plastic urn.

"Forget it, Mo. There's enough to see us through until tomorrow."

But Mo was already standing and making his way toward the door that led to the stone staircase and down one flight to the ground floor and building exit. "I get it anyway."

He was gone.

A queer feeling came over Joey. Mo was a lovely man, warm and friendly, who was always showing them photos of his wife and three teenage daughters. He had been their guide before and pulled them out of trouble several times when they'd come across anti-Western locals. But Joey knew she wasn't imagining it. These last few days he had been quiet. Too quiet.

She stepped back into the room. "What's wrong with Mo?"

"Dunno," Mitch said. The way he looked at her, she knew he'd noticed it too.

"He left a bit sharpish," Kurt added.

She nodded. "You don't think it was that banter we had the other night?"

"What?" Mitch asked.

"Where you guys were joshing me about all the women I've dated. He did go quiet."

"You think?" Mitch pushed fingers through his hair.

She shrugged. "I don't know…maybe he finds it offensive. His culture's moral code is different from ours."

"Nah," Kurt said. "I don't think so. Mo's pretty progressive."

"Maybe, but let's curb those chats just in case."

Both guys nodded.

She walked back toward the kitchen, crossing the ripped, faded linoleum as she moved across to the far wall where a basic stove and a sink were located. The sink sat on a poorly constructed wooden cabinet, its doors uneven, and the off-white paint peeling away. There was little else in the room except a table and four chairs that didn't match.

Joey grimaced. She hadn't said much, but she couldn't wait to leave this town either. They'd been here too long the minute they arrived. Everything about it was wrong. Most of its people had left, and it felt like a ghost town, or worse, a place waiting for something nasty to happen. These last few days she'd been on constant edge—as had the others.

She started pouring the water out of the urn and into a saucepan. They didn't even have the luxury of a kettle.

Joey did not finish her task.

The flash came first, then the explosion, its force slamming her hard against the metal edges of the sink, forcing her head down where it hit the faucets.

The smell of sulfur and an intense wave of heat had already assaulted her as she reclaimed her senses. She turned to look back toward the room she'd just left and where her colleagues were. All she could see was devastation—a room on fire, heavy smoke, debris. Joey could barely make out a gaping hole in the wall where the balcony had been. As she struggled to move back toward them, she heard gunfire and the unmistakable sound of AK-47 assault rifles. The sound grew louder. Whoever was behind the rifles, they were coming up the stone stairs toward her.

With a calculating calm Joey didn't recognize, she speed-checked the kitchen for a place to hide. There was none, except the cabinet under the sink. Not bothering to think if she could fit inside it, she threw herself in, cramming her long body into the unyielding small space. She pulled the doors shut.

She heard the shouting of the gunmen, their harsh words that made no sense to her, a language too alien. But she understood their intent. They were searching. She heard them discharging their weapons again. Bile rose in her stomach as she realized what they were firing at.

Her team.

Her colleagues.

Her friends.

The shouting grew louder, and she heard something heavy falling to the ground. Masonry? Then she knew they were in the kitchen. She froze, ordering every bodily function in her to cease. In her mind she became invisible—a speck of dust, a cobweb unseen as they searched.

She heard two voices, still shouting and on an adrenaline high. They were dragging something heavy. There was a smashing of glass and then laughter, its sound repellant and unnatural.

The tone of the voices changed and grew questioning. Shuffling footsteps moved toward her hiding place and stopped. Then with a rustle of movement, Joey saw a cabinet door open. She shut her eyes tight knowing what was to happen.

But it didn't.

The gunfire that followed came from the street below.

Someone shouted up, his voice commanding, guttural, and intolerant.

Orders.

Whoever was in the kitchen, they left abruptly. If they had opened the cabinet one second earlier, she would be dead now. But they hadn't, and for the moment, Joey was alive.

Joey didn't move from her hiding space. A toxic mixture of fear and common sense born of survival kept her there.

Gunfire surrounded her. She listened to the screaming in the streets below.

She heard gunmen in the stairwell and on the floors above her, their feet like rats scuttling. They were going from room to room, as she had reported earlier.

Several times, she thought they were in the room next to her, rifling for anything that survived the attack. She doubted anything had. They had either used a rocket or a grenade launcher. Nothing much ever survived either of those. She'd seen a weapon rocket launcher in the hands of a child some months back. It required little skill, and the enemy allowed their young to experience "the thrill."

She waited for them to come and search the kitchen, but they never did.

The cabinet became her unlikely friend. It protected and cocooned her, and had already saved her life. Joey would not abandon it. Not yet. Not until she knew she had a chance to escape and live. She had been in dreadful situations before and survived. She still had an old scar where a bullet had ricocheted off a wall and hit her in the arm. So she would wait.

But waiting came at a cost.

The heat was intolerable. There was a slit of light where the doors joined. It became her contact with the outside world. She knew when it was night and day. Only once did she dare to open the doors and peep out. Thirst demanded the action. The sun had shone directly in her face as she'd searched for the water urn, but it was gone. She saw the rubble and dust on the floor. If she moved, she would leave a trail. It wasn't worth the risk.

So she stayed put and suffered the confined space for another day. She'd always liked being tall. Now she wished she wasn't.

Then the cramp came and was unforgiving, but she could not scream. That was a death sentence, and she wasn't ready to die yet. Not here. Not like this.

Joey slowly moved a hand down to her left leg to attempt to massage the cramp out. Her fingers found wetness. Perhaps the pain wasn't cramp. Had the explosion hurt her? She moved her hand around the leg seeking the point of injury, but found none. Her fingers didn't feel sticky either, not like the blood from her head where it had hit the faucets.

She moved her hand back to her face and smelled it. Then she licked her fingers. It was water. A few dark forages later, she found a small leak in a pipe. She wrapped a handkerchief around it to soak the liquid. She knew what she was drinking was contaminated and that it would make her ill, but she had no choice. It became her lifeline, and for now, the water sustained her.

Time dragged but passed. The light through the cabinet door grew dark again. She waited many hours until the chanting and sounds of evil outside ceased. Even rebels slept.

Joey slowly pushed one of the doors open, her plan to simply stick her legs out and get circulation moving. As she extended one leg and began stretching it, something caught her eye. She saw the shadow of a man standing in the corridor that separated the kitchen from the room where her team had been. He had his back to her and she could just make out a rifle slung over a shoulder. In infinite slow motion, she drew her leg back into the cabinet and carefully pulled the door shut.

She heard him cough, then spit. She listened to the sound of rubble and debris crunching under his feet as he entered the kitchen. He stopped in the center of the room where the floor creaked as it had for her many times. Joey wondered if he knew she was here. Was he about to pounce and shoot her dead, or worse, drag her into the street for a ceremonial beheading of an infidel? Would pictures of her slaughter hit social media and air worldwide as many others had? How would her parents cope? It was their fear.

Her heartbeat grew fast and irregular, and her mouth went dry. She felt her muscles tense. Her mind focused, and she prepared for attack. She might get a chance to grab the gun before he fired. Better to die that way.

She heard the scraping of a chair as he sat down and the unambiguous sound of a match being struck to light a cigarette. She caught its smell and waited, like a deer caught in headlights, for him to finish his *down time*.

When he was done, he stood, but instead of leaving the room, Joey heard him walk over to the sink. Her adrenaline rose higher and made her lightheaded. He was inches from her but made no move to reveal her hiding spot. Instead she heard a rustling sound and then all went quiet. What the hell was he doing?

Then water trickled into the sink and down the drain. The bastard insurgent was urinating. Seconds later, he left.

Relief flooded Joey, but she couldn't stem her tears.

Kurt had called her Warrior Queen.

Fear made the Warrior Queen wet herself.

❖

The rebels seemed to have set up their HQ in the building. They were constantly in the stairwell, their comings and goings menacing. All day and late into the night, she would hear them talking, often ranting.

She continued to hide in her safe place, and another day passed where she wondered if she would ever stand up straight again.

It was the day after that when her situation worsened.

Her head hurt from where she'd hit it, and she was dizzy with the heat. Later, she threw up. Unable to do anything, she suffered the mess. Sweat ran down her face and her breathing became labored. Then the pains in her stomach started, and the diarrhea came.

Joey realized she'd lost count of what day it was, of how long she'd been under the sink. She began to drift into restless sleeps. If the insurgents didn't kill her, the contaminated water might.

After one agitated sleep, she awoke with a start. She became aware of an eerie silence outside. For the longest time, she searched for sound, but there was nothing. No rifles firing, nobody shouting or screaming. Nothing.

For the third time, she dared to push the cabinet open and welcomed the fresher air that met her. No one stood in the shadows waiting for her. At first, she couldn't move, her body was locked in position, but she pushed every ligament and tendon she had, forcing herself to crawl out of the space. It took time. Only when she was completely free of the cabinet did she try to stand, without success. So she pulled herself onto all fours and waited until she had sufficient strength to stand. When she could, the room spun, and she used a wall for support until the sensation passed.

Now she took stock of what was around her. Amid the mess and wreckage, she saw a trail of dried blood leading from the room where the explosion had been. The blood streaked across the linoleum and up to the broken kitchen window, its stains evident on the sill. Horror gripped her. She realized the dragging sounds had been either Kurt's or Mitch's body being thrown through it. Thrown like baggage.

Joey edged closer to the window, careful to avoid being seen or touching her friend's blood. There was nothing outside except devastation. She saw dead bodies. They had been left to rot where they fell. She didn't see her friends. The town was in ruins and its streets full of twisted metal and mounds of masonry where buildings had once stood. Nothing moved except a dog running around looking for food. She was hungry too.

She forced herself to enter the skeleton of the room where they had all last shared a laugh, afraid of what she might see. But there was nothing. No evidence that they'd ever been there. Nothing had survived. Even if it had, the rebels had picked it clean like locusts.

Joey crossed the room sticking close to the back wall since the floor looked unsafe, and there was no wall where the balcony had been. Fear flooded her, and her breath caught. What if all the rebels hadn't left? What if they saw her?

She started down the stairs toward the exit below. A wave of dizziness hit her, and she lost her footing and fell to the bottom. For a moment, she didn't move, and when she did, her shoulder hurt like crazy. Its pain bit into her, reminding her she was alive. It made her more determined to survive. She would get out of here. She would not die in this wasteland of a place.

She left the building, struggling to decide which way to go. Why couldn't she remember which direction led back to base camp?

Joey stumbled through the streets, her legs occasionally giving way. She fell to the ground often. Sometimes she saw an old man or woman who had survived the carnage. They looked shell-shocked and wandered about without direction or purpose. If they saw her, they showed nothing. They didn't try to approach her. It was as if she really was invisible. These last days, she had prayed for that.

She entered what once might have been termed a pretty market square. All she saw now were battered, blood-stained bodies, many hanging on poorly constructed crosses with handwritten placards around their necks. She couldn't read their words but knew their accusatory meaning.

Her vision blurred and her head hurt. A dense fog and a feeling of confusion swirled in her mind. But then she sensed she wasn't alone, and as she did, she remembered her purpose. She forced herself to stand erect.

"Are you getting this, Kurt?" she said. "Is the light okay? Stick with me…keep filming."

She turned to look at him, but no one was there. A cold steel blade of fear ran through her. She was becoming delusional. If she lost her mind, she would die. She breathed in deeply. "I must find the road home. I must find the road home," she started chanting the mantra. Surely if she said it enough times, the message would remain even if her mind didn't…some automatic homing message?

She dragged her feet as she moved around the square, the headache increasing.

"I'm Josephine Barry, and I'm here in the town of…I can't remember, Kurt. What's this place called?" She frowned. Why couldn't she recall that either? "It doesn't matter. We'll edit that later." She pointed out front. "This is the market square, and you can see the carnage. Just like…all the other places. They destroy everything."

She looked up. Familiarity and shock hit her.

Facing her was a decapitated head on a spike.

The face was Mo's, their guide. Bruised, battered, bloodied, but recognizably him.

She stepped back and fell to the ground.

The placard attached to the spike held one word. She knew this one. *Traitor*.

Beheading was for those who betrayed Allah, the ones who worked for the infidels. They had known he was their interpreter.

"Get this, Kurt. Everyone must see this. No one must forget." Her voice was hoarse.

She struggled to her feet.

"We're losing light, but keep filming. We're going to get out of here. We'll walk back if we have to."

Which way? I must find the road home.

She glanced up the main street to the left and then to the right. She still couldn't work out the route back to base camp. It was stupid. She'd driven them all here. She knew the route. Why couldn't she remember?

"We'll have to walk, guys. This way…we'll try this way."

She fell again and the dust rose and stuck to her sweating face.

She threw up before resting on all fours and waiting for another wave of dizziness to pass.

"We're not going to die here. We're going home."

I must find the road home.

Joey walked until the town disappeared behind her. She forced herself to put one foot in front of the other, but she was in bad shape and weakening. She should never have drunk the water.

Time distorted. Was it an hour later? Was it more? Was she still under the sink and this was an hallucination? Was she ever in Balshir? Would she wake in clean sheets to find this was a nightmare?

Joey saw something on the rough dirt road ahead of her. It looked like a dark blob on the horizon that shimmered in the heat of the sun like a mirage.

As she studied it, the blob grew bigger until she saw it was a large truck loaded with people. She could see them all over it, on its top, holding on to its sides.

The vehicle drew closer and she could see faces and make out their clothing. They wore fatigues and were brandishing weapons. They weren't Westerners. She was walking into the hands of the rebels.

She stopped.

They would see her now; she couldn't escape. But she wouldn't stand and wait to be slaughtered.

With the little energy left in her body, she turned off the road and headed into the rocky terrain to her side. It was a meaningless act since there was no cover, no shelter.

She tripped and fell to her knees. Another wave of dizziness hit her.

It occurred to her that this was it then.

This was where she was going to die.

"Guys, we can stop filming now."

Everything went black.

Chapter Two

The Reverend Samantha Savage, vicar of St. Mary and All
Saints, Ribbley, parked outside the church and got out of
her car.

She'd handed her life over to God's work when she was in her
teens, and until now, aged fifty-three years, the union had worked
well. But it wasn't today.

Sam leaned on the vehicle and looked at the imposing
structure before her.

This was the largest parish church in Worcestershire with
parts dating back to the eleventh century. It was a Grade One listed
building and very important to the history of Ribbley. It had fine
tower stands on the south side and niches for statues and paneled
battlements. Beyond the expected services, important civic events
took place here, and it was where organizations like the Scouts and
Guides held their own services. The church was rooted in the core
activities of the large town, which was why Sam was depressed.

As she looked across at the magnificent stained-glass
windows and small turret containing a staircase to the nave roof,
she growled.

Most of the roof was missing. There were structural defects
that could no longer be ignored, and urgent roof repairs were taking
place. The builders were in and had stripped half of the one side
of the roof to the extent that she could see timbers that probably

hadn't seen the light of day for centuries. It was expensive work, and despite several grants, there was still much money to be raised. An appeal had been launched, and Sam just hoped everything would come together in time.

The bishop was coming to see her today for an update. She sighed. At least she could tell him everything was now moving in the right direction. The survey was done. The repairs were progressing. The finance was…coming along. What else could go wrong?

There was an almighty creaking sound that grew louder. Sam stared in horror as the remaining half of the roof disappeared from sight. She heard the heavy timbers crashing inside the church. At the same time, a mushroom cloud of dust and debris pushed up into the air.

As she stood there pulverized and in shock, she saw a ladder appear through the dust and a man's face emerge. It was covered in white dust, and he looked like a ghostly apparition. He coughed a few times before waving to her. It was Bob Needham, the builder.

"It's all right, Rev," he shouted. "Bit of a setback, but looks worse than it is. No one hurt. We'll have the mess cleared up in a jiffy." He glanced back down into the building. "Well, it'll be okay for Sunday service." He smiled and threw her a thumbs-up before disappearing back down the ladder.

"Dear Lord, send me a miracle," she sighed, looking up into the blue sky. At least it wasn't raining. For that she was grateful.

Sam locked the car and made her way into the church, dreading what she would find. The scouts would be arriving in less than three hours, the choir was rehearsing later, and the bishop was due soon. It occurred to her that her ordination schooling many years ago had not stretched to broom skills. She was about to acquire on-the-job training.

❖

Two hours later, the church was starting to fill with expected visitors.

Sam heard footsteps behind her in the aisle and turned to see the builder ambling toward her. His face wore purpose. Her heart sank.

"Oi, Rev."

Sam reminded herself that his heart was in the right place even if his greetings etiquette wasn't. "Where is the respect built on eons?" she said not without humor.

"You what?"

She raised her hand in capitulation. "No matter. What delicacy of news do you bring me? I hope it isn't bad."

"It depends on your point of view." Bob sniffed and wiped his nose on his sleeve.

All God's children, she thought.

"You know that miracle you're always going on about?" he said.

"Yes?" Sam's spirits lifted.

"You're gonna need it."

She bit her lip.

"Good news, bad news," he continued.

Sam stiffened. "Spit it out."

"The rafters in the east wing are full of woodworm."

"Which will have to be treated," she said.

"Too late for that," he said. "They've been feasting for centuries. New timbers needed, I'm afraid."

Sam raised fingers to her temples and circled. A headache was starting. "This is awful."

"Doesn't God revel in feeding the multitude?"

Bob's attempt at humor fell flat. Sam was not impressed with his biblical knowledge.

"Not with church rafters, Bob. The bishop is not going to like this."

She paused. "And the good news is?"

"Look on the bright side, Rev. Your congregation has increased tenfold."

❖

The St. Mary Scouts converged on the church like a swarm of tiny uniformed bees on a busy mission.

Unusually, the entire group was present. There was the Scout Beaver Colony, the Scout Cub Pack, and the Scout Troop. They were all children of varying ages, and all very alive and boisterous. They were using the church hall, attached and accessed through the main church, to prepare for a Summer Day parade. Today they were making seed bombs that were part of a "creative challenge" of reforestation, a technique of introducing compressed bundles of soil containing seeds into the environment where needed.

Part of their Summer Day Parade involved singing jamboree songs, and Maude Simpson was present to play the organ. *Play* was not a word Sam really associated with Maude's musical abilities, but the partially deaf eighty-year-old woman tried hard. She was only supposed to be a temporary fix until a new organist could be found. The last incumbent had collapsed and died over the organ while playing, "Nearer my God to Thee."

Maude had just hit a wrong note, making Sam flinch, when the bishop arrived.

Bishop Neil Covey-Smartingdon walked confidently down the aisle. He was a huge bear of a man with a constant look of amusement always resting on his handsome features.

Sam liked him the minute she met him. They had trained and been ordained together many years ago. She considered him and his family her closest of friends.

He walked up to her and gave her a warm hug.

"You're looking well." His natural enthusiasm for life echoed in his voice. He glanced down at a pew and picked up a scout booklet. "Guerrilla Gardening Seed Bomb Guide," he read aloud. "Is this serious?"

Sam couldn't hide a smile. "Yes."

"They're not doing it here?"

"Yes."

"Actual bombing?" His confusion made her laugh.

"Yes."

"Why?"

"Practice," she said.

"Right." His focus changed. "I like what you've done to the roof."

Sam sighed. This was so typical of Neil. Nothing ever seemed to faze him. It was probably why he'd made bishop. He looked at her and must have seen the exasperation on her face.

"Okay, okay. Be calm, Sam."

"I'm having a bad day, Neil."

"What's wrong?"

"What's wrong? Everything is wrong. Look at the mess. It's going to cost a fortune."

"You've launched a public appeal for funds. Money's coming in." His calm voice resonated around the church.

It had no effect on Sam. "We'll never raise the sort of money to meet the costs of these repairs, Neil. You could probably build a cheaper church."

"Now you're being dramatic."

"I'm not, and you know it. This is a Grade One building. This baby eats money like…roof termites chomping wood." She grimaced at the irony.

The bishop rested an appeasing hand on her shoulder. "Emergency repairs will stave off the bigger jobs and give us time."

"You think? The rain's been running down the walls."

"But it's sunny now."

"It's got into the organ."

As if by provident timing, Maude hit a few wrong keys.

The bishop flinched. "Ah, so it has."

"No. That's Maude," she said. "I need a new organist."

They looked up onto a raised level where Maude was playing. She wore a multicolored shapeless hat, and a cigarette hung off her lips.

"Smoking's banned inside churches," Neil said without any real thought.

"You can tell her then," Sam scoffed. "She's already threatened to walk out unless we stop the leak and fix the organ."

More wrong notes filled the air.

Neil screwed his eyes shut as if in pain. "That might be a blessing. You need a miracle."

"I need several, but no one is listening." Sam cast her eyes to the heavens.

"God's backlog of work, I expect."

"I don't doubt it."

Sam was thinking of her own burgeoning list of things to do.

She took him through to the vestry where they could talk without interruption, and briefed him on the update of the roof, including the infestation of hungry mouths.

"That's not all, Neil. When am I going to get a treasurer?"

The post had been vacant for nearly five months. Peter Asprey had left her in the lurch when his lotto numbers came up and he won a decent amount of money. He left shortly after to go live with his sister in New Zealand.

Peter's gain had been Sam's loss.

The position of treasurer was pivotal. Appointed by the church council, treasurers were responsible for many thousands of pounds flowing through the church funds. They carried out the financial decisions made by the diocese and national church, and were also responsible for both raising and spending money. Until Peter had resigned, he had done all of this competently. Sam's problem was that no one wanted to replace him, especially as the task now involved the major project of renovation and all that entailed.

Sam was filling the gap. Drafting annual budgets and pro-posing financial objectives was not what she saw as her role as vicar. It gobbled up her time and placed no amount of stress on her shoulders.

The bishop shook his head. "I'm working on it and pushing the church council, but we haven't had many volunteers."

"How many?" Sam asked hopefully.

"None."

At least Neil showed remorse. She knew he was trying hard. It just didn't help her predicament.

"I'm no bookkeeper, Neil. Please keep trying. And I suppose now isn't a good time to ask about an increase in vicars for this parish?" She eyed him. "The bigger the parish, the more vicars needed."

Neil didn't bother to answer. They both knew there was a manpower shortage of clergy, and that many parishes were waiting for the newly ordained. It was happening all over the Christian world. Kids finished school and went straight into other careers to become lawyers, doctors, IT specialists, and so on. They weren't heading for theological college. Clergy now were mature men and women leaving their careers late to enter the church.

"How's the roof appeal going?" Neil asked.

"The local newspaper has run an article for me, and some money has trickled in. It's generated some interest in a radio station in Birmingham. They're going to send someone to interview me."

"Excellent."

"They want to know about the history of the church, its issues. I'll do anything that raises our profile and—"

Neil stopped her.

"You're letting this all get on top of you. If the money doesn't come in, then the diocese will have to raid their own coffers and fund the repairs. True, they won't be happy, but they'll just have to do it. Don't take all of this to heart." He paused. "Have you stopped the rain from getting into the organ?"

"Yes. Bob's sorted the roof leak above it."

"Good. I'll send a chap out to look at the damage to the organ. It might just be damp. We had similar issues with the one in the cathedral. Leave it to me."

His caring, reassuring touch was having an effect on her at last. She relaxed and allowed a grin to break through her current miserable outlook.

"Have you ever tried giving a Sunday sermon with no roof, with an organist who hits the wrong keys, and the sound of munching coming from what rafters are left?"

"See it as a challenge," Neil said. "Teach the termites to sing in tune. With luck they'll drown out the sound of the organist."

She gave him a playful arm punch.

"You're supposed to be empathetic and show understanding."

"That's actually the real reason for my visit, Sam. Sunday... as soon as you're finished here, get yourself over to my place for lunch."

Sam could only think of her workload and started to decline, but Neil interrupted.

"This is not an offer you can refuse. Miriam has requested your presence. If you don't come, my life will be misery. You know what she's like."

They looked at each with understanding. Miriam, Neil's wife, was a larger-than-life character with a huge heart and warm sense of humor. But she was not a woman to be messed with.

"What time?" Sam asked.

"About one."

Brandon Finch, head of production, stood in his office and stared at Joey. His face was a mixture of anger and disappointment.

"Fuck it, Joey. That was crap." Everything about his Barney Rubble stature oozed frustration.

"I froze."

"Again." Finch eyeballed her as he popped a small mint into his mouth. A look of disgust crossed his grizzled face. Joey didn't know if it was for her or the mint. He was a bear since he'd given up smoking.

She'd let him down in the live televised political show last night. It had been billed as an unmissable debate between the sharpest of minds on the role of the U.S. in the rapidly escalating problems in the Middle East and the rise of insurgents. Key opposition politicians, former advisors to Republican and Democratic secretaries of state, senior policy and program advisers, and a number of senior fellows at the Center for American Progress had all taken part. Joey's role had been to chair the debate. She'd make a complete mess of it, and the broadcast company had been overwhelmed by complaints.

"That was a live broadcast. I can't have that," Finch snapped.

"It's just a bad day. I'm sorry." Joey's apology was wet, and Finch knew it.

"Like before, eh, when you froze on national television while interviewing Senator Braddock? At least you eventually managed to ask him the most *inane* questions."

That time the public had been forgiving, the TV station less so. The previous night had been Joey's last chance to redeem herself and shine again.

"Not good enough. You were the ideal person as moderator. Public sympathy was with you and the respect of those debating. But fuck, I could have employed a sixteen-year-old studying political science and they would have done a better job." Finch shook his head and walked to the huge window that looked down over the city.

"When I took you on, I told you I'd never hired anyone so in tune with the public mood, so able to communicate with them. You reached out well. Shit, you were in their living rooms, sitting on their sofas."

"Past tense?"

"Whatever you had, you haven't got it now." Finch turned to face her and hesitated. "Look, what happened to you out there in Balshir was beyond hell, and I can't begin to imagine how you're coping with it, but—"

"You're firing me," Joey said.

"No. But I do want you to fuck off and go find your mojo again. When you do, come back, and we'll start over."

"And if I can't?"

"Adios, Joey. I'm not in this business as a charity. We make lots of money selling news. You know that. If you can't bring the bucks in, I don't need you."

"This isn't right."

"I'd have to agree with you, but that's life. I hired you to do a job which you now don't seem able to do." He spat the mint into his hand and threw it, along with the box it had come from, into the trash can. "Come on. This can't be entirely unexpected…not after last night."

Joey said nothing. She wasn't the same since her rescue by pro-Syrian forces fifteen months ago. Physically, she was fine, but mentally? Now she panicked every time she stood in front of a camera. She was on a downhill escalator and didn't know how to get off. Counseling wasn't helping.

"Okay." Finch reached into the trash can and retrieved the box of mints. He hesitated and then popped another mint into his mouth. He looked at her and the hardness on his face gave way to an uncustomary softness. "I'm not totally without heart. It's rare, but…" He moved back to his desk and leaned on it. "You've got family in England, right?"

The conversational move puzzled Joey. Where was this going?

"My mother's sister…my aunt. She lives in Worcestershire."

"I've got a contact in Birmingham…guy runs Stallion Films Production for the BBC. I've asked him if he wants a screwed up news correspondent on his team for a while." Finch shrugged. "He said yeah."

"Doing what?" It was difficult to keep the annoyance out of her voice when everything was falling around her.

"You'd be acting as consultant. They produce a lot of geopolitical documentaries."

For the first time, he looked at her with affection. "Go out there, Joey. Stay with your aunt…whatever. Study the English for a while. That'll take your mind off things and keep you busy. They're so far up their own asses they can't even flip eggs right, but I hear the natives are friendly."

"Do I have any say in this?"

"You do not. There are a lot of wolves out there baying for your blood right now. This'll keep them away…give you time."

Finch was protecting her.

"When do I leave?" she asked.

"Last night. Three seconds after the debate ended."

Chapter Three

Sam was dog-tired but didn't go straight to bed. It was that type of tired where she wouldn't sleep anyway. Instead she ran herself a glass of water from the kitchen sink and just stood there. She studied herself in the little mirror her housekeeper kept on the windowsill. It made Sam smile. Gloria was in her seventies and a conundrum, a riddle to be solved.

She'd been widowed twelve years ago when her husband had died of alcohol poisoning at a beer festival. She had answered the job advert for housekeeper to earn extra cash. The job didn't pay well, but Gloria stayed. Gloria didn't have a religious bone in her body and thought all church stuff was humbug. Yet she worked at the vicarage.

Four years ago when Sam came to this parish and asked the outgoing vicar about Gloria, he had simply held her hands in his and said, "God will reward you in heaven."

Sam never knew what mood Gloria would be in from hour to hour, but she worked like a Trojan and kept the small vicarage spick-and-span. She'd also started cooking for Sam on occasion, a requirement not in her terms of reference. Sam often felt she was being mothered. Gloria wasn't one to hesitate to chastise her for anything from leaving toothpaste on the porcelain sink to eating proper food at correct meal times. It seemed that they liked each other.

Sam stared at herself in the mirror. She was tired and it showed. Damn, she was at that age where everything was starting to show. She spotted a couple of gray hairs prodding out like beacons in her hair, and there was a mass of laughter lines, crow's feet, at the corners of her eyes. When had they appeared? But at least it was evidence that she could laugh. Her sense of humor had always been her greatest ally and something her parishioners seemed to like. She could even make Gloria laugh—sometimes. Not an easy task.

Sunday lunch with Neil, Miriam, and their four teenage offspring had been delightful. Her plans to return home late afternoon to work had been foiled. Lunch morphed into cozy drinks in the garden, and then an invite to stay for supper. Before she knew it, the day was over, and the time late.

But even the wonderful day did nothing to remove the emptiness she felt inside. Sam was feeling increasingly hopeless and trapped.

She'd heard the call of God early in her years and answered it. For that, she was a woman who had spent her life alone. Perhaps her busy work, dedication, or youthful energy had buffered and protected her from that fact, but lately the safety nets had weakened. For several years, a need grew in her. She wanted something more—for her. She wanted personal fulfillment beyond religion.

What had triggered that new calling?

The letter.

It was more of a note, handwritten and by someone struggling to hold a pen.

The letter had arrived one morning, its words scrawled and uneven.

And it had been unexpected.

Louise had written it.

She was asking to see Sam, but not as a parishioner seeking the comfort of religion before dying of incurable cancer. This was the call of a lover—a past lover.

Louise was the woman Sam had walked away from all those years ago when she finally made the choice between love and faith.

They had ended badly.

Louise had not taken Sam's choice well. She had told her to leave and never darken her doorstep again. Sam had tried many times to repair the damage but always failed.

This was the first time Louise had asked for her, and Sam had not hesitated in going to the hospice where she was in the last throes of life. The nurses told her she didn't have long.

"I didn't think you'd come," Louise had said.

"Why would you think that?" Sam answered with warmth as she sat beside the bed where Louise lay.

"I was awful to you that last time. I shouldn't have been."

Sam shook her head and smiled. "You had plenty to be upset about...and you were angry."

"You don't hate me then?"

"I could never hate *you*." She looked into Louise's eyes, once so full of spirit, but now dull. Everything Louise did was an effort—breathing, staying awake, talking.

"Thank you for coming. I wanted to see you again before..."

Sam reached out and held her hand.

"Are you in much pain?"

"Not really. Sometimes. The staff are good. For the most, they keep the pain away."

Sam felt Louise grip her hand tighter.

"Have you been happy?" Sam prayed she would say yes.

"I have. It's been a good life. Just wish it could be longer, but that's not to be. I've had a good run and met some wonderful people." Louise stopped as she labored for air. "But I've never loved as I loved you. I was so angry when you chose the church over me. The only woman I've ever *loved*, and I lose her to someone I can't even see...God. You can't compete with that." Her laugh was weak. It turned into a groan.

"Should I get someone?" Sam hated seeing her like this.

"No, it passes."

Louise couldn't speak after that, and Sam placed their conversation on hold. She stayed seated by her, hand in hand until Louise was able to talk again.

"Don't let it pass you by," Louise said.

"What?"

"Life and love, Sam." She gasped for air. "You must live life. God is fine, but make sure you leave a little in your heart for love." Louise looked at her with such softness. "I think God would be okay with that."

Sam was thinking how to reply when two nurses entered. They asked her to leave for a short while.

When she returned to the bedside, Louise was less responsive. Her breathing was more labored, and a nurse told Sam it wouldn't be long now. Louise never spoke again, but her eyes never left Sam's face.

"Would you like me to say a prayer?" Sam whispered.

A small shake of the head indicated no, but Louise moved her hand into Sam's.

Sam held it between both of hers and, as she stayed there waiting for the inevitable, she remembered the past and of how much she'd loved Louise. The decision to choose the church over Louise had not been easy. Sam pressed the hand to her lips and kissed it. She only left when the hand loosened its grip on hers, and she knew Louise was gone.

Sam wasn't the same after her death.

She went through the motions, did everything she always did. Outwardly, she remained the same upbeat vicar that made the parishioners laugh. But inside she was different. She closed down, and in the times when she wasn't administering to everyone else's problems and issues, she sat at home and stared at the walls.

Louise's words had hit home.

Sam loved God. She felt his power in all she did. There would not be a day in her life when she would doubt him. Her life was full...*really* full at the moment. She was respected by churchgoers, those she dealt with, and by the church. She'd been made a canon, an honorary title bestowed for faithful and valuable service to the church. There was no bigger accolade unless you sought the highest of position...bishop, and beyond. She never had. She liked the root contact with the masses.

But for all the room God occupied in her heart, there was a void. It was an empty space that was growing, and her vocation no longer filled it. Now she felt her calling was pulling her in the wrong direction.

"Leave a little space for life...and love." Louise's words echoed.

Sam placed the empty glass in the sink.

"Living life isn't that easy, Louise."

CHAPTER FOUR

Sam glanced at her watch and then pulled at her shirt. She was wearing a new black one along with a whiter than white clerical collar. The shirt was too tight and chafing at her neck. Wearing a cassock wasn't helping. The long robe was something she only wore for formal worship or ceremonial occasions. But the journalist from the radio station had said she wanted photos for the online magazine, and this forced Sam to put a little extra effort into her ecclesiastical attire.

She looked at her watch again. Damn, where was that reporter? Carrie Marlow had already canceled their first appointment a few days ago. The station had called at the last minute and given no reason. Now she was over an hour late for this one.

Normally, Sam wasn't a clock watcher, but she'd almost finished everything she wanted to do at the church before the wedding ceremony tomorrow. Her plan was to drop in at the local hospital on her way home to see a member of the congregation who wasn't doing so well. Apart from the interview, Sam was only hanging on until Elsa turned up with the flowers. Once she knew they were sorted, she could leave. She'd give Carrie another half an hour.

In the meantime, she studied the chancel area in the church which was now camouflaged to hide renovations. Bob had gone to huge lengths to conceal everything so tomorrow's matrimonial big day would not be spoilt. He was a rough diamond, and she was growing very fond of him. Despite his less than pitch-perfect sense of humor, he really was trying to make everything as painless as possible. Her volunteer helpers were doing the same. She watched them bouncing around the church like demented lemmings as they prepared it and laid out hymn books in the pews. She might not have much of a roof, but everything inside was beginning to look fantastic.

The sun was shining as Joey quick marched toward the huge arched porch and doorway into St. Mary's church. She was already regretting volunteering to help out her mom's sister, Auntie Elsa, a member of the church's congregation, and who she was now staying with. Joey had quickly discovered that Elsa had a gift. She could throw flowers together and create stunning feasts for the eyes which was why Joey was delivering a van load of flower arrangements for a wedding the next day. Elsa had taken a fall and Joey had wanted to help out, but it was the drive that was daunting.

She could have been here five minutes ago but for a chain of stupid "roundabouts" that left her figuring which way to go around them. The only rotary she knew was in DuPont Circle in DC, and she loathed that too. And why did the Brits have to drive on the wrong side of the road when most of Europe had gotten it right?

As she walked into the church, an austere looking woman who was attentively laying a crisp white cloth on a table looked at her over half-moon glasses balanced partway down a thin nose.

"Hi. I'm looking for Reverend Savage," Joey said.

"You're late," the woman said as she pointed out the vicar who stood at the far end of the aisle.

Joey didn't hover and made her way toward the dark, menacing shape farther down. The vicar had her back to her and appeared like a demonic apparition who was studying floor to ceiling thick plastic sheeting that was protecting the church from the restorations that were going on behind. As she drew closer, the vicar turned and Joey caught the sweep of shoulder-length auburn hair.

"I was expecting you earlier," the vicar said.

The statement took Joey back. Hell, these Brits were impatient. She'd driven here straightaway on Auntie Elsa's request.

"I came as soon as I could."

The vicar's eyes widened. "You're American. I didn't know."

They were also quick, Joey thought with sarcasm.

"You're a woman. I didn't know that either. I was expecting a man," Joey said.

The vicar looked taken aback but then shrugged.

"Well, no matter, you're here now and in one bit. I was getting a little worried that something might have happened to you."

"No. I'm all in one bit." Joey wasn't warming to her.

"It's just I'm on a bit of a tight schedule today, and I've got a lot to be getting on with."

"So have I," Joey said.

"You could have let me know you'd been delayed."

"I'm not, and I'm doing you the favor."

The Reverend Savage went to say something but thought better of it. Instead she nodded.

"I suppose you are. Where's your stuff?"

Joey thought of the mass of flowers. "Outside in the van."

"Okay. How do you want to play this?"

"I thought you'd tell me." Joey's answer seemed to confuse the vicar. How difficult was it to organize flowers?

"Well, would you like me to show you around the church first?"

"Not really, Reverend. I'll just bring it all in." She glanced down, and something about the vicar's attire caught her eye. "You're wearing jeans."

The statement seemed to amuse.

"I'm wearing a cassock *over* my jeans."

"Why?" Joey hadn't seen a denim wearing vicar in church before.

"Because of you."

"Me?"

"The photo."

"What photo?"

"I understand you want a photograph of me."

Joey straightened. Something wasn't quite right here. She started to smile. "Tempting, but not really."

Reverend Savage frowned. "You are from the BBC?"

"Yeah. How do you know that?" Joey had listened to Elsa's voice mail to the vicar. She hadn't mentioned that. Maybe Elsa had spoken of her new job with Stallion Productions earlier, but then surely she'd have also mentioned she was American.

"Your station called and arranged this appointment," the vicar clarified.

"My station?"

Joey was about to say that they must have their wires crossed when a man approached Reverend Savage and handed her a cell phone.

"You left it in the vestry, Sam."

"Thanks." The vicar stared at its flashing lights before turning gray eyes on Joey. "I've got a couple of messages. Would you mind if I check them? One of my parishioners is ill in hospital. It might be news."

"Please, go ahead."

Joey heard both messages as clear as if she'd held the cell to her own ear.

"Vicar, it's Elsa Morris. There's no problem, but I've sprained my ankle and can't drive. Don't worry. I'm getting my niece to drop the flower arrangements off. She should be at the church in about an hour. Lydia and Kelvin know where they are all going so they'll sort everything. The flowers look beautiful. They'll need a light spray of water in the morning and should look stunning for tomorrow's wedding. Again, Lydia knows what to do. Any dramas, just ring."

The vicar locked eyes with Joey.

"Hi. This is a message for Reverend Canon Savage. Reverend, this is Carrie from BBC Radio WM. I'm so sorry, but I'm going to

have to cancel the interview for a second time. I'm caught in a dreadful traffic jam on the motorway, and I don't think I'll be going anywhere fast. I don't want to mess you around so I'll get back to you later, and hopefully we can reschedule. Believe it or not, I'm really looking forward to meeting you, and hearing about the church. I'll be in touch. Bye."

When finished, the *emissary of God* looked at her again, this time her eyes twinkled.

"Let's start again," the vicar said. "Why are you here?"

Joey grinned. "I'm here to deliver flowers. I'm Elsa's niece, Josephine Barry. You didn't get her message, did you?"

"Nope." The vicar guiltily raised the phone and shook it in front of them. "I thought you were the reporter from BBC WM, here to interview me about the church appeal." She threw Joey a huge smile as she stuck her hand out. "I'm Samantha Savage, Josephine. Lovely to meet you, and please call me Sam…everyone else does."

Joey relaxed. She was beginning to recognize the frazzled look of stress around Sam's eyes. It made her more forgiving. "Call me Joey. I'm glad we've sorted the confusion out."

"Me, too. I see now why you didn't want my photograph. I felt quite slighted."

Joey started to laugh. "I didn't mean to upset you."

"No damage done. I have a hide like a buffalo." Sam's eyes narrowed in fun. "And I wear jeans because they're comfortable, and it doesn't pay to be too formal in this line of work. I think most parishioners prefer it to the more starchy appearance one normally expects of my lot. I stick to the shirt and dog collar, but the rest is relaxed."

"I see." Joey didn't really. Her mother was a churchgoer back home, and in all the countries her own work had taken her to, Joey had always found the different articles of clerical clothing like a personal assault course. She only knew she liked this vicar better when she smiled.

Sam was giving her a friendly tap on her arm.

"Shall we get those flowers in before they wilt in this heat?"

❖

Elsa answered the door with a smile and a walking stick. She leaned on it, and Sam could see the heavy bandaging on her foot. In the background was piano music. It was light and precise, expert fingers producing a calming effect.

Sam smiled back. "Elsa, what have you done?"

She was calling on her to make sure she was all right and to let her know her flower arrangements for the wedding had been spectacular. There were many compliments. She wanted Elsa to know.

Elsa beckoned her inside the small detached house and sighed in frustration.

"I tripped over the cat and sprained my ankle. The swelling's going down so I should be back to normal soon."

"I'm very glad to hear it. You're missed. And I can't tell you how much your flowers have been admired. Your ears must be burning."

"Only my ankle."

Elsa joked, but Sam noted the way she puffed up with pride. It warmed her. So often the little thank-yous were never said, yet they made a big difference.

"Shall I put the kettle on?" Elsa asked.

"No. I just wanted to check on you and make sure you're okay."

They sat down in the cozy sitting room.

Gentle music continued to drift in from next door.

"Joey," Elsa explained before Sam asked the question. "She loves to play, just like her mother. She's my youngest sister's daughter and staying with me. She's from America. I think you met her last week."

Sam grinned. Their introduction had been under confusing circumstances. "Yes, she stayed on and helped with the flowers."

"She's waiting to move into an apartment not far from you. She gets the keys later this week. But it's been lovely having her here, and she's taken the weight off my feet so to speak." Elsa tutted at her double entendre.

"Is she over here long?"

"I'm not sure. She's working here for a while, but I don't know the detail. For you to ask, I think."

Sam thought she heard an element of caution in Elsa's response but didn't have time to think on it at that moment, Joey entered the room. Sam was struck with how tall and slim she was. She hadn't really noticed before. She guessed she was in her mid to late forties, but she didn't look it. There was no gray in her long blond hair, and she appeared fit. There was a nasty scar on her forehead, and now Sam could see dark shadows under her eyes. While the shadows might be jetlag—Sam didn't know how long Joey had been here—the scar fed her natural curiosity. Joey was an attractive woman and the wound seemed to add a touch of mystery enhancing her allure.

Right now something else was more enticing about Joey. She was a piano player. A seed dropped with the weight of an anchor into Sam's thoughts.

After the usual array of friendly greetings, Sam blatantly allowed the seed to germinate.

"So, that was you playing the piano?"

"Yes, not too well I'm afraid, but I enjoy it."

Joey looked like an innocent for slaughter. Sam didn't care. She was beyond guilt after months of Maude's playing. She was desperate.

As if by telepathy, Elsa joined in. "How's Maude doing?"

"Killing my attendance numbers." Sam believed in truth. "Only the deaf appreciate her playing. God forgive me for complaining."

Elsa eyeballed Sam. "It's difficult to find someone these days."

"Yes, it is, Elsa." She smiled graciously at Joey who was now sitting opposite. "You know, Maude can't play next week due to other commitments, and I'm looking for someone to cover. Know anyone, Elsa?"

"Stop right there." Joey raised a hand. Sam noted the long thin fingers…pianist's fingers.

"We're not doing anything." Elsa played the sweet little old lady well.

"Yes, you are. You've both got collusion written across your faces," Joey said.

"No, no," Sam said.

"Yes, yes," Joey said.

Sam could see this would not be easy. "It's just you play so well."

"And it would only be for Sunday service, right, Reverend?" Elsa seldom addressed her as Sam.

"Absolutely."

"No, no, no." Joey grew more resistant.

"You're not doing anything better," Elsa said.

"No! Back off, you guys. I've started a new job and I need to focus. Besides, I'm moving into my place soon and I'll need time to settle."

"But it's only one Sunday," Elsa said.

"Two…three at most," Sam added.

"Why don't you play, Reverend?" Joey said evenly.

"I can't, and besides, I can't be in two places at once…doing the service, etcetera."

"My answer is unequivocally no. I'm too busy."

"My dear," Elsa said, "you can't work every day, and this will be good for you. Take your mind off things. You said yourself, music has such healing properties."

Sam reminded herself that she was intrigued. What was Joey healing from?

Joey dug her heels in. "No. Besides, I'm not religious."

"You don't have to be to play," Sam replied.

"And I've never played an organ in my life."

"Keyboards are the same. You can play one, you can play the other."

Joey stared at her hard. "It's obvious you don't play."

"There's a photo of me in this if you just play on Sunday." Sam resorted to begging.

"A photo?" Elsa looked confused.

"Long story," Sam and Joey answered in unison.

Joey stood. "Sorry, guys. I'm not doing it *and* I'm leaving now," she threw them a smile wrapped in warning, "so I don't have to keep looking at your pleading faces." As she exited, she eyeballed them through the door until it closed.

Elsa and Sam eyed each other as the door clicked shut.

"She'll break," Elsa said.

Sam hadn't thought she would, which was why it came as a surprise to find Joey sitting in a pew waiting for her several days later. Sam was returning from a meeting with the social services department. She noticed Joey the minute she entered the church.

There was a ray of sunlight, a beam that fell across Joey. It lit up her fair hair like warm golden sand. For a moment, Sam thought Joey was asleep; the sunbeam might have done that. But as she approached her, Joey turned and looked up with such keen blue eyes. Sam only saw a troubled face. Years of administering to people in all kinds of distress had honed her sensitivity. She suspected that Joey suffered and it made her wonder why.

"So, is it my vibrant personality or word of my dynamic pulpit skills that brings you into my church to pray?" Sam joked. She didn't dare hope it had anything to do with organ playing.

"I'm not praying."

Sam caught the breeze of defensiveness.

"But you're sitting in my church."

Joey shrugged. "I've been waiting for you."

"You looked like you were praying," Sam said softly.

"Looks can be deceiving, but I was enjoying the peace of this place. It's lovely to just be able to sit down and think."

"About anything in particular?"

Joey didn't answer, and Sam could hardly miss the shadow that crossed her face and the way she looked away, breaking eye contact. It made her intuitive antenna swing like a metronome. For someone she'd only just met, she was building an unexpected amount of data that hinted at one who really was troubled. But experience had also taught Sam that there were times when people needed to talk, and times when they didn't. She suspected this was one of those moments when they didn't as she sat down in the pew in front of her. Sam sensed a need to lighten something unquantifiable that had suddenly drawn Joey into a dark place. Sam applied humor. With a dramatic deep voice, she asked, "Are you in trouble, my child?"

Joey actually laughed, and Sam felt a glow of warmth. It was pure supposition, but she suspected Elsa's niece didn't laugh too much of late. An irrational urge rose in her that wanted to find out why. Its strength surprised Sam, and she assumed it was because she liked her. She had from the moment they'd met.

"Oh, Mother would love you," Joey said.

"She would?"

"She's big into religion."

"Ah, a believer." Sam loaded the comment with devout benevolence. Instinct told her she could *play* with Joey.

"Oh, yes."

Sam sensed the intelligence behind Joey's stare.

"But you're not," Sam said.

"I see myself as more spiritual."

"As do many."

"I've disappointed you." Joey wasn't apologetic.

"Not at all, I'm a realist. I gave up trying to entice people into the faith years ago. I merely leave the door open, and they can come in if they want."

Joey seemed to be brightening.

"I've changed my mind, Vicar. I'll play Sunday if you want."

"I want. And it's Sam."

"I'm only doing this once, *Sam*."

"Okay."

This was not the time to ask what had changed Joey's mind. Sam was too busy thanking her boss. When she finished groveling, she caught Joey looking at the impressive organ located to the side of the church. It was positioned on a raised level like a Juliet balcony and accessed by stone steps.

"Do you think I could practice now? I'm really a simple piano player and I don't want to mess up."

"Come on." Without thought, Sam grabbed Joey's hand and led her up to the mezzanine floor. "Practice away. The music's all here along with the order of service for Sunday. Take as long as you want. If you need me I'll be down there." Sam pointed to the pulpit. "John is setting up a new microphone and amplifier system so we'll be competing with you. Try to ignore it."

Joey managed.

Sam had a harder time.

When John finished testing the equipment for the umpteenth time, Sam just leaned on the pulpit and listened to the music. Joey was an accomplished player. It didn't matter that she was learning how the organ worked with all its pump mechanisms. There was no hiding ability *and* talent. It had been a long time since Sam had heard the church organ played so well. Its sound lifted her heart. When Joey finished, she told her so.

"My God," Sam gushed as she ran up the steps to where Joey was still sitting in front of the sheet music.

"What?"

"Magic. You play so well, and you got all the right notes."

"Doesn't Maude?" Joey closed the music in front of her and stood.

Sam scratched her head. "Yes, but not always in the right order."

"You have a way with words."

"Not everybody would agree with you." Sam took her hand again and led her down the steps. They were uneven and needed better lighting. Heavens forbid, Joey fell and broke a finger.

"That's it then. You're booked, Joey."

"Won't Maude be annoyed?"

"Not at all. She's not available Sunday. Besides, she's only temp, filling in until I can find a new permanent organist."

"What happened to the last one?"

"You don't want to know." Sam had hoped she wouldn't ask.

"What happened?"

Sam gave a dry cough. "He left unexpectedly."

Joey was about to ask more when Sam halted at the bottom of the steps and turned to her wearing a shifty look. Joey felt her strength drain. Professional intuition yelled at her.

"What?" Joey didn't have a suspicious nature for nothing.

Sam feigned shock. "What *what*?"

"Why do I know you're about to ask me something I'm not going to like."

Sam began a denial routine, but reneged at the last minute. "What are you doing Wednesday evening?"

"Why?"

"The scouts have got an event here and I desperately need someone to play—"

"Oh, no."

"It would only be for a couple of hours."

Joey stared at the desperation on Sam's face and her resistance vanished. Her new job was starting gently, and it wasn't like she had a load of furniture and possessions to move into the apartment. She was still awaiting their arrival.

"Okay," she caved in. "But this can't become a habit."

"Of course not."

"Remember, I'm not religious. This God stuff isn't my scene."

"You sound like my housekeeper."

"Your housekeeper?"

"Never mind." Sam grinned back at her.

"Why am I doing this?" Joey said. "You're walking all over me. I'm usually very strong."

Sam's grin widened. "The scouts will adore you."

"Don't they like Maude?"

"You're about fifty years younger."

"Ah."

Joey coughed awkwardly.

"What?" Sam asked.

"You're holding my hand."

Sam had grabbed it to help her down the poorly lit stone steps. She seemed in no hurry to release it.

"Sorry. I'm dangerously tactile." Sam let go.

Joey was surprised when Sam then grasped her arm.

"I don't suppose your *spiritual* needs require refreshment? I'm off to the vicarage for a bacon sandwich and a coffee. Want to join me?"

From the outside, the vicarage was hardly sizeable. Joey figured someone in power and holding the purse strings was economizing, figuring an unmarried vicar didn't need a large place. They hadn't disappointed. They had taken financial restraint to a whole new level. It wasn't what Joey expected.

They entered by a side door that led directly into the kitchen. It surprised her that the space was larger than she anticipated.

The first thing she noticed was the sturdy, sizeable, scrubbed oak table in the middle of a vast, echoing, tiled kitchen. The second was the motorbike leaning up against the table, and the assortment of bike bits all over it.

She was about to say something when she caught the look of fear on Sam's face.

"Shit," Sam said in un-reverend type fashion.

Before Joey could find out what was wrong, the *answer* walked into the room. A robust looking elderly woman wearing an apron and a sour face crossed her arms in disapproval as she stood before Sam.

"I thought you'd left." Sam looked like a burglar caught in a spotlight.

"Clearly. So you moved this…monstrosity into the kitchen. What is that?" The woman with the mildest Irish accent pointed to an oily piece of machinery sitting on newspaper on the table.

"A magneto," Sam answered flatly.

"What's it doing on the table?"

"I'm repairing it."

As Joey watched the two women interact and eyeball each other, a peculiar feeling came over her. Reverend Samantha Savage was a woman in control of all she surveyed. She was intelligent, articulate, and full of warmth. Yet here she was, some five feet seven inches of her, on her back hoof defending herself. Joey found it strangely appealing. Not for the first time she wondered why she had caved in to the vicar's pitiful request for an organist. Joey had a reputation for being resolute, with an unbendable streak of stubbornness. Yet she had given in almost at first hurdle. Auntie Elsa kept telling her to seek out company. It was unexpected to find that so quickly, and in ecclesiastical shape.

"Gloria, this is Joey. Joey, this is Gloria, my housekeeper."

Gloria acknowledged her, a small polite smile breaking the straight line of her lips.

"I had a parrot called Joey once." Gloria's smile deepened. It was probably for a much loved bird.

"My housekeeper has an endearing way." Sam's lyrical tones dripped with playful sarcasm. It brought the scowl back to Gloria's face.

"You'll see how endearing I can be if this *machine* is not back outside where it belongs when I return."

Sam splayed her hands in defense. "Gloria, you aren't supposed to be here. You said yesterday was your last day. You're supposed to be on holiday."

Gloria shrugged then stretched her neck. "I got my dates wrong. I leave later today." She glanced back at Joey. "My dear, would you like a cup of tea? I'm just off, but I can put the kettle on."

"I've got it," Sam said. "You get going."

Gloria was already hanging her apron and picking up her bag to leave.

"Now remember, there's a cottage pie in the deep freeze, enough for several nights, and I've left some nice chicken in the fridge. Don't leave it too long. It'll go off."

"Yes, yes, you told me yesterday." Sam affectionately squeezed Gloria's shoulders. "What would I do without you? You're golden."

Gloria was not appeased.

"I'll give you golden. If that bike is still in this kitchen when I get back off holiday, there's going to be trouble. You've a month to do that." As she left, she turned back to Joey. "Nice to meet you, Joey. Make yourself at home…if you can."

With a breeze of movement, Gloria was gone.

Sam exhaled. "Phew, a month…a wonderful month of freedom. This is the first time she's taken any real break since I've been here. Her lovely family want her to stay awhile…in Ireland. Wonderful people."

"You've met them?"

"Never." Sam eyeballed Joey. "But they want her for a month."

Joey grinned. "She's very fond of you." Despite Gloria's sharp tongue and chastisement toward Sam, there was no hiding the affection.

"The feeling's mutual. We do this all the time. It's like a game, but it's how we communicate best." Sam laughed as she put the kettle on and pulled bacon from the fridge, throwing it into a pan on the stove.

Joey studied the motorbike. "I haven't seen one of these for years. It's a BSA A10 Golden Flash, right?"

Sam turned, now more interested in the conversational topic than streaky bacon.

"Yes. It's a 1953, with plunger suspension."

With plunger suspension. Joey couldn't stop smiling. Only a real bike nut came out with statements like that. And the look on

Sam's face? Joey realized she could have spouted every word of the Bible from memory and Sam would have been less shocked.

"Dad used to have one," Joey explained. "Bit of an enthusiast."

"He hasn't got it anymore?" It was obvious Sam couldn't believe anyone would ever part with one.

"He's getting older and downsizing."

"I can't imagine anyone ever getting rid of a Beezer."

Joey smiled. Her father had called it a Beezer, too. It was an accepted nickname for the bike.

"Why did he do it?"

"Mother," Joey answered.

"Ah," Sam said.

"She just doesn't understand bikes."

"How terrible. Your poor father."

Sam reacted as if it were the worst news. Joey's smile grew. She was learning that Sam had a distinct way of seeing life. It was charming, and Joey knew she was in the presence of what Americans called an eccentric Brit.

Sam diverted her attention back to the bacon that was sizzling. "You work for the BBC then?"

"How do you—"

"You told me…when we met over the flowers."

"Ah, yes."

"Doing what?"

How Joey wished she hadn't mentioned it, but then it was the sort of question a person asked anyway. *"What do you do?"* And she was an American, and over here. The questions begged answers.

"I work for a production company that makes all sorts of documentaries for the BBC. I advise. I'm a consultant."

"It sounds important."

Joey was grateful Sam's back was toward her. She stopped smiling and didn't want to say why.

"I suppose so." She didn't feel it was. Nothing seemed important to her anymore where her job was concerned. Everyone was hoping she was going to "pull herself together" and get back to normal. How did she do that with the death of her friends weighing down on her? Her job had once been her life. She'd lived and breathed it. Now it was as if it was toxic, and poisoning her. If she could just get some balance back in her life. Maybe they were right. This move over to England—the change of air—might do her good.

"Are you over here long?"

Sam's persistent questioning added to her ever-present depression.

"Not sure. Maybe. See how it all works out. I'm looking for new challenges. It's why I'm here. I'll see how it pans out."

Sam was about to ask more when Joey changed the topic.

"What's wrong with the bike?"

Sam had already thrown everything they needed onto the table. She now dished bacon onto a plate and placed it next to the bike part before finally adding the pot of tea. They both sat down.

"Don't know," Sam answered. "It's a mystery." She stared at the magneto in disgust. What mystified her more was the reticence in Joey's voice when she spoke of why she was here, *and* why she was deflecting conversation to the bike. Sam knew not to push. For now they could talk motorcycles.

Sam bit into a bacon sandwich and washed it down with tea as she stared at the glossy livery that was her bike.

"It's been breaking down a lot, and now I can't get it to go." Sam sighed. The bike was normally her pride and joy. "You'd better not ask me anymore questions. Once I start talking bikes, it's difficult to stop me." How many eyes had glazed over on this topic?

"Don't worry about that. I grew up with Dad's obsession. I used to help him sometimes."

"Do you bike?"

"Not really. Sure, I can handle one, but I've never owned one or wanted to. I used to ride out with Dad occasionally when I was younger. If you want to talk bikes, go for it. I can cope."

Permission granted, Sam did not hold back.

"The bike's taken me to some interesting places, but lately it's been failing to convey me home afterward."

She thought of the first breakdown. It had involved the gear shafts breaking free. She'd had to call out roadside recovery. That, plus the repairs, had been an expensive day out. More recently, her broken down Beezer had stood forlornly at the roadside. All the kicking in the world couldn't get it to restart after it ground to a halt.

"I made the mistake of rushing her. She's got a truck full of torque and can pull like a train all the way up to seventy miles per hour with little effort. But the minute I go over that, the vibrations start. Last month, the bike started to shed a few parts. Even the kick-start lever fell off. It's my fault, Joey. These bikes aren't made to travel at high speeds for any length of time. It doesn't like motorways because there were no motorways when it was made. Anyway, now I can't restart her."

Sam looked over at Joey expecting to see rigid boredom on her face. Far from it, Joey was holding the magneto and studying it.

"What makes you think it's this?" Joey asked.

"I've tried everything else." Sam had worked herself into a right lather trying to assess the problem. So far, she had failed.

"Like?"

Sam had found a playmate. This was fun.

"The Internet BSA forum experts always seem to distrust the bike's electrics so, in anticipation of electrical Armageddon, I attacked my bank account and upgraded all the electrics."

"Did it work?"

"No."

"Have you checked the valve clearances?"

Sam leaned in, loving Joey's way with words.

"Yes, and what a messy, fiddly job that was, and for nothing. They all turned out to be within tolerance. I've also fitted new leads, plug caps, sparking plugs. I've even fitted an expensive twelve-volt conversion."

"Wow." Joey sounded impressed.

"But the problem's still there. I thought it was the magneto, but now I don't think it is."

There was a time when Sam probably wouldn't have recognized a magneto if it had smacked her in the face. Now after evenings frequenting online biking forums, and reading manuals, she could recognize one in complete darkness while wearing snow mittens.

"Why?"

"Because after much swearing and knuckle-bashing, I can confirm the stupid piece of metal is correctly adjusted." Sam grimaced. The piece of engine even had the audacity to look brand new, although it wasn't.

"It looks brand new." Joey read Sam's mind.

"It does, doesn't it?" Sam didn't hide her sarcasm, or frustration. "I love this bike, but right now it's broke, and I have no idea what to check next."

"Dad loved the Beezer as well. He called it his Brit bike. I'm pretty sure his was hell to start too, especially when it was hot, but I don't recall him actually replacing any parts." Joey was suddenly on her hands and knees examining the bike's engine. "In fact, if I remember right, all he did was remove something and give it a good clean."

"What?" Sam fell to her hands and knees alongside Joey.

"I can't remember."

"Yes, you can. Think."

Joey eyeballed Sam. "You're hindering my thought processes."

"No, I'm not. Would another cup of tea help?"

"You're being a nuisance."

"I'm just helping you to remember."

"It's not working. Go away."

Sam stood and walked over to the window, exasperated. She just wanted her bike back.

"Got it," Joey announced.

Sam flew back to her side.

"Carburetor," Joey said after a delayed pause. "That's what it was."

"The carb?"

"Not actually the carb, but the insulator which is—"

"—a thick gasket."

Joey sat back on her haunches. "I think once the engine gets hot you can get fuel vaporization…or something like that. Dad said something about the importance of having an insulation spacer or whatever it is, between the hot engine and the carb to keep it as cool as possible. It helps stop the gas from vaporizing before it's sucked into the engine."

"I looked at the carb." Sam was mystified.

"Did you do anything to it?"

"No. I just looked at it."

Joey rolled her eyes. "I'll Skype Dad and ask him. Then maybe I could come back and help?"

"You'd do that?"

"Yep."

Sam leaned back in amazement. "I am so beginning to like you, Josephine Barry."

She was rewarded with a smile.

Joey didn't see Sam again until Wednesday evening when she was organ playing for the scouts at their jamboree event at the church.

She had tried several times to see her earlier, as her father had given her loads of advice regarding the carburetor problem. The more she told him, the more he was sure it was a gasket issue. He'd even emailed her a diagram accompanied with copious instructions. Joey was eager to share what she'd found out with Sam. She wanted to go help solve the problem, but it seemed their schedules weren't compatible. When one was free, the other wasn't. They were going to have to wait till Saturday.

In the meantime, Joey settled at the organ and played. She listened to the angelic voices of the scouts. Earlier rehearsals, which the silvery tongued Sam had cajoled her into attending, had been chaos. The scoutmaster shouted his head off until he was hoarse trying to get the super-charged kids to stay in one place long enough to be organized. They made the Energizer Bunny look like a three-toed sloth.

But the concert was going great guns. She was glad Sam had sweet-talked her into playing. There was something about the music and being surrounded by youngsters that completely took her mind off the traumas of the Middle East. Though her respite was temporary, the release was golden.

She played the last song, and Joey watched as the audience, made up of the public, civic members, and parents of the scouts, moved around the church congratulating everyone. She turned to put the sheet music away.

There was a sudden loud bang, followed by crashing sounds that echoed around the church. Its source came from the other side of the plastic sheeting not far from her. She yelled, and her head went down in defense, her eyes shut tight. It felt like all the air was sucked out as her heart started racing. She started to shake and couldn't stop.

One of the scouts was there with her, shouting down into the aisle. "Reverend, something's wrong with Joey."

Joey wanted to tell him she was okay and not to worry, but the words wouldn't come.

"It's all right, miss." There was another scout there now. "One of the lads has knocked a builder's ladder over and it's fallen into some tools. He shouldn't have been there and everything's crashed down, that's all."

The simple explanation didn't help. Though her mind was telling her to be calm, her body was reacting badly, and she had no control.

Seconds later, she heard the soft, soothing voice of Sam. "It's okay, lads. I've got this." An arm went around her. "Take some deep breaths, Joey. You're safe."

She *knew* that, but it changed nothing. Joey felt humiliated, like she had when she was in front of the camera after they said she was better and ready again. They'd thought because her physical injuries had healed she was the old Josephine Barry once more. But she wasn't. She hadn't been ready. She'd never be ready. What was happening now only proved it. What was in her head was a mess, and she was useless. Brandon Finch had seen that. It was why he'd gotten rid of her. Now she was making a spectacle of herself *again*.

Her senses started to return to normal, and she realized it was quiet in the church. She glanced around and all eyes were on her. It was like the televised debates when she'd panicked. Everyone had stared at her. They were staring now. She felt shamed.

Somehow she managed to say, "I'm sorry."

The arm around her tightened.

Sam was rubbing her back, concern etched on her face. "Don't be. It frightened the shit out of me. I thought the roof was collapsing again."

Though Sam tried to lighten the moment, she couldn't hide her unease. It was a look Joey knew far too well. It was how everyone had looked at her at first. Later, when she didn't get better, they grew embarrassed and uncomfortable. They walked away.

"You've gone very pale. Are you okay?"

Joey answered with all the dignity she could. "It was just the shock, but I'm fine now." It wasn't really a lie. She was calming.

Sam didn't seem convinced and refused to let her leave straightaway. She even took her into the vestry, and one of the scouts made her a cup of tea. The Brits seemed to look on the drink as a cure-all. There was a lot of talk about letting someone drive her home, but Joey wouldn't be persuaded. All the concern only made her feel worse. Eventually, she succeeded in convincing Sam and the others that she was fine.

When Joey returned home to her newly moved in apartment, it felt lonely and empty. Much of her stuff was still in boxes, and the furniture she was renting wasn't arriving until tomorrow. It did nothing to lift her flagging spirits. She called Auntie Elsa. Seconds later, she was back in the car and driving to Elsa's to spend the night.

❖

Joey was alone, and yet she wasn't.

She was cold, but sweat ran down her face.

She held her breath, yet she was panting.

The carpet beneath her bare feet cut like blades into her skin as she stood without motion.

The door in front of her was shut, but she felt no protection.

There was something on the other side, and she sensed its evil menacing presence. All it had to do was push and the door would open for there was no lock.

She still held her breath and prayed it couldn't hear her. If it did, it would come to her and she had no defense.

She kept watching the door. As long as she could see it she was safe.

But the light was fading.

What lay on the other side grew in the dark.

She moved back into the room and looked for somewhere to hide. There was nowhere.

The door disappeared, and the wall began to shimmer.

Its solidity altered, and it grew semitranslucent. As it did, she saw a black, wispy hand of smoke with long, extended fingers push through. A weightless, sinewy arm followed, and the beginnings of a body behind it. It slithered to the ground.

And it sensed her.

It turned.

She screamed.

Joey awoke from the nightmare shouting.

She switched the bedside lamp on and checked the room. Her heart beat wildly as she waited to see if she'd woken her aunt. Only when she knew she hadn't, she turned the light off and tried to go back to sleep.

❖

Joey was organizing the arrival of her furniture.

The delivery men had removed everything out of the protective cardboard and thick plastic wrapping, but Joey was still left with the enormous decisions of where to place everything. She was in the middle of her apartment figuring where she wanted the three-seater couch when the doorbell rang.

She was amazed to find Sam on the other side of the door holding flowers.

"These are for you," Sam said as she handed over a bunch of red carnations. "A belated *welcome to your new place* gift."

"You shouldn't have." Joey beckoned Sam in. "This is it." She proudly showed off the room. "Bit of a mess. Furniture has just arrived. But what do you think?" She closed the door.

Sam tilted her head in studious contemplation. "I like the concept of all the furniture in the middle of the room. It saves movement and will make hoovering easier. On reflection, perhaps you could space it out a bit."

Joey was getting used to Sam's dry humor.

"The delivery guys did ask if I wanted them to put it in place. They sorted the bedroom furniture, but the rest needs my deepest thoughts. I'm not one for domesticity, and I want to get it right the first time. I'm not into shifting stuff around the room like a tango. Once it's down, it stays there." She looked at Sam. "I thought you were busy?"

"I am, but as I was passing, I thought I'd be right neighborly and bring you some flowers."

Joey didn't believe her.

"You thought you'd check up on me after my meltdown yesterday in church."

"I thought no such thing," Sam said.

"Yes, yes."

"No, no." Sam was adamant.

"Yes," Joey repeated. "But that's okay, and you don't have to worry, I'm fine. Besides, I've got other problems to cope with."

"Such as?"

"Where to put this couch."

It rested like a huge carbuncle in the middle of the room.

They studied it.

"What about shoving it up against that wall?" Sam eyed an area to the left.

"Not that side?" Joey was briefly favoring the opposite wall.

"No. It'll take up all the room and you'll want space for side lamps."

"Good point." Joey made a decision. "You're right. Now how strong are you?"

"Did I mention I was just passing?" Then Sam grinned. "Okay, you take that end and let's shift it."

A few minutes later, the couch was where it needed to be.

"That little table will look great in the corner with a lamp on," Sam said.

Joey hadn't thought of Sam as the domestic goddess type, but her idea was sound. She agreed. "I've got my eye on a cheap Tiffany style lamp in a shop down the road. I think it's about to get bought."

"Sounds good."

"Can you stay for coffee?"

"Alas, no. I really am passing and have a meeting to get to. I just wanted to bring you the flowers—"

"—check up on me," Joey interrupted in a lighthearted manner.

Sam smiled back politely.

As she got to the door, Sam said, "You still up to getting deep and dirty on Saturday? We've a bike to fix."

"I'll be there."

"Bring all those notes and suggestions your father sent."

"If I can find them." Joey looked at the mess surrounding her.

Sam feigned serious. "Forget the *if*. You find, you bring. Get it?"

"Got it." Joey grinned.

"Good. I'll give you a call and let you know what time I'll be back at the vicarage." Sam opened the door. "Are you going to be all right with this?" She was looking at the disorder before her.

"I'll cope."

"Good luck." Sam left.

Joey turned and leaned up against the closed door staring at the chaos awaiting her attention. But she felt happy. It was a nice caring touch for Sam to drop in. She *was* busy and yet she'd found time to buy her flowers. She thought about the arrangements for Saturday. She was looking forward to tinkering with the bike and spending time with Sam. It amused her that her first friend over here was a vicar. She'd told her mother the other night when they'd Skyped. It had amused her to no end.

Joey picked the flowers up off the chair she'd set them down on. Where was she going to put them? More important, in *what* was she going to put them? She didn't have anything. She decided the flowers would take center stage in the middle of the dining room table and that she needed to go buy a vase, along with that lamp she was eyeing. She'd do it now.

As she left the apartment to go shopping she thought how nice it would be to invite Sam over for a meal sometime.

Chapter Five

S am and Joey were seated cross-legged on a mat in the vicarage kitchen in front of the motorbike. They were surrounded by an array of engine bits as their noses almost touched the bike casing.

The air was still, the moment serious.

Neither of them talked.

They barely breathed.

When they opened the bike up, it was clear the old gasket was in a bad state and beyond repair. They eyed each other without words, knowing what they had to do. It was touch-and-go, but they managed to replace it with little difficulty. No oil was spilled. But now they needed to replace the magneto. It was a tricky task.

Sam psyched herself up, stretched her fingers, and rotated her neck. She took a deep breath.

"Magneto." Her voice was a whisper as she held her hand out.

Until now, the magneto had been on a metal tray resting on Joey's legs. She placed the item into the palm of Sam's hand who took it gingerly and slowly pushed it into position. When she was sure it was where it needed to be she held her hand out again.

"Bolt One," she said.

"Bolt One," Joey repeated, handing it over.

"Spanner."

"Spanner?"

Sam glanced at her, then at the spanner and pointed to it.

"We call that a wrench." Joey tutted.

Seconds later. "Bolt Two." Everything was going well, but it was a fiddly operation. Sam knew that one slip could lose a valuable part somewhere in the engine casing. Would it ever be recovered? Not without removing more parts. She could not afford to get this wrong.

"Bolt Three," she said.

Its name was whispered back and handed over.

Sam nearly dropped it and heard Joey's breath catch. Sam caught it before it hit the floor. Joey watched her intently as she wiped the sweat from her eyes.

Seconds later, Sam leaned back. "Attach the multimeter and test the wiring."

Joey's long fingers moved fast. "Attached," she breathed quietly.

"Do we have output?"

"Yes!" Joey couldn't hide her elation.

Sam stared at her, unable to hide her respect. "Would you like to close?"

Joey gave a quick serious nod and moved into position.

"Clean spark plugs," she ordered, and Sam passed them to her one by one without delay. They had checked the gap clearances with a gauge earlier. She watched in awe as Joey's nimble fingers placed them into position and tightened them.

"Ouch," Joey suddenly bleated. "Band-Aid."

"One Band-Aid." Sam handed it over, noticing it was the last one. The tin had been half full when they started. There had been setbacks. "Can you go on?" she asked Joey.

"We must."

Sam nodded in admiration. Joey was good. Her bike was in safe hands.

"Oily rag," Joey said finally as she then proceeded to wipe around the area of operation. She leaned back. "We're done. We can't do more."

"Let's hope we've done enough."

"We've tried." Joey sounded sympathetic.

They rose together, stretching their limbs.

"What if it doesn't work?" Sam asked.

"You can always get a new bike."

"A new bike?" Sam broke the reverent surgical mood. "Are you mad, woman?"

Didn't Joey understand? She hoped she was joking. "I could never part with her. She's the one thing that gets me through. Without her, I'm lost. She keeps me sane, even if she does break down and leave me stranded."

When everything got on top of her, Sam would come home, saddle up, and ride out. Even when the damn thing didn't work, she loved getting her hands dirty and tinkering with the engine.

Work really was pushing her to her limits.

The church had bestowed upon her the title of canon.

The Reverend Canon Samantha Savage.

Such a mouthful and she seldom used it. It was supposed to recognize honorable work within the diocese, for faithful and valuable service. What it really meant was being given more responsibility. There was too much work before. Now it was ridiculous. She was in charge of several other vicars, one of whom she had no respect for, nor he for her. She found working with him, the Reverend Nicolas Bentley, stressful. She couldn't call him old school, but some of his values were antiquated at best, and wrong at worst. But that was another issue.

She was without a treasurer, and having to do all the tasks that involved. Then there was the roof, or lack of it. Her list of tasks was endless, but she tried to obliterate them all from her mind and stay focused. It didn't help when her day seemed to start almost as soon as the last one ended.

Sam was amazed she hadn't been called out today. She was at the end of her tether. No one could keep going like this forever. Maybe her gasket was about to blow. She felt more like an accountant than a cleric. Even before she saw Louise, everything had been gnawing away inside. She simply wasn't happy, and hadn't been for some time for she was being pulled in the wrong direction. And now Joey had the audacity to suggest she might consider parting with her bike if it didn't work?

"I can't imagine *you* have problems," Joey said. "You seem so in control and loving what you do. I doubt anything rocks your cradle."

"You think? Believe me, even vicars have issues."

"Like?"

"Like I have absolutely no intention of spoiling this enjoyable moment by whining about work. I'm having a wonderful time and don't want to ruin it."

Joey apparently understood and let the subject drop as she stretched her long limbs again. Then she looked at Sam and her face wore a tight smile.

"Tell me, *Vicar*. Are you in a habit of bringing strangers back to your home?"

The slant of the question was unexpected.

"You're not a stranger. You're my organist."

"Temporary." Joey tilted her head.

"Perhaps." As Sam joked, she couldn't help noticing the ever-present dark shadows around Joey's eyes.

"Temporary. Don't get any ideas." Joey hesitated. "So are you?"

Sam squinted. "Not usually."

It was true. She didn't often bring people back here. Any official business was usually conducted in the church offices. As for real friends beyond acquaintances, she didn't seem to have many. She was too busy. Any spare time she had, she coveted it. It was unusual that she'd invited Joey back to her sanctuary. She wondered why. Apparently, so did Joey.

"Why me, then?" Joey asked.

"I don't know." Sam did find it curious, and it was too easy to say it was the biking connection. She liked Joey from the moment she met her, and the more she was with her, the more she grew on her. "Maybe it's your accent." But the simplistic lighthearted answer didn't appease Joey. Something was on her mind. It didn't stay there long.

Joey's face grew serious, and Sam wondered what was coming.

"I want you to know I'm gay."

Sam didn't see *this* coming. "Are you in the habit of telling everyone your sexuality?"

Joey's gaze was intense. "Only when I think it might matter. When I think the person in question matters…and when I want to be dumped quickly before I get hurt. I've found it pays to sort these issues out early. I don't hide who I am, and this allows people to back off."

"That's not going to happen," Sam said.

"There are people out there who don't like people like me."

"I'm not one of them." Sam stared back at her.

Joey said nothing.

"Okay?" Sam said pointedly.

"Okay."

"I'm glad that's sorted. Now come and sit on my bike."

Sam straddled the motorcycle and indicated Joey get on behind. She stretched her arms out, resting her hands on the handles. It felt good, and she closed her eyes, imagining she was out on the road, totally in control and cruising fast. She felt Joey snuggle up behind her. Several thoughts ran through her mind. Most were to do with the intimacy Joey's physical closeness brought, and how Sam was surprisingly comfortable with it. But the dominant one was of the pale Joey seated in the church only a few days earlier, agitated and sweating brought about by the unexpected crash of building equipment. Joey's reaction had been extreme, and it was adding to Sam's concerns and curiosity.

Sam removed her hands from the handles and placed them in her lap. She straightened her back.

"Joey, since you've aired your sexuality, and the ground hasn't opened and swallowed you, would you mind if I ask you something of a personal nature?"

"You can ask."

"What is it that puts those dark shadows under your eyes?"

"You think they take away from my flawless beauty?" Joey played superficial.

Sam saw it as a defense mechanism.

"Your flawless beauty remains intact, my child. But the shadows?"

"I don't sleep well."

It was an honest answer and one Sam didn't doubt.

"Why would that be?" she asked.

"I suffer from nightmares."

"May I ask what fuels those nightmares?"

Sam felt Joey tense.

"It's not something I like to talk about."

"Something happened?"

There was a pause before Joey answered, "Yes."

"And you don't like to think about it."

"When I do, everything gets tense and I can't breathe. I try not to revisit it."

"But you do."

"Memories keep coming back at me unexpectedly. They're always intense. The nights are worse. It's when the nightmares come."

"Are you seeing a counselor?"

"No." Joey's answer was quick. "It was a waste of time. She made me feel worse."

Speech is silver, but silence is golden. Sam believed the saying and she waited. She was rewarded when she felt Joey rest her head on her back.

Sam sensed a window in Joey's defenses. She played her ace and hoped she wasn't misjudging the situation. If she was, Joey might run.

"Is this about what happened to you and your team in Syria?"

Joey sat up. "You know?"

"Only what I've read on the Internet," Sam said softly, "and what has ended up in the media."

"You never said anything."

"No. I've been waiting for you to."

Sam sensed Joey's discomfort.

"How long have you known?" Joey asked.

"I've known something was wrong for a while now. Elsa said something about you needing to heal, and when that scout knocked the ladder over in church, your reaction wasn't simple shock. That's when I hit the Internet and did some research." Sam paused. "I hope you don't mind."

"Oh, Sam." Joey rested her head again on Sam's back, this time wrapping her arms around her waist.

Sam's attention was briefly distracted by the action. She forced herself to focus.

She thought of what she'd read on the Web, of what had happened to Joey and her colleagues. It was painful reading. That Joey had survived and been rescued was a miracle. The fact she was haunted by the event was expected. Sam was treading on delicate ground. She didn't want to ruin anything. She hoped her words would encourage Joey to talk, that they would be a bridge she might cross. Sam sensed she needed to.

"What I read scared me, Joey. What happened to you out there defies all civilized explanation. I pray such incidents are isolated events, but they never are. History shows their recurrence regardless of what we do. And for those who get caught up in the vileness of it?" She looked down at Joey's arms wrapped around her and her own hands covering hers. A fierce streak of protectiveness ran through her.

"Joey, we grow up in some leafy, safe place where everything that happens is predicted, assumed, and we know how to act. When we end up somewhere and experience carnage and atrocities beyond our imagination, we place standards on ourselves and we think we have to carry on as normal, and take it all in our stride. When we don't, we punish ourselves, and we become confused.

Our brain tries to rationalize what's happened. If we can't, we break down. We can no longer do the things that once seemed simple."

Sam turned her head to speak over her shoulder.

"I can't imagine what you've been through or the nightmares that haunt you. What I read fills me with fear, and I'm over here, thousands of miles away, safe in rural sleepy England."

Joey's arms tightened around Sam as she spoke.

"I thought I was above it all, Sam. I thought I was invincible and that nothing would happen…not to me, or to anyone with me. But it did. And it's shattered my world. I'm scared shitless. I'm scared to be what I was before, in case this happens again."

Sam wanted to tell her that was unlikely, but Joey spoke first.

"I know, I know. It's unlikely to happen to me again, but it doesn't stop the fear. And I'm ashamed."

"Why?" Sam whispered.

"I'm ashamed because I shouldn't be like this. I'm an investigative journalist. It's my job, my career. It's something I've done all my working life. I'm supposed to be tenacious, indomitable, and relentless in the search for revelation, and for truth. Not cowering away like this."

"You've been traumatized. You've lost your confidence."

"I've lost faith in myself, Sam. I've lost my belief. Without that, I'm nothing."

Sam rose from the motorbike, turned around, and sat down again facing her. She took her hands back into hers.

"I fear being successful." Joey paused. "When I went back to work, they put me in front of the camera again. It was easy stuff for me, but I kept breaking down. It was almost a deliberate thing, like I wanted to fail."

"Why do you think you did that?"

"So the wonderful Josephine Barry won't be expected to go back out there. They wanted me to." Joey stared hard at Sam. "You must think I'm a coward."

"I don't. It takes guts to have done what you have. But bravery isn't a bottomless pit." Sam shook Joey's hands, lightened her voice, and smiled. "If you were a believer, this is the part where I tell you that God does not give us the power to think and rationalize for nothing."

"I lost my friends, Sam, all of them. I was the only one that got out. They were murdered."

"Yes, they were, but it wasn't your fault."

"It *was* my fault. I don't want to talk about this anymore."

Sam saw survivor's guilt on Joey's face. She also saw a barrier descend and watched as Joey distanced herself from the memories. Sam wouldn't push.

"It feels like there's a liquid inside me, Sam, that is sloshing around violently. I can't control it and it's hitting the sides all the time, knocking me around."

"Then stop moving. Stand still and stop setting yourself standards. Be kind to yourself and give it time. Liquid settles and finds its level. Don't fight it."

Unexpectedly, Joey smiled. "You have a very calming influence."

"That's because I'm a vicar. It's what we do." Sam rubbed Joey's hands "None of us are as strong as we make out...as we'd like to be."

"You are."

Sam laughed and shook her head. "No, I'm not."

"Well, you look it."

"Inside I'm crying," Sam said.

Joey looked as if she wanted to hear more, but Sam thought it hardly the time. "A conversation for another day," she said. She gave Joey's hands a squeeze. As she did so, for an infinitesimal moment, a look passed between them. Whatever it was, it was mutual and they both grew self-conscious and suddenly ill at ease in such close proximity.

Sam distanced herself and hopped off the motorcycle.

"When will you test the bike?" Joey remained seated.

"I can't today, no time. But maybe tomorrow, after Sunday service."

"You'll have to let me know how it goes."

Sam was shocked. "I'm not testing her without you. Are you free? Say, about twelve thirty? I don't have evening prayers until after six. We could ride out somewhere and have lunch."

Joey wasn't playing the organ tomorrow; Maude was back in town. She had no arrangements. A bike trip would be fun.

"What if it breaks down?" she asked.

"It won't. I have faith." Sam grinned. "But if it does, we'll have a long walk home."

"I'll put my walking shoes on."

Sam stepped back and trod on something.

"Oh, not good." She bent down and picked something up. It was a bolt. A bright shiny new bolt.

Joey and Sam shared a glance.

"Call me suspicious, but isn't that supposed to be in the bike somewhere?" Joey said.

Sam took a deep breath. "Well, it isn't now, and I'm not going back into the casing." She studied it before handing it over to Joey. "Here, put this in your pocket. It's your lucky bolt. Keep it on you."

"A lucky bolt? Isn't it supposed to be a rabbit's foot?"

"Dare to be different."

Joey placed the unused bolt into her pocket. "I'll treasure it."

The earlier embarrassment forgotten, Joey eventually left leaving Sam to prepare for evening service.

Sam tidied the tools up. As she did, her mind was awash with conflicting thoughts.

She didn't doubt that Joey was traumatized by what had happened on the Syrian border. She didn't doubt she was drowning in guilt and suffering from PTSD. That was all to be expected. But Joey seemed *too* intent on blaming herself for the death of her colleagues. The fact was the rebels had fired on them and all but Joey had died. Those actions had not been Joey's to control.

Sam wasn't sure why, but she sensed there was something else that plagued Joey. Right or wrong, Sam wanted to help. All she could do was wait, be patient, and listen.

The second issue on her mind was more complicated.

Sam knew Joey was a lesbian before she'd told her. She'd read it on the Internet. Joey hadn't lied when she said she didn't hide who she was. The consequences of that had been some particularly nasty and vitriolic discussion on social media from the loony squad about God's retribution on homosexuals and lesbians. It had enraged Sam, and even more when some of it was written by so-called ministers of the church. That certainly answered part of why Sam was keen to be with Joey, to protect and help her. But it didn't answer what had made her invite her back so quickly in the beginning. And why was it she heard Louise's voice in the background whenever Joey was around?

Joey wasn't lying when she told Sam she had problems sleeping.

When she managed to fall asleep, she had nightmares.

She would be back near the Syrian border and often inside the cramped cabinet under the sink. There was always something menacing and faceless hovering nearby that would fill her so full of fear, she would wake gasping for breath and terrified.

When she was awake, the slightest sound, word, or smell could bring intrusive, upsetting memories that played on her mind like an infection that would not go away.

She took to wandering around her apartment at night, grateful she was no longer at Auntie Elsa's where she would disturb and worry her.

A surprising highlight in her life was the job with Stallion Film Productions. She hadn't wanted to come here, but everything was working out well. It seemed they were impressed with her experience and knowledge. They liked her take on issues and her ideas for documentary angles. As much as she could, she was able to relax. No one demanded she stand in front of a camera. She was firmly a "behind the scenes" specialist.

Her work colleagues were nice too. They knew what had happened to her, but she never felt it was an issue—that people were watching her, looking for the cracks like they had back home. If stress reared its head with *any* of them—the BBC had demanding and tight deadlines—their answer was always a pot of therapeutic tea, then back to the grindstone.

It was three in the morning as she looked out her sitting room window. Her apartment was in an urban, built-up area, and by day, the view was unappealing. At night however, as she looked down the street and at the line of parked cars below, life seemed different. Nothing moved, and everywhere was lit by tall streetlamps that gave off a strange green hue. Their light made the place seem different, as if the quiet, unassuming road before her might lead to a mythical land, another world.

She shivered. It was summer, but the nights were cool.

She rubbed her hands and thought of Sam yesterday on the motorbike.

Sam had held her hands.

Joey stared at them now as if there was still some visible residue of where Sam had touched her. She remembered the softness of her hands and their warmth. Was she overreacting, making a song and dance about it? It was a small matter, but to have such physical connection with another human being—it had been too long. Always before, it had been there, but when she'd needed it most, it wasn't.

Before she went to Balshir, she never wanted for female company. They lined up. When she came back, they were still there. But after she started to fall apart, when she broke down on live national television and the press discussed her "mental state," they dropped away like autumn leaves. Suddenly, they were sorry, they were busy. Hadn't they mentioned they would be out of town—for months? If they saw her out, they diverted their eyes and pretended not to see her.

Josephine Barry was no longer the person to be seen with—the journalist who held an impressive array of awards and honorary doctorates. Now she was an embarrassment.

Joey was getting a painful, late lesson in life. You get out of life what you put in. She would go through women like a kid through a bag of jelly beans. Now when she needed someone, anyone, in her life, no one was there.

Maybe it was because her professional life consumed everything she did, leaving her with little time for real relationships. Maybe it was because she was shallow. Whatever the answer, it hadn't mattered before Syria. Somehow the lack of correlation had produced balance. But now her career was in tatters, the stability was gone, and she swayed in the air like untethered rope in the wind.

For once in her life, she was lonely. There was no one to turn to except family. They were there for her and tried to protect her, but it only made her feel smothered. Now she was a stranger in a strange land. And yet she was beginning to feel at home.

She knew it had much to do with Sam.

The enigmatic Reverend Samantha Savage was in her life. A denim wearing, occasional cursing vicar with a huge passion for motorbikes, and lost souls. She wondered if that was why Sam bothered with her. In her vocation, she was privy to all kinds of private information, encountering people with every sort of issue. Joey was no different. She was someone with an issue right now. Sam's professional sensitivity picked up on that almost immediately. Joey was probably just another person on Sam's list of "things to do, people to sort."

She hoped it was more than that. She liked Sam very much. Joey connected with her and found her a comforting influence; she was quieter and calmer when she was in Sam's company. But she couldn't ignore the fact that Sam was a vicar first and foremost. Her natural concern and benevolence was built into her job.

But it didn't matter to Joey. Not really. Someone—someone nice—was bothering to get to know her, include her in their life, and listen. Sam really listened and heard the subtext. She was also non-judgmental. Joey was sick of those back home who labeled her and never hesitated to tell her she'd brought everything down on herself because of her lifestyle. No one seemed to care about people's personal lives over here.

She wrapped her arms around herself and shivered as she looked at the clock on the sideboard. It was after three thirty. She needed to try to get some sleep. She had something to look forward to. Sam was picking her up for lunch, and they were going for a bike ride. Joey started to smile. Maybe her excitement would chase away her guilt and the nightmares would leave her alone for once.

She ambled back to bed.

Chapter Six

L et's go for a spin," Sam said.
    She was sitting on her bike outside Joey's apartment as she threw her a helmet. Joey caught it with the seasoned panache of an England fielding cricketer.

God forgive her, but Sam had prayed all morning that her two Sunday services would pass quickly and without the usual string of parishioners waiting afterward to chat. Her prayers were answered. Not a single person approached her, and she'd left church in record time, getting home to change and fire up the motorbike.

Sam was in high spirits. She wanted to test the bike out and see if the recent irritating problems were resolved. But more, she was looking forward to spending time with Joey. Her bonhomie had peaked when Joey had approached her waving. Sam didn't miss the surge of pleasure that crossed Joey's face. She was excited too. Sam found herself hoping that the emotion was more for her than the joy of a bike ride on a hot sunny day.

Joey climbed on behind her.

"We're going Bridgnorth way," Sam said through the lifted visor. "I know a great place for lunch."

She dropped the dark plastic back down over her face.

Then they were off.

Sam took it easy until they were out of town. Once onto the longer country roads, the biker demon took over. With a flick of her hand, she increased speed and heard the corresponding power kick in beneath her. She felt Joey behind her, closeup, like she had been in the kitchen. Her arms were wrapped tight around her waist, and something deep inside Sam warmed.

It didn't take her long to realize Joey was no newcomer to biking. She'd said she'd ridden with her father a lot. It showed. As Sam veered left on a tight corner, so did Joey. The two of them were like liquid fusion.

The sun glittered through a copse of trees in the distance as they passed Shatterford and Bellman's Cross. They rode past the old wood mill to the left and a fancy home that had once been a school hall. The road forked, and Sam turned right and up the sloping hill. At the top, she could see the country pub she was heading for in the distance. She increased speed again, wanting to put the bike through its paces. She dared the bike to let her down. But nothing fell off. Nothing went clank. No engine power loss. All the old signs of misery were missing. Another of Sam's prayers might have been answered.

The pub grew larger and Sam finally came to a halt under a large oak tree in the parking lot. Shade was a necessity on a hot day like today. She removed her helmet before alighting.

Joey's was already off and she was shaking her long hair loose. As she ran her fingers through her locks, Sam's breath caught and something inside her tingled. Joey was throwing her head back and actually laughing.

"God, that was exhilarating. I've missed rides like this." She set her blue eyes on Sam. "And you, you're an accomplished rider. I loved every minute of that."

Sam wasn't used to such praise. She hid her pride with humor. "Translated...*I didn't fall off.*"

Joey bowed her head graciously. "Not even close."

Sam patted her on the arm in a friendly gesture, nudging her into the pub before her own head grew too large to get through the door.

"Do you think we've fixed her?" Joey said.

"She sounds good. The test will come when we leave. I see you have your walking shoes on."

"I never take chances."

"All the kicking on the planet won't start her if we've failed. Let's get a drink and order. We may need the sustenance."

The drinks were barely in their hands when Joey said, "Yesterday, you said you're crying inside."

"I did?"

"You did. It was when I asked if you had issues."

"It was only a figure of speech." Sam tried to make nothing of it.

"It was said with meaning."

"It wasn't anything important." They'd only just arrived and Joey was straight into the serious stuff.

"It's important. I heard it in your voice." Joey wasn't going to let this drop.

Sam sighed. "I haven't even sipped my drink and you're into this like an attack ferret."

"Forget at your peril that you're dining with an investigative journalist. I don't hang around. I like to get straight to the point."

Sam nodded. "How could I forget?"

They moved outside to a rectangular picnic table and back into the sunshine.

Sam didn't want to bleat, but Joey was persistent.

"If you really must know, I have no church treasurer. The last incumbent left some months ago, and *I've* been doing the job since. It's a big enough task at the best of times, but now? You might have noticed that I have an impressive church with no roof. I have no money at this time for repairing the roof so I'm also spearheading the appeal. I'm also down one curate so there's no one to assist me in my admin, pastoral, and liturgical responsibilities. I'm actually supposed to have two given the size of the parish. Sorry you asked?"

Joey shook her head so Sam continued.

"What I do have is a growing congregation with increasing needs. I have builders in my church at all hours. I have dust everywhere, and I have woodworm. I have one particular vicar who gives me nothing but issues. We clash. And finally, I have a phone that rings off the hook and I think I'm going mad."

"But apart from that everything's fine," Joey responded dryly. Sam smiled.

"I guess it's the recession and the church is not immune. They need us to do more with less. The powers that be seem to forget we're human too. When I started at St. Mary's I was given a large geographical area with a sizable population. Now that parish is half the size again, and with increased responsibility. There are times I meet myself coming back from places. I hate moaning, but things get depressing sometimes." Sam took a long drink. "But I have a wonderful team of willing volunteers, and for that I'm grateful. But they're not permanent and they can't baptize, marry, or bury people, or administer to religious needs."

Sam gave a throaty groan. "Oh, and as of this morning, Maude, my organist, has given me one month's notice. She says she's too old to do this anymore."

The real reason was more painful. Poor Maude had overheard some detrimental comments about her playing. While the remarks had been accurate, the way they'd been said was harsh. They'd not been meant for Maude's ears, but she'd heard them anyway. Now her feelings were irreparably hurt. Sam's attempts to soften the criticism had failed. Maude would not play for much longer.

"If this is the bit where you attempt to blackmail me into becoming your permanent organist—"

Sam cut her dead. "Relax. I think I've found someone. There's a young scout leader who's just moved into the area. He's been the organist for his last church and is more than keen to take over from Maude. He's ready to start as soon as she steps down. So something is going right."

Sam was grateful. The young man had overheard Maude's resignation and sensitively mentioned his desire to take over. He even suggested asking Maude to "show him the ropes" later in the week, and allow him to shadow her. Sam thought this a great idea.

It would give Maude some dignity back, helping—training—the replacement. She hoped he wouldn't pick up any of her musical abilities.

Their meals arrived and they started eating.

"Can't anybody help?" Joey asked.

"Yes. Neil…Bishop of the diocese…he's working on all the staff shortages and doing the best he can. The trouble is people aren't joining the church like they used to and everything is getting spread thinly. I'm sure all will improve."

Sam wasn't sure at all, but let the subject drop.

"On a lighter note, Carrie Marlow is turning up tomorrow to do that interview for the local radio station. I'm hoping some airtime might bring money into the appeal fund. So how's your new job going?"

"All right, I think. We get along well together and they like my ideas. I enjoy going to work so it's a good start."

Sam was pleased Joey was settling in.

"Did you buy the Tiffany lamp?"

"I did. It's now sitting on the small table you and I placed by the side of the couch."

"Sounds homey."

"I'm nesting. You'll have to come over one night for dinner."

"I'd love to." Sam would look forward to that. When she was around Joey, it didn't feel like work. She could leave her *dog collar* behind and be plain old Sam for once. Even when she was with Neil and his family, she was always aware that he was the bishop. Her time with Joey was beginning to feel like she had a real life.

But she couldn't entirely walk away from her concerns for Joey. It wasn't her job talking; it was a growing friendship. She wanted to see if Joey would talk some more about what had happened out in Syria. Joey continued to look exhausted and in need of quality sleep. Sam was glad they'd shared something of a conversation about what had happened to her, but she was under no illusions that Joey kept emotions tight and would only talk so much before the barriers came down. They'd been down for too long now, and Sam knew the dangers of lids sealing and contents festering beneath. But she wouldn't raise the topic today. Joey was having fun, and Sam didn't want to ruin anything. She could wait.

"I'm going to miss not playing for you," Joey broke Sam's chain of thought.

"Bless you." Sam beamed. "I'm sure you have more pressing matters for your time now, but I've loved having you play...as have the congregation," she said, not without humor. "If you feel the need to tinkle the ivories again, you have only to say the word. I'm sure we can accommodate a guest spot."

They were interrupted by Sam's cell. She tried to ignore it, but Joey insisted she answer.

It was Stephen Bell. His mother was in the local hospital and had taken a turn for the worst. She was not expected to last the day, and Stephen was asking if Sam could see his mother. She told Stephen she would be there as soon as she could.

"I'm sorry, Joey." Sam couldn't hide her disappointment.

"Something's happened?"

"One of my flock isn't well. She's in hospital and not expected to see the day out. Her son wants me to go see her. I really have to."

"Of course. You must."

Sam was thankful for Joey's understanding.

"I can get a taxi home," Joey added.

"No need for that. I have to go home and change, grab a few bits and bobs, so I can drop you off. That is if the bike starts."

The BSA A10 Golden Flash motorbike fired into life at the first kick, and they made it back in record time.

Sam dropped Joey off.

"I'm sorry. I hope I haven't ruined your day," Sam said.

"You haven't. It's been great, and you did warn me that your phone rings off the hook."

"Yes, I just wish it hadn't today."

Just before Sam left, Joey said, "You're a nice person, you know? The lady in the hospital will be glad you're there."

The compliment sent a tingle down Sam's spine. As she rode back to the vicarage to change, she wished that cell phones had never been invented.

❖

Joey's reprieve from organ playing was short.

Sam's begging phone messages were now becoming routine. She needed Joey to play at the church yet again because no one else was available. This time it was for a couple of hours one evening later that week.

It was for the bishop's certificate course, a weekly event which was led by Bishop Neil Covey-Smartingdon. It was for those who wanted to learn more about the Bible and the greater theories of Christian faith. Sam needed her at St. Mary's to play a couple of short old hymns to show symbolic interpretation of prayer in song. Joey had no idea what that meant, but playing held dual opportunity. She would see Sam again and get to meet the bishop Sam spoke of with such warmth.

Joey raced to the church from work and arrived just in time.

Sam's welcome was warm if a little hurried. "Thanks, Joey. I owe you. Neil is about to start. The music's up there," she indicated the organ, "along with the program. I think it's straightforward, but I'll give you a nod when you need to play. Your two pieces are short. I'm giving a brief talk on an area of diocese history which Carrie, the lady from the BBC radio station, is going to record. She interviewed me yesterday but wants more. She's already here. I must dash. See you later."

As Joey made her way up on to the mezzanine level to play, she could see Carrie seated a few pews behind the students with a recording device on her lap. As if by instinct and knowing she was being observed, Carrie turned and looked up at Joey. She smiled and waved. Joey nodded back.

As she settled at the organ, she couldn't resist a sneaky glance back at Carrie who was now occupied with the recorder. She was not an unattractive woman, probably in her mid thirties. A healthy mop of shiny brown curly hair fell to shoulder length, and she wore a vivid bright lipstick that contrasted with her pale skin. She would have studied her more, but the bishop started to talk.

For the next ninety minutes, Joey's attention was firmly rested on the evening's proceedings, and it took minimal time for her to realize what Sam saw in Bishop Neil. He was nothing like she expected a bishop to be. There was no stuffiness or formality. This man was handsome in a friendly sort of way, and when he laughed, everyone laughed with him. He made everything he spoke of interesting, and you wanted to listen.

Sam didn't disappoint either. She spoke of Danish Vikings coming up the River Severn on their way to Bridgnorth, and of the possibility of monastic ruins beneath the current St. Mary's. Her lively delivery engaged all of the twenty attendees whose ages ranged from mid twenties to late seventies, and her handling of some in-depth questions at the end was good. Joey felt a strange sense of pride.

Everything drew to a close, and she headed down to meet with Sam. As she stood waiting, Carrie came over to talk. For a reporter, she was in no rush to leave.

"You play very well." Carrie's voice was light and chirpy. "Do you mind if I use some of it in the background of the interview I'm putting together? I'll give your name a mention."

"I'm not the resident player. I'm covering for absences."

"That doesn't matter. It'll all add to the sentiment of the piece." Carrie subconsciously head flicked her dark hair before locking intense eyes on Joey. "So, what's an American doing over here in Worcestershire?"

"I'm doing some consulting work with a company called Stallion Film Productions. They do work for the BBC and produce—"

"Wonderful documentaries," Carrie interrupted, clearly impressed. "I know them. Who doesn't? They've won plenty of awards. If you're working for them, you must be good."

She was a woman who oozed confidence and charm. Joey got the distinct impression she was flirting with her. She knew the signs, and they were flashing away like beacons. She was the type Joey had gone for in the past, but she wasn't interested now. Something major had shifted in her since Syria, a constant whispering in her head that she needed to be more than she had been. If she was the survivor, she needed to deserve that. She found herself looking over to where Sam was, down the far end of the aisle. She was deep in conversation with Neil.

Sam was pleased with how well the evening had gone. Neil didn't attend every session but when he did, it was clear the students appreciated his presence and his dry wit. Tonight was no exception. Only now were the students beginning to drift away leaving the two of them able to talk.

"Do you want to stay for coffee?" Sam asked.

Neil shook his head. "Better not. I've an early start tomorrow and will be driving down to London. I'm off to Lambeth Palace for a meeting with the archbishop."

Sam shook her head and smiled. Neil said it as if he was popping into the local chemist for a quick consultation with the pharmacist. The Archbishop of Canterbury was the head of the Anglican Church.

"Anything important?" she asked.

As usual, Neil was flippant and wrapped everything in humor. "He needs my guidance. I can never refuse him."

The last person on earth to need any guidance was the new archbishop. He was a man with drive and plenty of fresh ideas. The church was torn over issues of power and sexuality. There was never going to be agreement, especially with some of the overseas churches. The archbishop was looking for fresh ways to solve emotional concerns. Neil had strong opinions of what was needed to modernize the church and make it more appealing to the young. He'd often met with resistance from the old school, but it seemed he and the new archbishop shared a common vision.

"You do realize you're destined for higher places, Neil. He doesn't keep asking you down to London because he likes your

jokes. He's sussing out his new team to help him forge changes…
and you're going to be one of them."

Neil grew serious. "Miriam says that."

"She's right. He values your opinion. Any transformations
will have to be driven by good minds. He wants the right team
around him so he gets the best help."

"Talking of best help, your new organist plays delightfully.
And I hope I won't get hit by a bolt of lightning for saying this, but
Maude's absence is a blessing from heaven."

"Don't. She overheard some unpleasant comments about her
playing and has taken them to heart."

"Well—" Neil started to say, but Sam interrupted.

"No, Neil. It was cruel and she doesn't deserve them. She's
only ever tried to do her best, and frankly, without her, we wouldn't
have had anyone."

Neil looked chastised. "You're right. Maybe you could let me
know when she's around next. I'd like to thank her…spoil her. I'll
do a little presentation in church in front of everyone."

"She'd like that. It'll mean a lot."

"Can you come to lunch next Sunday?"

"Love to."

"What about your American…Joey? You said she's from
Baltimore? I did a sabbatical there years ago and had a wonderful
time. Do you think we can ask her to lunch, too? The more the
merrier. Miriam always cooks for the five thousand anyway."

"I'm sure she'd love that."

"Good," Neil said. "I'll ask her in a minute. She seems busy."

Sam looked down the aisle and saw Carrie and Joey standing
together chatting away like old friends. Carrie was grinning like an
inmate out on a day pass. It was plain to see she was smitten with
Joey. An odd flicker of resentment passed through Sam. It didn't
help when she saw her pass Joey a card…which she took.

Neil started talking to someone, and Sam chose the opportunity
to walk down to Joey and Carrie. As she approached them, she
caught the end of their conversation.

"If you need anything, information or whatever, you give me a call. We BBC people should stick together," Carrie said. "I can also show you around the place if you want."

"Thanks, but it's always difficult finding the time."

Unexpected satisfaction filled Sam, knowing Joey wasn't interested. It unsettled her to realize she was showing a measure of possessiveness toward Joey. Sam was self-examining her unusual behavior when Carrie turned to her.

"Reverend Savage, thank you. This has been great and I've got everything I want. I'll be in touch and let you know when the program airs." Her attention shifted back to Joey. "If you change your mind, you know where I am."

Sam didn't miss the coquettish look on Carrie's face. She was glad when she left.

"Found a new friend?" Sam said.

"No."

"Looks like you have to me."

"I haven't. It's just the BBC connection."

"Really?"

"Really."

Sam faked casual indifference, but Joey's eyes narrowed. They would have disappeared into slits but for Neil's appearance.

"Ah, the wonderful organist." He bounced up to them in energetic manner, thrusting his hand forward. "Hello, Joey, I'm Neil, Sam's friend and resident bishop of the diocese."

Joey shook his hand and smiled back.

"I was wondering if you'd like to come to lunch on Sunday. Sam's coming too. She tells me you're from Baltimore? I was out there once and would love to talk about the place. You can meet my wife. She loves Americans!"

"I'd be delighted," Joey answered. "It'll give me a chance to catch up with Sam too."

Sam noted the shrewd look Joey cast her.

❖

Sam returned to the vicarage after lunch at Miriam and Neil's. It had been a wonderful time, and the laughter had flowed with abandon.

As usual, it was a feast, and Sam always left feeling ten pounds heavier. Miriam was a born socialite who enjoyed nothing better than entertaining. If Neil was destined for higher places, Miriam would be a blessing. She could cook and hold conversation with anyone. Even the most reserved opened up to her and started chirping like a budgie.

It was because of that gift that Sam had been full of reservations when she and Joey arrived. Miriam's usual sharp cutting twenty questions aimed at getting to know someone had the potential to backfire with Joey. She would not want to talk about herself, and Miriam would view it as a challenge. Sam was becoming aware that Joey hid her trauma well, and that what Sam saw and heard was only the tip of the problem. Miriam was damn nosey, and Sam often thought she had missed her true vocation and would have made a splendid journalist. She didn't want Miriam stomping around Joey's fragile psyche.

But from the moment they arrived, Miriam avoided all the hotspots with the precision of a human landmine detector. Sam felt guilty. Neil's wife was a perceptive woman, and Sam should have given her more credit for spotting signs. The outcome was Sam's fears did not materialize. Miriam and Joey hit it off straightaway.

As for Neil, he talked animatedly about his time in Baltimore, and at St. Basil's. Joey listened and laughed, and even knew a few of the people he mentioned through her mother's church connections.

Though Sam enjoyed every lunch she came to here and was always made to feel one of the family, this one was special.

"So, how are you settling in, Joey?" Miriam asked.

"Really well, thanks. I love the job and the people I work with. I wasn't too sure I would, but they're smart people with vision."

"And living arrangements?" Miriam asked.

"The apartment is nice."

"You're not lonely?"

"I'm making friends, and some of them are turning out to be exceptionally nice"—Joey turned and rested a hand on Sam's shoulder—"even if they do have hidden musical agendas."

Everyone had laughed. Sam had too. It covered the strange nervousness she suddenly felt as Joey touched her. Many of her congregation were tactile and she was used to it, but none of them made her feel like this, sensitive to every movement Joey made. She was becoming keenly aware of everything physical about Joey—her laughter, the intonations of her voice, her scent. Many times throughout lunch, Joey continued to touch her. It was always light and innocent, but it always produced the same effect on Sam. Only one other person had held that power. Louise.

"I hear you're good with the motorbike too," Miriam said.

Joey flicked her chin in response.

"Now I see why Sam thinks you're wonderful." Miriam stood. "I'll go get dessert. Darling, we need another bottle of wine."

Neil disappeared too, leaving Sam and Joey alone.

"So you think I'm wonderful?" Joey arched an eyebrow Sam's way.

God help her, Sam felt her face redden. Joey didn't seem to notice.

"There's something very nice," Joey said, "about being a twosome at a lunch table, isn't there? I'm usually by myself."

Joey was voicing exactly what Sam felt.

Sam thought of her own experiences at social functions. She was always alone. Ecclesiastical dinners and church soirees often seated her next to someone with the personality of a dead fish. Not that she objected, but it seemed that was her role. Today at lunch, it was different. She didn't feel alone, and she was amazed at how much more alive she felt. It was all because Joey was here.

The other night in church, Neil referred to Joey as "your American." The sentiment had stuck in Sam's mind. An array of new feelings ran through her. She couldn't stop thinking of her own strange behavior toward Carrie, resenting her apparent interest in Joey.

She thought also of Louise and her words "not to let life and love pass her by." Had Louise sensed Sam's growing fear? She was right. It was what made her unhappy, and why she no longer felt fulfilled by her vocation.

The strangest seed germinated in Sam's mind. What if she found someone? Was it really too late for her? Reality kicked her in the gut as it reminded her she was a vicar and that any relationship of her choosing would be lesbian. The church was making huge strides forward. There were many in it who announced their sexuality, but it always came with great rancor and bitterness. The church was still divided regardless of what anyone decreed. Did Sam want to get caught up in that? People would leave her congregation in a show of resistance. She'd seen it happen. This was not why she'd chosen to follow God. She didn't want to be the source of people *leaving* the church. She wanted to welcome them to it.

But why couldn't she love and be loved back?

Her thoughts strayed to Joey.

She was a true woman of the world, not someone who existed in a parochial narrow channel such as Sam's. But it didn't stop Sam recognizing how attractive Joey was both inside and out. Sam also knew she *was* attracted to her. Of course, she'd invited her back to the vicarage. Not with any intentions but just to pass time with someone she enjoyed being with. Joey would have no interest in the likes of her. Who would look twice at a fifty-something-year-old, a religious minister who had the onslaught of gray hair? Joey was a renowned journalist.

But Sam could dream.

Chapter Seven

Half a dozen cigarette ends lay on the ground around the more sheltered side of the church. They weren't there yesterday evening.

Sam studied them with a forensic eye. They weren't the same brand. She noticed several different boot imprints in the soil by a freshly dug grave. She also noticed tire marks in the grass over by the far end of the church. It must have been a vehicle of some height because there was a newly broken tree branch now lying on the ground, its sap still wet.

It was morning, and one of the builders had called her outside to the foot of the scaffolding.

"Someone's been up on the roof," he said. "They haven't taken anything, but tools have been moved." The young lad was one of Robert's workers. He was tanned and looked strong.

"Bob's away today, but I thought you ought to know. I think they've been scouting around looking for lead."

Sam didn't doubt it. Other churches had recently been targeted—alas successfully.

"Can't think why they didn't take it," the lad said.

"Full moon," Sam answered. "They might have been seen. It's too light. They'll return when the moon wanes."

"I'll remove all the ladders before we leave tonight…lock them up. It won't stop them, Vicar, but it'll make their life more difficult."

She thanked him and went back into the church to phone the police. They weren't as helpful as she hoped. They talked about not having the resources to stake out the church on an off chance that thieves might turn up. All they could do was get a patrol car to pass by regularly and keep an eye out.

Later, when Sam returned to the vicarage, she checked out the lunar cycle on the Internet. The full moon was waning, and last night hadn't been as bright as the night before. Might the light-fingered crooks return tonight? Sam wasn't taking chances. She would stake out the church herself. She was already missing half a roof and was damned if anyone was going to steal what was left.

Joey grabbed a pint of milk from the supermarket refrigerator and was surprised to see Sam doing the same. Dressed in her motorcycle gear, Sam looked exhausted and her hair stuck out at odd angles, but the smile she threw Joey was genuine.

"Hey," Joey said. "I stopped at the vicarage on my way home from work last night. You weren't in."

"I was out."

Joey grinned. "I know that. It was late."

"I spent the night at church." Sam yawned.

"All of it?"

"Yes. I've got potential lead roof thieves, and I'm waiting for them to come back."

"They've left a calling card?"

"They've been up on what roof I have left scouting about," Sam said with no enthusiasm.

"Why haven't you told the police?"

"I have, but they work on a 'catch them while they're doing it or catch them when they've done it' system. Manpower issues," Sam explained. "So I'm going back there again tonight. That way, if they strike, I'll be there and can call the police, and hopefully get them *lead*-handed as it were."

Sam seemed to brighten at her own joke.

"You're crazy!" Joey exclaimed.

"No, I just love my lead." Sam blinked the tiredness out of her eyes. "Why did you call? Anything wrong?"

"No. I just wanted to say hey. I haven't seen you for over a week. The job's been busy—nice busy—but busy. And so have you by the sound of it. I just wanted to touch base."

Sam looked genuinely pleased, and Joey relaxed. She didn't want Sam to think she was needy.

"I wish I'd been in, but as you see, life is happening at the moment."

Joey *had* called with a reason. Now was an opportune moment. "I also wanted to ask, when you can, if you'd like to come over for dinner one night."

"What, to your place?"

Joey raised her eyebrows. "No, I was thinking the graveyard. Yes, Sam, to my place."

Sam grinned. "I'd love that. I'll bring wine. Can I just sort my roof thieves out first?"

"Sure, but don't go doing anything brave like tackling them or anything."

"No chance of that. I'll just call the police. Promise."

"Yeah." Joey didn't really believe her.

It was probably what made her turn up at the church later that night. She wasn't going to sleep anyway so she might as well go help Sam, and make sure she didn't get herself into any trouble.

"What are you doing here?" Sam said as Joey crept into the side door of the church, the one she used to gain access when the main church door was shut. "I thought you were a thief."

"You didn't think I was going to let you do this by yourself. It's dangerous."

"It's gone midnight!" Sam exclaimed.

Inside the church was dark and quiet. There was the smallest of residue light from an outside lamp. Joey could just make Sam out. She was dressed in black from tip to toe, and with a dark wool beanie on her head. "You look like a thug," she whispered.

"I'm blending in," Sam whispered back.

Joey was in dark clothing too. "What time do you think they'll come?"

"No idea. I'm thinking after one. They'll assume all nice people are in bed. Of course, they may not turn up. Where have you parked?"

"Next road down. I thought I might give the game away turning up this time of night dressed like a poacher and carrying a flashlight."

Sam giggled like a kid. "If this wasn't so serious, it'd be fun."

"I've brought coffee." Joey produced a thermos. "Stakeouts can take time."

"I'm really beginning to like you," Sam said wryly. "Let's go through to the vestry. If anyone gets onto the roof, we can hear better."

They settled in and drank the coffee, talking in low whispers.

"Shit, Sam, I can't believe you spent last night here alone. This is a spooky place at best, but at night? It gives me the creeps."

"I can't argue with that, but I suppose over the years I've got used to the place, and the ghosts haven't bothered me yet."

"You have ghosts?"

"Yes, the place is full of them," Sam said.

Joey wrapped her jacket around her.

"During the English Civil War, the church was invaded by Roundhead troops who came to ransack it for valuables. An Anglican bishop tried to protect the church but ended up having his throat cut. He bled to death just where you're sitting."

Joey looked down and shifted uncomfortably.

"Countless people have seen him, Joey, mostly at night and after concerts. And there are many who swear they've seen that slab beneath your chair turn blood red. Others say they've heard a man's voice chanting prayers in old English. Sometimes I—" Sam stopped dead.

"Sometimes you what?"

"No, I don't want to frighten you. You're here to help me."

"I don't scare easy. I'm American."

Sam scrutinized her, then made up her mind. "Sometimes I think I've felt his breath on my neck as I've been giving a sermon. Of course, it might be a draft. This is a big old place. But once, when I was here alone, I'm damn sure someone touched my arm."

There was a loud noise above them, and Joey leapt with shock. "Someone's on the roof."

"No guesses who." Sam rose to go outside.

Joey put an arm out to stop her. "You can't go out there. You might get hurt."

"I just need to make sure it's the thieves."

"Who else is likely to be on the roof at this hour?"

"It could be a squirrel," Sam said.

"Damn big squirrel!" Joey said.

More noises came from above, and it was clear there was a colony of *squirrels* on the roof and they were all wearing heavy boots.

Joey couldn't stop Sam from marching to the door.

"I know what I'm doing. I just need to see it's them, and then…" she waved her cell phone in the air, "we dial 999 and call the big boys in."

"I'm coming with you."

"You might get hurt."

"And you won't?" Joey said.

Sam gave up. She nodded and put a finger to her lips to signal silence. They crept out and around the other side of the church using bushes as cover. They crept up behind one larger bush and squatted down. There they could see a large dark colored van that had reversed down the narrow path from the far end of the church. Its rear doors were already open. They could also make out the shadows of two or three men up on the roof, and hear them pulling at the lead.

"Bastards," Sam muttered. "They've brought their own ladders."

Joey could just make out a series of ladders leading up through the different levels of the scaffolding allowing access to the roof. The thieves had come prepared and were daring.

Sam whispered to Joey. "Take the cell. Go back into the church and call the police."

"What are you going to do?"

"I'm going to wait here. If it looks like they're leaving, I'm going to push that bloody ladder to the ground so they can't make their escape." There was one long ladder at the base that provided the final part of the burglars' exit strategy.

"You're what?" Joey mouthed. "You're a lunatic."

Sam frowned and started pushing her. Relief surged through her as Joey did as she was told.

When Sam knew Joey was safely gone, she edged up closer to the van. She wanted to be in place if she needed to push the ladder. She hoped she wouldn't have to and that the police would turn up in time. But her heart sank as she realized one of the men was coming down from the roof.

Shit. I'm going to have to do something.

"I hope you're ready for this, God," she sighed.

She moved from behind the van and crept toward the ladder giving it an almighty shove and sending it crashing to the ground. At about the same time, she heard the driver's door open. The first thing she saw was a dot of red light. This was one of her smokers. The second thing she saw was the stocky, overweight shadow of the man behind the cigarette as he exited the vehicle.

She froze and at first she didn't think he'd seen her, but then she realized he had. He was coming at her and cursing.

"Oh, bugger." Her ordination training had been lacking in lead protection techniques and hand-to-hand combat. She must mention that to Neil when she next saw him.

Sam smelled the tobacco on his breath as he reached out for her.

Trapped up against the scaffolding, he'd just got hold of her by the shoulders when a large lump of dark matter moving at speed pushed him away from her and forced him to the ground. He fell heavily, and the fall sounded as if it had winded him. He seemed in no fit state to get up. The *lump* turned to her and spoke. It was Joey. She was sitting on top of the man.

"I thought you said you were just going to look." Joey was angry.

Sam was about to help Joey and was in the act of moving forward when a pair of hands grabbed her from behind and pulled her back by the shoulders. A deep male voice resonated.

"Got you, you little thug."

Sam turned to see a police officer. He was about to cuff her as Joey shouted, "No, she's the vicar."

The officer removed Sam's beanie allowing her hair to fall free. He looked at Joey. "And who the hell are you?"

"I'm an investigative journalist."

Sam heard the pride in her voice.

"God help us," the officer muttered.

A voice in the darkness said, "Got one, Sergeant. I think it's Wesley Chaste."

Another police officer appeared out of the shadows. He looked far too young for his profession and was dragging a cuffed skinny man who had tried to shimmy down a scaffolding pole but landed straight into the waiting hands of the law.

"Mike's chasing another down out the front," the same young officer added.

"And I'm sitting on one," Joey said with all the dignity she could muster.

Amidst an array of flashlights, Sam saw the sergeant beckon to one of his team to cuff the driver.

"There's one still up on the roof, Sergeant."

"Go, fetch," his superior ordered dourly before turning to Sam. "So what's your name, Vicar? Death?"

"Savage."

"That figures." The sergeant wasn't impressed. "You two could have been hurt. These aren't the types you find in any church congregation. They're violent and got plenty of form. You should have left them to us."

"They were after my lead." Sam was indignant.

The sergeant still wasn't impressed, and by the time the police left, it was nearly four in the morning.

Sam and Joey made their way back into the vestry. Sam put the lights on.

Joey sat down wearily. She had a feeling she would sleep when she got home although she had to be up before six thirty. It probably wasn't worth the effort. "We're idiots, Sam," she said. "That could all have gone very wrong."

"They could have got my lead roofing." Sam seemed pleased with herself.

"They could have really kicked our ass."

"I didn't see you hesitating."

"I was following your lead. You were very brave, Sam."

"So were you, and the way you tackled that man was impressive. I thought I was in big trouble."

"Just as well I came back out then. You were lucky."

"Thanks to you." Sam collapsed onto a plain wooden chair and stretched her legs.

Joey grinned. "It sure feels good though, yeah?"

"It does. The bastards are off the street *and* off my roof. They'll be in custody by now."

As Joey nodded, the collar of her jacket rubbed against her face and she flinched.

Sam saw. "Are you okay?"

Joey realized she'd hurt herself in the fall. Her face was stinging and she rubbed it. "Sure, but I think I grazed my chin when I took that guy down."

Sam picked up her chair and moved closer to Joey.

"Let me have a look."

She leaned in to look at the abrasion, and Joey was aware of how close their faces were. Sam had her finger and thumb on her chin evaluating the damage. Her touch made Joey's heart beat faster, and she fought to control her breath.

Sam seemed innocent of the affect she was having on Joey. "I'm aware," she said as she continued to inspect the graze, "that I flung you in the deep end tonight. I placed you in some danger. I hope you're okay."

"Why wouldn't I be?"

"Well, you've been through a lot the past few years and this might have upset you." Sam was pouring bottled water over a handkerchief and starting to wipe the wound clean.

"No, I'm good." Joey's mind was not on past experiences. Her present concerns were more to do with how cozy this moment was. She was struggling to maintain her composure.

"Oh, you're better than that," Sam whispered. Her gray eyes fixed on Joey who was reminded that it was the same look that had passed between them on the bike in the kitchen.

"I'm glad you're here," Sam added, her voice soft.

Joey found the moment intimate, and under normal circumstances she might have leaned forward and kissed Sam. She realized she wanted to. But she held back. These weren't usual circumstances. This was a vicar in front of her, and one who was very grateful for her assistance tonight. Joey was on dangerous ground. She didn't even know Sam's sexual leaning. An internal klaxon warned her that this was not the place or time to test theory. It might go horribly wrong.

"I couldn't let you handle this by yourself." Joey played safe.

Sam seemed to scrutinize her for a moment before diverting her eyes toward the slabbed flooring. "No, I mean…I'm glad you're here. I'm glad that you've moved into the area. I like having you around. Life seems better. Sweeter."

Their faces were so close, and for a moment, when Sam looked back at her, Joey thought *Sam* was going to kiss *her*. Instead Sam leaned back.

Joey's heart had been beating wildly with the excitement of the evening. Now it was beating wildly again but for different reasons. All her experience told her what was going on here, and yet she couldn't believe it. She had to be wrong. Sam was too important to mess with. This wasn't one of her casual follies, the "love them and leave them" type. Even if she was right and Sam was attracted to her, she didn't want to ruin anything and she might. Her track record wasn't good. It occurred to her that she thought more of Sam than any other woman she'd met. It also occurred to her that she might just be falling in love with her. She kept her response measured and meaningful.

"Thank you, Sam."

Sam unexpectedly stood. Whatever Joey thought she'd sensed was gone and Sam was all business again. Her manner turned oddly distant.

"Well, it's time to draw this exciting night to an end. I've robbed you of too much time already, Joey. You've work tomorrow…today, and I have an early service." Sam was already putting her chair back against a desk and tidying up.

"Sure." Joey stood too and gathered her belongings. She should leave.

As she moved toward the exit, Sam stopped her.

"By the way, about the ghost of the murdered bishop?"

"Yes?"

"There isn't one," Sam declared. A slow smile appeared on her face. "I was stringing you along. You're too gullible."

"You had me looking for blood stains on the floor," Joey said.

"Good night, Joey, and thanks for everything. You've been a wonderful ally. Drive carefully."

Joey headed into the night air once more and toward her car. She wasn't sure what had just happened, but something had passed between them. Her own feelings were interesting too. When had they changed toward Sam? She didn't know, but they had.

But you didn't fall in love with a vicar, and if you did, you weren't going to win. Competing with God was one thing, but adding a lesbian relationship to the mix was another. This was unexplored ground. Sam might not feel the same way. It was completely possible that Sam was only expressing her thanks. She was an overworked vicar who might be a little lonely and looking for simple friendship.

Joey glanced at her watch. There was no point in going to bed. The thought of a long shower appealed more to her than sleep now. Maybe it would sharpen up her thought processes. Despite all her confusion of the night, she knew what she'd seen as Sam closed the church door. Sam's face had held the look of disappointment.

"Can we talk?" Joey stood at the vicarage door.

She and Sam hadn't spoken since their night's adventure in the church grounds four days ago. This wasn't unusual. They weren't in the habit of calling each other all the time, and yet, since then, the lack of contact between them felt wrong.

Joey guessed something had passed between them that night, and the way Sam looked now, she could tell Sam had felt it too.

Normally, Sam's face lit up when Joey put in an appearance, but there was no welcoming smile for her this evening. Sam was not her usual self, and Joey sensed she was ill at ease. Joey definitely was.

"Are you alone?" Joey asked.

Sam nodded, and without saying anything, stepped back to let her in. Joey entered and waited till the door closed. She placed her car keys on the table, hoping Sam would say something, but when she didn't, Joey crushed the silence.

"I haven't heard from you."

"I've been busy and just trying to catch up on things," Sam said.

Joey knew it for the excuse it was.

"I wondered if everything was okay."

"Everything's okay. We got our thieves," Sam said.

"That's not really what I was asking."

Sam nodded, and though she smiled, Joey sensed nothing but tension, something that had never existed between them before. It had everything to do with that look Joey had seen as she'd left the church—the look of loss, of disappointment. She knew now she was right. Sam had wanted something to happen, and it hadn't. Joey thought she knew what that was, but wasn't sure.

"Sam, about what happened at church…after the police left, and we went back into the vestry. Is it me, or did you feel it, too?"

Sam didn't answer.

"I'm guessing you did *and* I'm guessing that's why you haven't been in touch. And I don't know if it's because of something I did…or didn't do. You know so much about me, but I know nothing about you, the *you* behind the vicar." Joey sighed.

"I guess this is unfair of me coming to your place like this, but I wanted to say something, and I wanted to say it without a whole heap of congregation listening in. It's kinda private." Joey tried to smile.

"I really like you, Sam. Hell, I like you more than that. That night I was real close to kissing you when you were fixing my face. I didn't because I didn't know if you wanted that, if you *could* want that being a vicar and all or whether you sensed what I wanted and were disappointed in me for daring to overstep friendship."

Sam's face was unreadable, and Joey wondered if she was making a huge mistake. Something inside her started sinking. She wondered if Sam knew the power she had over her, a strange indefinable sway that pulled Joey toward her with such force. Joey had never felt this before. She had never looked at any woman and thought of something prolonged and enduring. And to find this was happening with a vicar was, until now, unimaginable.

"You've shown me nothing but kindness and friendship, Sam, and I can't tell you what that means to me, and I'm damned afraid that what I'm standing here saying is going to ruin that. But I'm Joey who is falling in love with Sam. I warned you who I was. And I just want to see if you *might* feel something for me…beyond kindness and friendship."

Sam's continued silence stretched like elastic, and Joey felt sick.

"I'm sorry if I've screwed this up. I didn't come here to make you uncomfortable." She was desperate for Sam to say something, anything, but when she didn't, Joey knew it was time to leave.

"Okay. Let's whizz past the awkward bit. I'll go, and you just forget I've been here." Joey reached for her keys, but Sam stopped her.

Sam capped her hand tight over Joey's and locked eyes.

"You haven't," Sam said. "You haven't got this wrong."

"No?"

Sam moved a step forward and placed a hand to Joey's face letting it rest there. Joey's unannounced arrival had taken her by surprise. Until now she'd been trying to make sense of all the crazy thoughts and emotions going through her. She *had* avoided Joey. Sam had been shocked by the power of what she'd felt for her in the vestry, and what it might mean. Joey's arrival tonight meant Sam now had to address these feelings. Meditation *and prayer* were no longer options.

Sam had done nothing but replay that night over and over. If Joey hadn't turned up this evening, Sam wondered if she'd have found the courage to approach her and voice what she felt. She didn't know the answer. All she did know was that she wanted to banish the doubts, worries, confusion she could see written across Joey's strained face. She kissed her lightly on the lips.

"I should have kissed *you* that night, Joey. I wanted to."

She watched Joey close her eyes, and when she opened them, they were moist.

"I've never felt like this before, Sam. I've been scared that I was getting this all wrong, and even if I wasn't…what this might mean for you. I've never fallen in love with a vicar before. I'm not sure I've ever *been* in love before. I've never felt like this."

They stared at each other and smiled, and Sam wasn't sure who initiated the next kiss, but it didn't matter. It was less chaste and lasted longer.

"What happens now?" Joey asked.

Sam couldn't help but laugh as she wrapped her arms around Joey and pulled her close. "I think this is where two people who like each other decide they want to get to know each other better."

"I *mean*," Joey said, "I turn up on your doorstep and declare the whole enchilada. I don't want you to do anything you don't want to...or can't."

"You're fretting because of my day job."

"I'm worried. This is happening fast."

"Yes, it is," Sam said. "But sometimes that's how love happens. It doesn't make it any less real."

"I don't want to rush you."

Sam broke the embrace and leaned back to look at her. "You're worried for me. Don't be. I've waited a long time for someone to come into my life again and make me feel like this...alive. The minute I saw you, I think I felt it then. It's grown ever since. I don't do this lightly."

"When I didn't hear from you..." Joey said.

"I didn't know how you felt about me. I'm a vicar. Was I about to overstep the trust you placed in me? How sinful would that have been?"

Joey pulled Sam close. "I'm damned happy we've cleared this up. I thought I had this wrong. I would have lost everything. I would have lost you."

Sam wasn't sure how long they held each other, but it felt as if time stood still as she soaked up the warmth and happiness that flooded through her like the elixir of life. Yes, things were moving fast, but she knew she was tired of waiting.

"I guess I should leave...let you sort yourself out for tomorrow. Give you think time too," Joey said as they finally pulled apart.

"Is that what you want?" Sam said.

"I thought we might want to take things slow...a step at a time."

Joey's honorable intentions meant much to Sam, the words perfect sense, but it wasn't what she wanted.

"Is that what you want?" Joey asked.

Sam had missed Joey. She'd done nothing but think about consequences and possibilities. Now that Joey was here, she knew she didn't want her to go.

"No," Sam said.

"Oh."

Sam couldn't help smiling at Joey's apparent moral dilemma. She was trying so hard to do the right thing, but Sam sensed she didn't want to go either. She knew if she didn't leave it would change all between them.

"Would you like to stay?" Sam asked.

"The night?"

"Yes."

"With you?" Joey said.

"Kind of the idea, Joey." Sam paused. "We both know what is happening here. We both know what it means. I want you to know I'm not in a habit of asking anyone to stay the night with me." She ran her hand down Joey's face again, loving the softness of her skin. It had been a long time since Sam had connected like this with anyone. "These moments in life are rare, and when they come your way, you should hold on to them."

Joey hesitated for a few seconds, then answered, "Yes. Yes, I'd like to stay."

Joey had made love many times before. It was always hot passion, often fueled by alcohol, and an almost desperate need for the fiery, sweaty escalation of lust to get them both to climax as soon as possible, and if they could repeat the excitement, all the better. The end product always left her with the satisfaction that she was alive and fully out there *playing the field*, something she could wear like a badge of honor. It was her way of connecting with life, a reassurance that she was desired and wanted. Her many partners were always "grateful" and left wanting more. They would tell her she was good in bed. But after they left, she couldn't have told you their names.

Sex. That's all it ever was to her, the attainment of a physical high. No emotions involved. She never felt protective or caring toward her partners. There was nothing there that bonded them together, made her, or them, want to hang around with each other for too long. They would in time recognize the shallowness of each other and not like what they saw. They would move on.

Being with Sam was different. This was a slower, gentle and respectful exploration of each other, and its excitement was keener, the joy of knowing what was to come.

Surprisingly, Sam led.

Her hands moved over Joey, exploring every part of her—her face, her neck, her breasts, her sex. Their warmth as they caressed and probed made Joey tingle and shiver. At times she felt vulnerable as if this was her first time. Perhaps it was. Syria *had* changed her. Here with Sam, she was discovering what it was to be made *love* to, that inexplicable mixture of physical and mental. With Sam, Joey felt her desire to please and to reach into her, to be one with her. This wasn't the hard sell of plain sex. This was a slower path to reward paved with intense, adoring stimulation. Joey's breath would catch, and Sam would slow, looking into her eyes as if checking all was okay. Sam would kiss her before continuing, a caressing of tongues, a melding of bodies.

Joey felt only protected and safe with Sam. She wanted to let down all the protective barriers she'd put in place over the years, ones she hadn't known existed until now.

When her climax drew close and their bodies quickened in rhythm, a voice deep inside her whispered that she'd found the one. Her mother would love the irony, her agnostic daughter falling for a woman of the cloth.

A burst of ecstasy flooded through Joey taking her to the waterfall's edge where she teetered on the abyss for what seemed like an eternity. When it passed, they held each other tight, saying nothing and listening only to each other's fast breathing.

Joey began to pleasure Sam, and uncharacteristically took care to learn what pleased her. She mirrored Sam's patient buildup, only changing pace when asked to or to linger longer where Sam needed her. She wondered how long it had been since Sam had made love to a woman—to anyone. She'd said she'd waited a long time for someone to come into her life again. Joey wondered who that had been.

Joey had no point of reference with vicars, but Sam was quick to respond, her excitement building fast and strong. She whimpered with every touch of Joey's hands and lips. Her nipples stood erect, and she welcomed Joey deep into her mouth where their tongues danced. Her appetite became voracious, a hunger that needed attention, and Joey sensed it had been a long time waiting for Sam.

Sam cried out in delight as she came. She pushed herself close into Joey who felt ripple after ripple rush through Sam. She was filled with such satisfaction of giving back pleasure, thinking only of Sam's enjoyment.

When Sam collapsed backward, drawing Joey with her, she laughed with joy.

Joey found this bonding intense, overpowering, and above all sincere. She felt the mantle of superficiality drop away from her.

Joey was receiving the greatest lesson—how to love.

Afterward, as they lay together, they spoke of intimate matters. Joey wanted to know who that "someone" was Sam had hinted at.

"Who was in your life before?" she asked.

"Her name was Louise. It was before I joined the church and was ordained. We were school friends who grew up together. As we became older, both of us realized we were more than friends. We had fallen in love and became lovers. We went to the same university."

"What happened?"

"I made a choice, Joey. I chose the church and let Louise go. I couldn't see how I could walk that path as a lesbian. We parted badly, and despite my attempts to see her over the years, it was always a bitter time and wounds didn't heal. She wrote me a letter

I. BEACHAM

a few years ago. She was dying and in a hospice. She wanted to see me. I went, and it was a gentler time. We spoke about the past. We healed our wounds, and I was with her when she died."

Joey reached an arm over Sam who covered it with hers.

"It was a sad time, Joey, but I'm so glad we parted friends."

"Do you have regrets?" Joey asked.

"None. Only lessons learned. It's what made me want to be with you tonight. You've come into my life, and you're very special to me. I want you to know that." Sam ran a hand gently down Joey's face. "What about you? Has there ever been anyone special in your life?"

Joey's laugh was cynical. "Hardly. I've been too driven by my career and had little time for anything else except quick, meaningless sex. My perceived powerful woman image has attracted women like magnetic polarity, but I've never wanted commitment and they haven't been the type for that either." Joey turned her head toward Sam. "It's different with you. You make me feel that I can be someone real. I've never felt this depth of connection with anyone. You might just be changing me into an honest woman, Sam. It'll be a miracle if you are because you're with someone who hasn't got a good track record." She heard the regret in her own voice.

"I'll be the judge of that," Sam said without hesitation. "How did you get that scar?"

There was a nasty old wound on the upper arm Joey rested across Sam.

"I was in Sarajevo. A bullet ricocheted off a wall and hit me. Hurt like hell."

"And that one?" Sam pointed to the newer scar on her forehead. It was where her head had pushed into the kitchen faucets during the explosion. The memory sent a chill through her.

"You don't have to answer if you don't want to," Sam said.

"It was in Balshir. The rebels fired a missile into our quarters. I was in another room, but I got hit by its force."

"It must have been painful."

"I lived. My colleagues didn't."

"Want to talk?"

"No."

Sam hated that Joey was repressing her experiences. Sam knew she'd tried counseling but had given it up because *"it didn't work and was a waste of time."* Joey had stopped going to the sessions. This was dangerous. Repressed memories were like a boiling pot with a lid on. Eventually, the lid blew under the pressure. Memories that were forced down behaved the same way. They would fester and manifest themselves again later with unwelcome consequences. Sam was a firm believer that the earlier the intervention, the better the outcome.

She knew Joey needed help. She needed more than a friend— or lover—listening. She needed professional support. How she could convince Joey of that was a different matter. She'd dug her heels in and wouldn't talk. Sam tactically changed the subject.

"What made you turn up today?"

She felt Joey relax.

"When I left St. Mary's after our great roof adventure, I saw something in your face. I acted on it."

"What did you see?"

"Attraction…love." Joey bent over and gave her a chaste kiss.

"I'm glad you did."

When Joey had left the church that night, the door closing had felt like it was slamming down on Sam's life. She had wanted to reach out to Joey but didn't know how. Her ecclesiastical persona had stood in her way. "I'm very glad you're here," Sam whispered.

"I'm very glad Gloria isn't," Joey laughed.

Something crossed Sam's mind. Gloria had phoned to say she had a new date when she'd be back. Sam hadn't paid attention and had forgotten it all. It wasn't important anyway. Gloria would turn up when she was back.

"How did you get that?" Joey pointed to a scar on Sam's chin.

"I was putting a chalice away after service. It fell off the top shelf as I was looking up."

Joey didn't look impressed.

Sam sighed. "I must seem very dull to you. The most action I get is baptizing infants and trying not to drop them in the font."

"Dull is not a word I associate with you. I don't often come across a motor biking vicar who chases thieves off her roof."

"Yes, but you tackled the driver to the ground."

"I did, didn't I? We make quite a pair." Joey laughed. "Tell me, Sam. Have you gone all this time without sex? Since Louise?"

Sam turned. "I'm a vicar not a nun."

Joey shifted and raised herself up to study Sam. It made Sam realize that maybe she wasn't so dull. Joey's hair fell across Sam's breasts, and the simple act produced such a feeling of happiness in her. She thanked God she'd met Joey and that they'd been given this chance of love.

"Well?" Joey nudged her.

Sam feigned world-weariness. "I admit that I've taken myself away on breaks sometimes and allowed myself to indulge in carnal matters."

Joey looked shocked.

"It's true. Not too many times…and I've never had to pay for anything."

"You've done this? Really?"

"I have." Sam wasn't lying. "You're disappointed."

"No." Joey's eyes were wide open. "I'm fascinated. When was the last time?"

"Several years ago in Weston-super-Mare. It was after Louise died. I desperately needed to connect with someone."

Joey nudged her again. "You won't have to go anywhere tonight. You've got me." Her eyes were full of love as she moved across to cover Sam.

Their lovemaking began once more.

❖

"I've got to get up." Sam stared at the bedside clock wishing she could make it freeze time.

"But it's Saturday."

"Time waits for no man…or vicar. Neither does God. I have a ten o'clock service."

Joey moaned and stretched.

Sam bent and kissed her. "Sorry." She swung her legs off the bed and onto the floor. "I'll go and put the kettle on."

There was lightness to her step as she moved downstairs, but it disappeared the minute she entered the kitchen. Gloria was there unpacking shopping and decanting it into the cupboards and fridge. Sam couldn't hide her shock, and her usual greeting etiquette fell short.

"You're back," she spluttered.

"I am." Gloria responded in her normal cheerless manner that hid her real warmth. It occurred to Sam that the vacation might not have lived up to Gloria's expectations.

"You're back early," Sam added, wondering how she could keep Joey's presence upstairs a secret. Now she wished she'd paid attention to Gloria's phone call.

"No, I'm not. I rang and told you when I'd be back." Gloria's cheerlessness turned to despair. "You forgot, didn't you?"

"Yes." Sam didn't lie. "How was the break?"

"I enjoyed it, but I missed home. The family has grown too large and noisy. While it's been lovely seeing my sister and cousins again, I'm glad to be back and to my routine." She glanced around. "I see you kept the place clean and that the motorbike has disappeared from the kitchen."

"There's been a miracle," Sam said wryly.

At that moment, a thunder of feet sounded behind them and Joey appeared in the kitchen half dressed.

Sam flinched. Joey blanched.

"Other miracles too, I see." Gloria's left eyebrow raised an inch.

There was a moment of awkwardness before Gloria said, "Breakfast for two, then?" She started moving around the kitchen in preparation.

"Doesn't this upset her religious code?" Joey whispered.

"She hasn't got one," Sam whispered back. "You two have a lot in common."

CHAPTER EIGHT

"That's the new beams in, Rev," Bob said. He wiped dust off his hands as he stood inside the church with Sam looking up at the church roof. "There's still a lot to do, but now those babies are in, everything will move faster."

"Am I allowed to ask how fast *fast* is?"

He stared at her as if she'd grown a new head. "You can't hurry something like this. This is a job that has to be done right and with great attention to detail. I want to honor the craftsmen who originally built all this. I want their ghosts to know that mankind has progressed and expanded in ability and knowledge...at least in the building trade."

Sam noted how his eyes filled with humility and respect. It wasn't something she often saw in his tanned chiseled features.

"This church is a structure of beauty. The craftsmanship I'm finding takes my breath away, and they never had the fancy tools we do today. Oh, if only I could walk in their shadows for a few days."

"Careful, Bob, you're beginning to sound like a zealot."

He smiled. "I know I'm a bit rough round the edges, but me and the family, we go to church most Sundays."

"Most?"

"Gotta be honest, Rev. Sometimes it's a bugger getting out of bed, especially in the winter. These bones aren't as young as they used to be."

"Don't let it worry you, Bob. Sometimes I struggle too."

She realized that of late, her aches and pains had much to do with unaccustomed lovemaking. Conversely, despite the stiffness, she felt younger.

She was walking back down the aisle smiling when Carrie, the BBC reporter, walked into the church and down the aisle to greet her.

"Hello, what brings you here?"

Carrie sauntered up to her, self-confidence oozing. It was difficult not to admire her shapely form in the tight pencil skirt that showed off long lean legs. She wore a ribbed, body clinging cashmere jumper set off with a pretty pink flowered silk neck scarf. With her abundant curly hair that dripped alluringly over her face and shoulders, she dressed to enhance the gifts nature bestowed on her. They were in abundance, especially on her chest. Sam could not deny she was an attractive woman.

"Thought you might like to know our piece on the church has gone down very well with the listeners. We've had lots of positive feedback online, and people are chatting about how much they like you. You've got a great radio presence." She swept her hair to the side, a habit Sam had noted the other evening.

"Thank you, that's good to hear. But you didn't have to come all this way. You could have phoned."

"Yes, I know, I know, but I was passing and thought the personal touch was better." Carrie's smile was rakish. "Actually, a colleague asked me to propose something to you…sound you out. WM runs a radio series called *Forgotten Worcestershire*. I think he's wondering if you'd be interested in coming into the studio and talking about some of the other stuff you mentioned to me."

"Like what?"

"Those interesting artifacts found during the excavation some years ago. You also talked about the radar survey of the churchyard and the Saxon Monastery, and the church mentioned in the *Domesday Book*. Civil War skirmishes. And I'm sure you have lots of other interesting information of historical relevance you could talk about. I'm not on that team, but it's perfect material for their series."

Sam began to dismiss the idea.

"I know you're busy," Carrie said, "but do give it some thought. You really know your history, and people like hearing it. Any airtime highlights the church appeal. It could work in your favor." She didn't give Sam time to say no. "I'll get the editor to give you a call in a week or two, okay? You can deal with him as to whether you want to do it or not."

Carrie was no longer interested in the conversation. She scanned the church, plainly looking for something. Sam had a hunch as to what.

"Looking for anything in particular?"

"Joey not here?" Carrie asked.

"No service. No organist." Sam's response came out blunt. She softened. "Joey only helps when we've no organist. We have now. Besides, she works during the week."

Carrie pursed her full lips.

Sam's curiosity was killing her. "Something you want to see her about?"

"I thought I'd take her out, show her around. We BBC people have to stick together, and I expect she's lonely over here." Carrie was straightforward if not irritating. "Don't you agree? It must be a bit boring for her. Nothing very exciting happens around here. It's all a bit dull."

"It depends what you want." Sam forced a smile onto her face and then ordered it to stay there.

Carrie immediately balked and offered a meager apology. "I wasn't implying *this* is all dull, but she's a fast lane sort of woman. This parochial living must be very insular for her." Carrie flicked her hair. "Anyway, I must dash. I'm really glad I got to see you and tell you the news. Give the suggestion some thought."

Carrie pivoted on her high heels and left.

Sam watched her leave. She stopped smiling, and irritation coursed through her.

What the shit is dull about here?

She listened to the builders hammering away and their radio tuned into heavy rock music.

God was becoming pretty progressive of late, she thought.

A tinge of uncertainty ran through her. Was this life all a bit parochial and insular for someone like Joey? She was, or had been, living in the fast lane.

Somewhere in the distance, she heard one of the builder's singing words from "Another One Bites the Dust."

She hoped he was killing woodworm.

What the shit is dull about here?

"Considering this is what can loosely be defined as our first date, it hasn't started well," Joey said, deadpan.

Sam cringed. She was an hour late.

They were supposed to meet at six thirty, have something to eat, and then catch a movie. Work had held Sam up, and she'd only just arrived at the mall.

But Joey understood. She knew only too well how the day job could edge into personal life and mess up everything. Sam had run from the parking lot to get to her, unable to hide her frustration and now panting like the winner of the Boston Marathon.

"I tried to phone you, but you didn't answer," Sam wheezed.

Joey held her hands up. "My fault. I've left the cell in the car. I didn't think I'd need it."

Sam deflated like a flatulent balloon.

"Now I've ruined the evening, what shall we do?"

Joey kissed her before answering. "Let's go eat. The movie can wait." She placed a hand on Sam's shoulder and pushed her toward a place she'd seen earlier. "Steak house?"

"Perfect."

Once they'd sat down and ordered, Joey asked, "So what kept you?"

"Bit of an ugly affair." Sam didn't look happy. "Two gay guys have asked for a church blessing at St. George's which is a small country church in this diocese. It's one of the parishes I oversee."

Joey thought Sam looked tired. She was definitely annoyed.

"There's a vicar there who isn't gay friendly. He's blatantly told them he wouldn't do a blessing even if he could because he doesn't believe in marriage being denigrated."

"Ouch. That isn't nice."

"A simple '*sorry I can't do that*,' would have sufficed, but he has to be aggressive about it."

"I thought there were same sex marriages over here?"

"Civil marriages, yes. At the moment, the Church of England isn't carrying out same-sex marriages, and there's no *authorized* service for blessings. The church is moving in the right direction, but it's taking matters slowly, giving everyone time to readjust." Sam didn't hide her irritation. "He's upset them, which is sad."

"What do you mean by no authorized services?"

"There are some maverick vicars willing to conduct blessings of civil marriages in church."

"Are you one?"

"I think I'm about to be."

"Is this the vicar who gives you *issues*?"

Sam nodded. "I won't lie. I don't like the man. It's not like it's the occasional issue. It's everything. We're always at different points of the compass. I suppose I should be grateful; all the other vicars are first class."

"Well, maybe a good bloody steak and a beer will help."

Sam stretched her hand across the table and took Joey's.

"*You* help." Sam gave a weary smile. It warmed Joey.

The food arrived, and for a while they ate, and the conversation was limited.

Then Sam asked, "Am I dull?"

Joey choked on a garlic mushroom. "Where's this coming from?"

"Nowhere," Sam said quietly. "It's just this area's a bit parochial and insular."

"No, it isn't. It's peaceful and normal with real people in real life."

"But you're used to excitement."

Joey set her knife and fork down on her plate and stared at Sam. "Am I really having this conversation with the Slayer of Lead Thieves?"

It was the first grin she'd got out of Sam since she'd arrived. Joey relaxed and picked her fork back up. "You are not dull, Reverend Samantha Savage. This topic of conversation is over. Period." She was pleased to see Sam yield to her authority.

The food on their plates disappeared, and coffee arrived.

"Carrie Marlow came into church a few days ago," Sam said.

"Yeah?"

"Yes. She came to tell me that the piece has aired and gone down very well. They've had some good feedback."

"That's nice."

"Apparently, the station wants me to do some more recordings for a series called *Forgotten Worcestershire*. They want me to talk about local historical events."

Joey was both pleased and worried. Sam's historical knowledge was impressive, and she made it interesting, but when was she going to find time to do this?

"Will you?"

"I love talking about local history, but I'm not keen. I don't have the time, but Neil's told me to find it, and he'll get cover. He sees the value. It's a subtle way of getting the church into the mainstream, and hopefully—"

"Free advertising for the church appeal."

"Something like that."

Joey studied Sam's crestfallen features. She really was under too much pressure. Neil ought to know better. "I think you need another coffee." Joey beckoned the waiter.

"Carrie could have phoned. I thought she was busy."

"I told her that," Sam said.

"She strikes me as a woman who doesn't do anything without reason."

Joey watched Sam's grimace as her eyes narrowed. "I think her real modus operandi was to see you."

"Me?"

"Yes."

"Why?"

"She said something about showing you around, that you might want some excitement in your life," Sam said.

Now Joey understood what lay behind the *dull* topic. Carrie had made Sam feel inadequate, as if Sam might be compared to the voluptuous Carrie, a *younger model*, and be found wanting. If it was, Sam had nothing to worry about.

"I'm not interested. *You* show me around. I'm happy with that." This time it was Joey who reached across the table to touch Sam's hand.

"The right answer," Sam whispered.

"Which reminds me." Joey dug into her jeans pocket and handed a key over to Sam. "It's to my place. Not that you ever have any spare time, but I'm working at home for the next few days. They're doing some refurbishment of the offices, taking down ceilings that contain asbestos or something. They want us out of the way. Drop in for coffee...use the key, and don't make me walk to the door to let you in."

It was a couple of days later when Sam got the chance to test the key out. It was late afternoon and she was on her way back from a local hospice. She always tried to drop in there on a weekly basis regardless of whether anyone had asked for her or not. Sometimes the people there would talk, irrespective of whether they held religious belief. Her visits were often more for the families than the patients. The staff appreciated her presence too. They were often the forgotten army, the ones that dealt with life's endings on a daily basis.

It was about four in the afternoon when Sam pushed the key into the lock and opened Joey's door. She half expected to find her seated at the dining room table, its surface covered with paperwork and drawings. But while the latter was there, Joey wasn't. There was just a cold half-full mug of coffee.

Sam called out her name but got no reply.

She crept toward her bedroom. Perhaps Joey was sleeping. Sam knew she suffered from nightmares and that a good night's sleep was not part of Joey's life anymore. Joey mentioned she grabbed sleep whenever she could.

As Sam quietly pushed the door open, she could see the curtains were partially closed and that the room was in shade. It looked as if Joey had taken a nap. The bed had been slept on, its top covers in disarray, but Joey wasn't there. Sam was just beginning to think she might have popped out when she saw something move in the shadows of the far corner of the room. As her eyes grew accustomed to the dark, she saw someone crouched up tight on the floor with a blanket over their head.

"Joey?"

Warning bells played in her head, and a sense of alarm pulsed through her. They didn't vanish when Joey's head appeared from beneath the blanket.

"Are you all right?" Sam moved swiftly to her. Joey looked frightened to death.

"I think I had a panic attack." Her voice trembled.

Sam sat down beside her. "What brought it on?" she asked quietly.

"I don't know. I lay down on the bed. I didn't sleep well last night."

You never sleep well, Sam thought. She waited for Joey to tell her more. She didn't wait long.

"I was back there. I was inside the cabinet under the sink, but I wasn't alone. Kurt, Mitch, and Mo were with me. We were all squeezed into this tight unforgiving space. It was dark, but I could see their faces. We were hiding. We knew something was the other side of the door. It kept scratching at it and making this noise. It was horrible. I couldn't breathe, and I was scared. I had wet myself and was ashamed. I was trying to hide it, not let the others know what I'd done.

"Then Mo was opening the door saying he had to go and get us water. Kurt was trying to stop him. I was frightened that whatever was out there would see where we were and come for us. Mo left. And then Mitch pointed to something. I saw the shape of a hand coming through the semi opened door. The hand covered Mitch's face. I heard him scream. Then I was by myself. I was alone. As I reached out to close the door, something hard hit me in the face."

Joey touched the scar on her forehead. "I screamed. I woke myself up, and I couldn't stop the panic."

Sam could make out Joey's eyes. They were wild, like a cornered animal. She could see she was still shaking as if she was cold.

"Has the panic stopped?"

"No." Joey looked at her in desperation.

"Does this help?" Sam fingered the blanket.

"I feel safe," Joey whispered.

Sam took a deep breath before nudging closer to Joey. She placed an arm around her and then pulled the blanket back over both of them.

"What are you doing?" Joey said.

"We're going to wait until this passes. We'll wait together until you feel safe again."

Sam pulled Joey close and felt her lean into her.

"I'm sorry, Sam. I don't mean to be like this."

Sam kissed the top of her head. "Don't ever say sorry to me, Joey. I love you."

Sam held Joey and patiently waited for the attack to finish.

It frustrated her because she didn't know what to do. Joey was so anti any counseling. Sam knew Joey had PTSD, an extremely debilitating disorder which produced anxiety attacks, flashbacks, and nightmares, all brought on by seeing or living through a dangerous event. But knowing what someone had wasn't the same as *knowing* what to do.

Sam didn't really understand the complex disorder. The closest she'd come to it were newspaper articles and superficial conversations with Milo Granger, a warden at one of the churches within her diocese. His son had been medically discharged from the army after serving in Afghanistan. Harry suffered from PTSD, and its consequences had wreaked havoc on his family and friends. Now Sam wanted to talk to Milo again. Maybe he could shine a light on an otherwise bleak situation.

As Joey's attack passed, they had moved into the sitting room where they were now huddled together on the sofa. Sam had canceled a meeting she was attending that afternoon. She wouldn't leave Joey like this.

"You need help," Sam said.

"I don't want help."

"Why don't you see someone, Joey, a professional?"

"We've had this conversation before. It didn't work."

Sam felt her stiffen. She ignored it.

"Maybe you need to see someone different," Sam said.

"I'm coping."

"But the panic attacks…"

"They're bad dreams, that's all." Joey was digging in her heels.

"But they're not," Sam said. "You've got PTSD. This isn't going to go away."

"It *will* go away. I just need time." Joey was getting agitated. "I don't need anyone sitting in front of me asking me to tell them how I feel. I know how I *feel*. I'll cope with this my own way."

The last thing Sam wanted to do was make Joey feel like she was ganging up on her. She let it pass. "I just want to help, Joey."

Joey relaxed and turned to rest her head on Sam's shoulder. "I know you do, Sam. I know. I'm sorry I'm like this."

"What can I do?" Sam said.

"Take me out for a ride, Sam? I don't mean now, but maybe when you're next free. I love it, the sense of freedom, the fresh air in my face. I can forget anything when we're out on the road. When I'm with you…"

CHAPTER NINE

The lush green scenery sped past them as they rode on the motorbike into the Shropshire countryside.

Sam was beginning to love Saturdays. It was the only day she could guarantee spending time with Joey. Where she'd always been available to her parishioners, she was keeping Saturdays safe now. The new arrangement was working. She was able to shoehorn anything that came up into other days. The earth hadn't opened and swallowed her in punishment.

Riding her motorbike today with Joey up close behind her seemed like heaven on earth. She felt her tighten her hold as they took a corner. Sam was like a kid at Christmas. She found herself thinking of Joey all the time and wanting to be with her. Sometimes Joey's work schedule got in the way, but never too much. More often it was Sam's. The work continued to hit her at a relentless pace, and there seemed no light on the horizon. Neil was trying to get her a treasurer and more staff, but as yet nothing and no one was coming forward. She did the only thing she could. She waited.

She found it hard to believe that Joey had been in her life now for over four months. More surprising was the way they had connected and become *an item*.

The last few years had been hard on Sam. There was this growing awareness inside that life was passing her by. More frightening was the feeling that her calling to the church was weakening and that she was no longer fulfilled. Something else was out there calling her. But she didn't know what.

These foundation quakes were there before she saw Louise, but seeing her old lover, her old school friend, dying, everything depressing heightened. At times, if she let her feelings loose, it was like her own personal panic attack.

Joey's presence placed those feelings on hold. But now, as they spent more time together, other questions rose. Did she and Joey have a future together? Is that what Sam wanted? If it was, how would she balance her clerical life with a partner who happened to be another woman? How would the church handle that? How would her congregation handle that? How would *she* handle that? She mentally kicked herself for getting ahead of it all. Joey might not feel the same way. It was early days, and commitment might not be on her agenda. These were matters they had yet to talk of.

Sam accelerated up a long hill and let the exhilaration of speed fill her. She knew Joey would be feeling the same for they were like twins on the bike. Sam was thrilled to discover how much Joey enjoyed biking, but until recently, she hadn't understood how much it helped Joey whose experiences in the Middle East were never far away. It worried Sam. She wanted Joey to open up, but she wouldn't. She would allow Sam so far in but then bring the shutters down.

Sam hadn't missed what Joey had said the other day. Sam had said she needed help. Joey had replied she didn't *want* help. Not that she didn't *need* it. The difference was subtle, but to Sam it was meaningful. Sometimes Sam felt Joey was hiding something, that she was carrying an unspoken guilt. If this was true, then it was rotting away inside her. Joey would say everything had been her fault. When Sam asked what she meant, Joey closed up. It only made Sam more determined to see Milo, but he was out of town for a few days.

Sam dropped speed as they rode into Ludlow. She took a side road that skirted the boundaries of the old medieval market town.

Several minutes later, she pulled over on the roadside and removed her helmet. "This is one of my favorite views," she said.

Joey got off the bike and crossed over the road to stand on the riverbank. They were looking at an old arched stone bridge that crossed the River Teme. The other side was a steep hill where the ruins of Ludlow Castle rested. Sam watched the awe on Joey's face. It probably mirrored hers. This view never failed to impress. Winter was the best time to be here when the snow was about and covering the mass of trees at the foot of the castle. She prayed Joey would still be here to see it. Sam hated the thought that Joey might return to America; she was only here on a temporary basis.

Joey walked back over the road and flung her arms around Sam, kissing her cheek. "I love you," she whispered as she put her helmet back on and straddled the bike.

Not half as much as I love you, Sam thought.

They continued into the center of the town, a thriving community with its centuries old black and white timbered buildings. The place was packed with people, teaming with foreign tourists. After a walk around the town, they found a quaint tea shop.

"I'd love to go to the castle," Joey said.

"Not today you don't," Sam replied. "Saturdays are bad. There are too many others with the same idea. We'll come back when it's quieter."

"Promise?"

"I promise." Sam smiled.

"Reverend Savage?" They were interrupted by an elderly couple who were just leaving the shop. "I thought it was you. What are you doing up here?"

Joey watched as they smiled and greeted Sam with such affection. Sam returned their warmth, standing to shake their hands. The conversation was short and delivered in informative bullets. They were parishioners from the previous church where Sam had been vicar. They were delighted to hear she was now at St. Mary's Church. They saw Sam's move as a promotion. Sam was missed. The old man was now retired. His wife had had open-heart surgery. They had recently moved to Shropshire to be closer to their son. He was still in the civil service. They beamed when Sam said she'd be delighted to see them if they were ever down her way. They then apologized for interrupting, smiled very happily, and left.

It occurred to Joey that this was something that happened a lot when she was out with Sam. People always seemed to know her, and they always wanted to say hello.

"Your notoriety is legend," Joey joked.

"I'm sorry. I thought we were far away enough to be safe."

"You're pretty popular. They just wanted to say howdy."

"I know. They're good people too, but it's nice to get away sometimes."

"Think yourself lucky, Sam. How do you think I feel back home? Being on national television, there aren't many places I can go without being recognized."

Sam made a face. "It must be awful."

Joey nodded. "Fame comes at a price."

"I'll never complain again."

After they left the tea shop, they returned to the bike and rode back to Joey's apartment.

They'd only just entered when the phone rang.

It was Carrie.

Joey listened to Carrie as she watched Sam pretend not to be interested.

"Do you fancy dinner tonight?" Carrie said.

"I'm busy I'm afraid."

"How about lunch sometime this week? I'm around your area."

"Bad week, Carrie. Work is full on."

"Okay. I understand busy. I'll give you a ring later. You take care."

"Carrie Marlow?" Sam said.

Joey liked the way Sam feigned indifference.

"She's persistent if nothing else." Joey didn't mention the several other texts she'd received. "The woman doesn't know what 'no' means. Can you stay?" Joey asked. An evening with Sam over a decent bottle of wine held attraction, but Sam was shaking her head.

"I've a sermon to fine tune for tomorrow. I've kept putting it off, but it won't wait any longer."

"You know I'm disappointed," Joey said.

"Me, too."

Joey heard Sam's motorbike roar off into the distance.

She wished Sam could have stayed. She felt safe when she was around.

CHAPTER TEN

Surprise! I've got two weeks vacation to take. How about we go somewhere?"

Joey was standing in Sam's kitchen barely able to contain herself. She was a mature woman in her forties who'd seen more of life than most people, but today she felt like a teenager. She couldn't keep the excitement out of her voice. All she needed was Sam's thumbs-up, and she could start barraging her with ideas as to what they could do. Their options were limitless—a bike trip north or south. Or they could book an overseas vacation. Or they could go hill walking, something she'd discovered they both enjoyed. Joey didn't care what they did as long as they were together.

But as she gazed at Sam's face, her excitement and enthusiasm drained. Sam looked crushed.

"When?" Sam asked.

"I don't have a huge window of opportunity because of Stallion contract demands and deadlines, but anytime in September."

Sam shook her head.

"I can't."

"Are you sure?" The answer hit Joey like a rock hammer. "You haven't looked at your calendar yet."

"I don't have to. I can't. I've several ministers away in September on seminars, and I'm covering. It's been agreed for ages, way before you came over. I can't renege now."

Joey could see Sam was upset. She was too, but she understood. How often had her own work intervened to mess up her personal life? She'd lost count. Sam's situation was no different.

"Hey, it's okay." Joey's heart strings tugged. Sam looked like her favorite hymn book had been stolen. "You can't help this. You're a busy person. I understand."

"I feel awful," Sam said.

"I know."

"Can you slip your leave to another time?" Sam asked.

"No." Joey couldn't. "The production team's small, and it doesn't leave room to maneuver."

"And this was meant to be a wonderful surprise, and I've spoilt it, Joey. If I could rearrange this, I would."

"I know." Joey wrapped her arms around Sam. "There will be plenty of time for other surprises. Don't eat yourself up."

Joey left shortly after.

"Damn. Why do we both have to be such busy folk?" Joey sighed as she drove home. She wanted to kick herself. She'd been so excited, but all she'd done was upset Sam. Poor stressed out Sam was already being pulled in every direction by work. Joey hated having made it worse.

Monday arrived, and Joey stepped into her office.

She was glad the weekend was over. She hadn't seen Sam at all. Even their usual Saturday jaunt was ruined because of a wedding and reception. Sunday was no better with two christenings.

Joey felt low. She was anxious and panicky for no real reason. She'd bolted out of bed early this morning and started pacing to the point of exhaustion. She had managed to get some sleep later, and without nightmares, but she didn't like the lack of control that was becoming more and more the norm. But she would see Sam tonight. That would make her feel better. It always did.

Only minutes after sitting down with a coffee, Brian Mortimer entered her office. In his fifties and full of boyish charm, he was constantly on fast forward sporting a perpetual bounce in his step and with a demeanor that always oozed enthusiasm. He had a moustache that twirled and circled at the ends making him look like part of a circus strongman act. As he stepped inside the door, he held out both palms in front of him.

"Hey, hey, lovely American. How are you this bright sunny day?"

As ever, he made her laugh. His style was different. It was sometimes difficult to accept that he was an academic with a long list of Oxford degrees and awards that ran off the page. He was the CEO and driving force behind Stallion Productions, and essentially the man she worked for.

"I'm well, Brian," she lied. "How are you?"

"All the better for seeing you."

He swerved at speed into a chair beside her. "Can we chat?"

Brian looked serious. Joey wondered what was coming.

"Sure."

"Your project..."

Joey had finished her ideas on a proposed documentary. It was detailed and precise. She'd sent it to him early last week and hadn't heard back.

"Problems?" she asked.

"Problems?" He looked astounded, and then he broke into a huge grin as he quickly allayed her fears. "Outstanding, Joey. Frankly, exactly what I expect from someone of your experience and caliber." He got down to business. "I love the angle you propose. I like the edge of debate. We're going to run with it."

"I was worried when—"

"You didn't get my impressive speedy feedback." He nodded mock serious. "That's because I took your proposals to London, to see the Big Cheese at BBC HQ...Darth Vader himself. I presented your plans." Brian paused. "He was impressed, Joey. I saw him smile. He really likes your ideas and the potential spin-offs you suggest. They see money. I see money. Everyone is happy." Brian splayed his hands again. "He wants to speak to you personally.

Yes." He nodded again. "Darth Vader is offering you an audience, Joey. One to one."

"Christ," she laughed. "This is like working—"

"For the master race. Yes, I know. Exciting, isn't it? Which brings me to the important reason I'm here."

How anything could be more important than their previous topic she couldn't imagine. She was being summoned by the BBC's controller of programs.

"Would you like a coffee, Brian?"

Brian was dismissive. "No time, wonderful American. I've paperwork to move across my desk."

He really did make her feel better. No one could be depressed when Brian was in the room, especially if you were the focus of his attention.

"Let's talk contracts. We have you here until Christmas. I'd like to suggest something you can think about. I'm keen to hang on to you and either extend your time here, or turn the contract into something more permanent."

"What about visas, work permits?"

"Hey! You're working for the British Broadcasting Service. They're second only to the Mafia."

"Hang on a minute. Why does *Darth Vader* want to see me?"

"Two reasons. I think he really wants to meet *you*. You have an incredible reputation, deservedly so, and which shone out of your project like a beacon. The second reason is, I think, he wants you back in front of the camera again."

"I can't do that." Joey's heart pounded.

Brian put a hand on her arm. "I know, Joey. I told him. He's not going to force anything, but I guess he feels his awe and presence might make you keel over and bend his way if he asks you personally. It's the power of the dark side and all that."

Joey shook her head. It was like all her nightmares entering the room.

Brian saw. "Okay. Leave it with me. I'll sort it."

"Please, Brian. I'm not ready…I'm not sure I'll ever be ready."

"Wonderful American." He clicked his fingers. "The problem is gone." He stood and pointed a finger at her. "Give the contract some thought. No rush. Let me know when you're ready."

He moved swiftly to the door but paused for a second before leaving. "Have a great day."

He was gone.

Joey leaned back into her chair and sipped her coffee which was going cold.

Much was floating in her head of late.

Joey thought of Sam. They were growing closer and she was starting to wonder if Sam was the woman she wanted to spend the rest of her life with. Assuming Sam felt the same way, there would be hurdles. Which side of the Atlantic would they live? Sam was a vicar whose role in life was firmly over here. There was the question of her *being* a vicar. How difficult was that going to be? Could a vicar be *out and proud*? Joey could only imagine the press back home when they got news of this. Sam was a private woman who would hate the media interest. Of course, Sam might not want any of this anyway. She might not see settling down as an option. She had walked away from love once before in favor of the church.

But Brian's offer of an extended contract, with the added carrot of permanent employment, removed the pressure. It would give them time to see what they wanted. Joey also liked the idea of staying with Stallion Productions. It was a young business with fresh ideas, and a man driving it with the energy of a hurricane. She didn't feel as if she was being carried. She had felt that back home. She'd heard the whispers behind her back, that she was washed up...her career over. The media had been bolder, putting it in black and white.

But Brian's news lifted her. It meant she didn't have to go home in the New Year.

Her first instinct was to tell Sam, but then she decided not to. Not yet. She wanted to think everything through first. Maybe she also needed to talk to Brandon Finch. He might have objections. In truth, she suspected he'd be relieved.

Her day improved and became even better an hour before she left.

Brian popped his head around the door.

"I've spoken with the controller. He's dropped the topic of putting you in front of the camera. Good guy. But he still wants to see you. His secretary will call you later in the week. Okay?"

"Thank you, Brian." Joey was relieved. Even though he'd promised to sort this issue, she'd had her doubts.

"No problemo. This is what we call excellent Anglo-American diplomacy."

He grinned and disappeared.

Joey left the office feeling a damn sight better than when she'd arrived.

She headed into the municipal parking lot. Parking space was limited at work and was first come, first park. She'd lost out this morning.

As she arrived at the car, she heard someone call out her name. It was Carrie.

"Hey, fancy seeing you here," she said as she sauntered over to Joey.

"I'm just leaving work." Joey eyed Carrie. She was smartly dressed. She was also sexy, and she knew it.

Joey was reminded, and not for the first time, that her old self wouldn't have wasted any time getting to know her better...much better. But she had different values now. Carrie on the other hand didn't and seemed eager to impress. She pouted her lips before smiling.

"Want to go for a drink? There are some great pubs around here."

"I'm sorry, Carrie, but I'm busy this evening." Joey thought of Sam. Her heart lifted.

Carrie looked crestfallen. "You keep turning me down. I'm going to get a complex."

Joey laughed. Carrie's expression was alluring. She let her down gently.

"You just catch me at all the wrong times."

"You do realize that all work, no play, makes Joey a dull girl. And I do know how to play. But okay," Carrie said. "I'll just have to keep trying. I might get lucky." Her green eyes twinkled with naughtiness.

Joey got into her car and watched Carrie in the rearview mirror as she walked away. She had a feeling Carrie knew she was watching. The woman swayed her hips a fraction too much, as if advertising her wares. Joey smiled. Carrie was wasting her time.

She waited and saw her get into her car and leave.

Joey glanced at her watch. She was going to get caught in rush hour traffic. It would turn a one-hour drive into two. As she exited out onto the busy road, she longed for a helicopter where she could rise above the congestion. It would get her to Sam quicker. Suddenly, the distance between them was vast, and she desperately needed to be with her. She made a calculated decision to go to the church instead of the vicarage. Sam led evening worship on Mondays, and by the time Joey got back, that's where she'd be.

She made the right choice. The traffic was worse than usual because some idiot had the audacity to run into the rear of another vehicle at a big intersection and block it. By the time she arrived at the church, Sam was already conducting the service, so Joey sat in a pew at the back and waited. She didn't miss the several times that Sam glanced over to her as she read prayers. She'd spotted Joey's arrival within seconds as if she possessed some internal sensor.

When the service was over and the last member of the congregation had left, Joey walked down the aisle toward Sam. Sam was waiting, her features impassive, her manner reserved. Without speaking, Sam pointed toward the vestry.

Once they were inside, Sam smiled, but Joey thought she looked nervous. She stepped forward and wrapped her arms around Sam who melted into them. Joey felt her warmth.

"I've wanted to do this all day," Joey whispered into Sam's neck. She knew Sam still felt bad for not being able to get time off. "I come into your life and give you nothing but problems," she joked.

Sam kissed her. It was long and passionate.

Joey's state of anxiety lessened.

"I love you being in my life, and I love the problems you present me with." Sam's husky voice was a whisper. "I'm just trying to work out how I can solve them."

Though her last words were sprinkled with humor, Joey heard the vulnerability in them. She took Sam's face in her hands and kissed her again. When she withdrew she saw such love looking back at her.

"Is kissing appropriate in the house of God?" Joey asked.

Sam put a finger to an ear. "I don't hear any complaints. I guess he's okay with the odd show of affection."

Joey tingled when Sam ran a finger down the side of her face and said, "I'm going to find more time to be with you."

Joey smiled. "You may need one of those miracles you're always talking about."

"I know." Sam exhaled loudly. "How about we go out for dinner on Wednesday evening? And a week on Saturday, *very early*, we bike up to Ludlow and do the castle. We can get there before the multitude do and be first in the queue."

Sam was trying, and Joey loved her for it. It didn't hinder things when Sam pulled her close and hugged her tight again.

"Do you want to come back to my place? Spend the night?" Joey asked.

"Yes."

❖

Sam stayed the night.

They joked and laughed and made love. The tension that seemed to accompany Joey all the time now almost disappeared. When she was with Sam, nothing worried her. Sam cocooned her from everything. Even her nightmares lessened when she slept in her arms.

Wednesday evening came, and they went out to dinner. Nothing interrupted. No one called. No parishioner approached the table delighted to see Sam. It was Joey and Sam's night together. It was a wonderful dinner.

Everything was going fine. But then Saturday came, the day of their expected bike ride to Ludlow. It was the day Joey learned that Sam's promises could not be kept and that church business had a way of constantly ruining their plans. Sam was already thirty minutes late as Joey waited inside her apartment. The phone rang.

"I'm sorry, Joey."

Joey knew what was coming. Sam's voice concealed nothing.

"John Alistair, the vicar of St. Barnabas is ill, and he can't do a wedding ceremony today. I have to cover."

"Why you?" Joey couldn't hide her disappointment.

"Everyone else is committed. I can hardly let the couple down. It's their big day."

"Sam, you have other commitments, too."

She heard Sam pause, but she didn't answer directly. "Do you want to come along?"

"No, Sam, I don't."

"You're angry," Sam said.

"No, I'm not."

"You sound it."

"I'm just disappointed, Sam."

"I can't help this."

The fact that Joey knew Sam couldn't didn't make her feel any better. "God damn it, Sam, Neil had better hurry and find you some more staff. You can't keep filling in the gaps. It's gonna kill you." *And me.*

"I've got to go. I'll ring you later," Sam said.

When the call ended, Joey refused to wallow in self-pity. It wasn't her style and she wasn't going to start now. Sam was caught between a nail and a hammer head. Things *would* improve once Neil worked his magic and sorted out staffing issues. Until then, she and Sam would simply have to cope.

Joey turned her energy into halfheartedly cleaning her apartment and repositioning furniture. By mid afternoon she was done. She'd just made her mind up that a walk was a good idea when the landline rang.

She half expected it to be Sam, but it was Carrie.

"Hey, recluse. Why are you in on a Saturday?"

Joey closed her eyes. She was disappointed it wasn't Sam, and Carrie's question was bad timing.

"Last-minute changes to plans," Joey responded dryly.

"At a loose end?"

Joey hesitated for too long.

"Maybe I can offer you an alternative to that, and I can promise you it's way more exciting," Carrie said.

Joey winced. She didn't doubt Carrie was making a move on her. It was the last thing she wanted.

"I know this great gay club in Birmingham," Carrie said. "It's private membership only, so selective. It caters to the boys and girls, and it's the place to be for lively, wired people on a Saturday night. You can let your hair down and not worry about being seen. It's rated one of the best clubs in the country…great music to dance to, and a place to forget all your troubles."

"Who says I have troubles?"

"Not me. If you don't have any then you'll get into the mood faster. I'm a member, and I'm planning on going tonight so the question is, do you want to sit home alone on a Saturday evening, or do you want to party and have some fun?"

"Carrie, thanks for the offer, but I'm not looking for anyone… I'm taken."

A moment's hesitation, and Carrie bounced back. "Well, I can't say I'm not disappointed but I understand. But hey, you can still have a night out with a friend, can't you?" Her voice turned sincere, more genuine. "Seriously, Joey, just come along. If you don't like it, you don't have to stay. It's just an opportunity to get out and meet new people. I could do with the company too. I've had a dreadful week at work. How about I pick you up at seven tonight? We can go eat and then hit the club."

Something about Carrie's change of approach—less the vamp, more the human being looking for escape—altered Joey's mind. She didn't want to stay in tonight. She envisioned the usual sleepless night interspersed with the usual nightmares. A change of surroundings and a chance to let off some steam might do her good.

"Okay, you win," Joey said.

"Good decision, girl. We're going to have fun, fun, fun. Wear dancing shoes."

❖

Joey awoke to the sound of her doorbell.

Her eyes focused on the bottle of pills sitting on the bedside table, and she vaguely remembered taking them when she'd come home. It was probably why her head felt fuzzy and heavy. She hated taking the medication because of this. It stripped her of mental sharpness and made her every thought sluggish and slow.

The doorbell rang again.

"Don't worry, I'll get it."

It was Carrie's voice.

Joey turned to see her semi-naked, searching the room for her clothing. Unsuccessful, Carrie grabbed a cover off the bed, wrapped it around herself, and left the room.

What the hell is she doing in my bed?

The answer didn't come, only a surge of ice-cold panic before she recalled that nothing had happened between them. She dimly remembered Carrie bringing her home last night from the club. She hadn't been well.

Joey struggled to get up. As she did, the room spun, and she felt nauseous. She looked around the room for her clothing, but it wasn't there. Where was it? She had so many questions and precious few answers. Was this all a bizarre dream?

Joey heard voices in the distance, but she didn't hear the words. She wobbled into the sitting room.

"I'm sorry I've disturbed you both."

The caller's voice sounded familiar, but too soon, Carrie was closing the door, and whoever had been the other side was gone.

Carrie was scrutinizing her, a look of concern on her face.
"Hey, you. How are you feeling?"

Joey had to think. It didn't take her long to realize she felt like shit. The memories of last night started to seep back. They weren't good. She remembered the noise of the night club, the flashing strobe lighting, and the unbearable heat. She blinked hard.

"What happened?" she asked.

"We were at the club, and you had some sort of hallucination. You kept going on about *finding the road home* and asking why you couldn't remember the route back. You were really sick. I had to bring you home. Don't you remember?"

When Joey didn't answer, Carrie said, "I couldn't leave you, Joey. You kept throwing up. I put you to bed, but I stayed in case you were sick in your sleep. I didn't want you to choke."

Joey looked around her. Her clothing was scattered all over the floor in the sitting room. It smelled. It was the smell of vomit. It wasn't a pretty sight. And Carrie had brought her home and stayed.

"Thanks." Joey couldn't think what else to say. She was embarrassed. She'd lost control again, and in public, like she'd done back home in the States. "I'm sorry, Carrie. I guess this hasn't been your idea of a good night out."

Carrie showed only concern. "Sod that," she said. "I'm only glad you seem better now...but I think you ought to see someone, Joey. You scared me. You were talking gibberish and..."

Joey saw the same look in Carrie's eyes that she'd seen on all the others. It was the look that showed how uncomfortable people had become being around her. It was the look that silently said they thought she was mad. Normally they ran. Carrie hadn't, and that surprised her. Joey knew her type. Carrie was an amorous vixen who lusted after women. She was one-night fodder that required no love, no commitment, and no promises. She hankered only for sex. Joey had been like that once. It shocked her that Carrie was showing redeeming virtues.

"Who was at the door?" Joey asked.

Carrie shrugged. "Reverend Savage. It shocked me at first. I thought why would a vicar turn up here unless it was bad news. I half expected her to say someone had died. But she said it was just a passing call and nothing important."

I'm sorry I've disturbed you both.

Those were the words Joey had heard...Sam's.

Joey went cold. She looked at Carrie who had answered the door wearing nothing but a blanket and showing way too much flesh. From the door, Sam would see Joey's clothing, stripped off quickly last night, scattered all over. Joey's heart was beating fast. Sam would be making assumptions...horribly wrong ones.

"I told her you were still asleep," Carrie said.

Joey winced.

Carrie didn't see for she was already heading back to the bedroom. When she reemerged, she was dressed. Joey couldn't help thinking she was the fastest dresser she'd come across.

"Hey look, girl. I'm going to dash. It's past noon, and I've got some work to do for tomorrow. Are you going to be okay?"

Joey guessed Carrie would be praying she would. It was clear she wanted to leave. She couldn't imagine Carrie doing any work on a Sunday.

In truth, it was a hidden blessing for Joey. She wanted her gone too. Joey needed to go find Sam. She could only imagine what was going through her head and how she was feeling.

As soon as Carrie had gone, Joey gathered up the stinking clothing and threw them into the wash. She tried calling Sam's cell, but it kept going to voice mail.

Joey showered, dressed, and went to find her.

She tried the church first because it was closest. Sam wasn't there, only one of her worker bees.

"I haven't seen her since church service this morning, Joey. If I do, would you like me to say you're looking for her?"

"No, it's okay. I'm just passing. I can catch her later."

Joey hated the forced casualness, as if there was no important reason to see her.

Her heart was in her throat as she returned to her car. On an off chance, she phoned Neil and Miriam.

Miriam answered. "Not here I'm afraid. We've got extended family with us this weekend, which I wouldn't wish on my enemies, let alone people I love. Anything wrong?"

"No. I just wanted to run something by her, but it can wait. It's not an emergency."

Joey felt like she was going to implode. She was desperate to find Sam.

She looked at her watch. It was nearly two o'clock. She headed for the vicarage.

No one was there except Gloria who instantly felt she had to explain why she was present on a Sunday afternoon. Her Irish tones filled the kitchen with rhythm.

"I wasn't here at all on Friday as I'd a dental appointment in the morning, and an optician's appointment in the afternoon. I didn't have anything better to do today, so I thought I'd come over and change the bedding…which I normally do on the Friday."

Joey nodded politely as Gloria prattled on about the appointments and how she should have thrown in one for her hair and made it a complete day of *fix me*. Joey wanted to shake Gloria quiet and get her to tell her where Sam was.

"Have you seen Sam?" she asked once Gloria shut up.

"I saw her about one thirty when I arrived. She was just leaving."

"Do you know where she went?"

"I do not. I only know she—" Gloria stopped mid-sentence, as though she didn't want to say more.

"What?"

"Nothing. She just looked tired."

"Oh."

"I'd have left ten minutes ago, but I can't find my glasses." Gloria was prattling again, this time about her glasses. She was looking around the kitchen. Joey felt obliged to help her, but they didn't find them.

"Just as well I'm having a new pair," Gloria said.

Joey was stepping through the door to leave when Gloria stopped her. She started to say something but didn't finish.

"What is it, Gloria?"

Gloria hesitated before she declared, "Nothing."

"You were about to say something."

Gloria shook her head. "No, it can wait."

"What can?"

Gloria's eyes narrowed. She donned what Sam affectionately called her *clam* look. Nothing would make her say more until she wanted to. Joey sighed and left. As she did, she noticed Sam's bike was gone. Her heart sank. Sam could be anywhere. She'd never find her.

She was just contemplating her next move when she spotted something on the ground by the bus stop. It was a pair of glasses. She picked them up and headed back to the vicarage.

She knocked on the door again.

"You've only just left," Gloria said. "She still isn't back."

Joey managed a smile. "Are your glasses gold rimmed?"

"They are."

"Then these are yours." She handed over the glasses and was heading back to the car when Gloria spoke.

"Why are you looking for Sam?"

"I need to talk to her."

Gloria frowned. "You know I like you, Joey, don't you?"

It was an odd statement that sent a chill through her. She waited for what was coming. The clam was opening.

"I'm not a religious woman, and I'm not one for interfering in others' lives. But don't hurt Reverend Savage, Joey. She's a special woman who does much for the people, regardless of their religious beliefs. She's hugely respected...and I don't want her getting hurt."

It was said in such a tender way, Joey reached out and placed a hand on Gloria's arm. "I would never deliberately hurt Sam."

"I'm not saying you would, but...just be careful. Behind the clerical uniform, she's a gentle type lacking in personal experience...you *know* what I mean. She fights in everybody else's corner, but when it comes to her own battles, she's got no suit of armor to protect her."

Gloria stared at Joey for a second before closing the door.

As Joey drove away, she wondered what had happened that had made Gloria come out of her shell and give away how much she cared for Sam.

Joey had to find Sam.

❖

Sam rode the bike hard.

A straight piece of road opened up in front of her that stretched way beyond, and she accelerated into it, feeling the power roar beneath her. Way ahead, she caught sight of a Sunday driver crawling along. She spotted the crest of the hill farther in the distance. Was there room to overtake, or should she drop speed until she was safely over the brow?

Common sense and survival told Sam to play it safe and wait. It would add another ten seconds to her journey. But Sam wasn't in the mood to be sensible, and she revved the bike and increased speed. She overtook the car, just missing an oncoming vehicle as it crested the hill. She caught the look of fear on the driver's face, a man in a car with kids. Horns blew as she swerved onto her side of the road and left the scene behind.

Undeterred by the close call, she rode on at speed, ignoring the voice in her head calling her an idiot and accusing her of trying to kill, if not herself, then others on the road. The shock brought her to her senses.

She turned left, off the main road, and onto a quieter country lane where she dropped her speed and eventually pulled over into a lay-by. She removed her visor. She was shaking as she stared out across the fields and hedges.

Sam hoped her bike ride would bring some peace and clarity, but it had been anything but a relaxing ride. All she could think about was Carrie opening Joey's door wearing not very much, and the array of clothing all over the sitting room floor. Carrie's voice was in her head again. *She's still asleep.*

Her cell phone buzzed inside her jacket. She unzipped it and removed the phone. There were several messages from Joey and some others. She put the phone back in her jacket. She waited another ten minutes before restarting the bike and heading back to the vicarage at a more sedate speed.

When she got back, Gloria had gone.

Sam was glad. She'd made a fool of herself earlier. Gloria had asked her a question twice, and Sam hadn't been able to answer. Gloria had looked at her in alarm, asking what was wrong, but Sam had remained mute. It hadn't really mattered. Gloria seemed to guess it had something to do with Joey and didn't push further. When Sam left for her bike ride, she hadn't even been able to say good-bye.

This time Sam left the vicarage more in control of her emotions.

She rode to Joey's for the second time in the day. The first she'd been full of anticipation and nervous at having disappointed Joey. Now she felt nothing.

When she got there, she could see Joey's car was gone. She waited outside in the parking lot across the road.

Eventually, Joey turned up. She spotted Sam immediately.

Sam, still on her bike, waved her over.

"What are you doing here?" Joey asked.

Sam thought she saw relief on her face. It was the last emotion she expected to see.

"I hear you've been looking for me," Sam said.

Joey looked confused.

"You've been leaving clues all over the place. John rang from church…said you'd turned up. Then Miriam said you'd phoned. Gloria left me a note on the kitchen table saying you'd been there. You've been busy," Sam said.

"Aren't you supposed to be doing evening prayers?"

Joey's concern for her schedule hardly seemed relevant, and Sam could only respond with a halfhearted smile.

"Yes, but I couldn't face it so I thought I'd test the system out and get someone to cover for me for a change." She paused. "It works."

Sam's success didn't register on Joey's pale face.

"So, why are you looking for me?" Sam asked.

"I've tried to phone you. I've left messages."

Sam had listened to all three voice mails asking her to ring back. She'd ignored them.

"Why are you looking for me?" she repeated. Sam felt cold inside. She assumed it was shock. Her world was crushed.

"Because you've got it all wrong. Because you left before I knew you were there…before I could explain," Joey said.

"What is there to explain? You slept with her."

"No, Sam. I didn't." Joey's eyes never left hers as she shook her head. "I didn't kiss her or hold her or whisper sweet nothings in her ear." Joey straightened. "I know what you think you saw and what you think happened, but you're wrong. I want to put this right. I want you to know what happened." Joey shivered. "Can we discuss this inside?"

"No." Sam would hear Joey's excuse and then leave.

"Carrie called me yesterday afternoon and asked if I wanted to go out for dinner and then to a night club. I'm sure she had more on her mind than friendship. I told her I wasn't looking for anyone and that I was already involved with someone. She accepted that and asked me out anyway. So we did. Just as friends."

"You're telling me *nothing* happened?" Sam said.

"I am. Sure, she came on to me once, but I made it clear I wasn't interested. I told her to stop wasting her time. And do you know why, Sam? Because it isn't what I want. Because she isn't you. You're who I want. You're the one I love."

Sam watched as Joey ran a hand through her hair.

"We spent time dancing in this really noisy, overcrowded club. I didn't feel too good. It was hot so we stepped out the back to get some air. There was a group of guys there having some argument over who knows what. One of them struck a match to light a cigarette." Joey paused. "Then do you know what happened? It must have been the smell of sulfur. I went into meltdown…a flashback. I was back in Syria as we were hit. All I can remember is falling to my knees and being violently sick. I created what you guys call *a scene*."

Sam saw the shame on her face.

"And do you know what Carrie does?" Joey said. "This is the same Carrie who reminds me so much of my former self? She brings me home and puts me to bed. You know, I'm not sure because I don't remember much after stripping off my vomit covered clothing in the sitting room…but yes, I think she slept with me. *Slept.* She was afraid I'd throw up again and choke to death. She lay beside me on the bed to make sure I was safe. Nothing happened, Sam. And why would it? Why would she want anything to do with me after a stellar performance like that? In your typical Brit reserved wording, Carrie *conducted herself admirably*. She made sure I was okay. What you saw…the scattered clothing on the floor, that wasn't foreplay.

"And my error in all of this? I shouldn't have gone out with her in the first place, but I wasn't thinking straight. I was feeling anxious and on edge. I kept thinking about things I just want to forget. One of the coping strategies the counselor told me was to get out and occupy my mind…to do something. I was feeling isolated, Sam. Frankly, the Harlem Gospel Choir of New York City could have invited me out, and I'd have gone."

The look on Joey's face told her this was the truth. Sam groaned and dropped her head to rest on the handlebars. All that ridiculous angst she'd been through. It was misplaced. Joey had done nothing wrong. Far from it, Joey had suffered. Sam lifted her head and looked at her.

"I leapt to the wrong conclusion."

"Yes, you did."

"I should have let you explain."

"Yes, you should, but the picture looked kinda skewed, didn't it?" Joey said.

Sam shook her head in disbelief. She was the one to feel ashamed, not Joey.

"Oh, Joey, I'm sorry. Some minister I am. I'm supposed to see the good in people, not leap to conclusions, and not be judgmental. What a crap vicar I am."

"I'd never cheat on you, Sam."

Sam wished she could erase the entire day. "I'm sorry I've doubted you."

"You know my past. It was easy to connect the dots." Joey was forgiving.

Sam wasn't the only one in shock. She saw Joey shivering, and her pale face was almost translucent. She hopped off the bike and grabbed Joey's hand. "Let's get you inside."

It warmed her when Joey smiled back at her.

When they got to the door, Sam took her key out. It was the one Joey had given her.

"Why didn't you use it earlier?" Joey asked.

Sam opened the door. "Because I felt bad for letting you down yesterday. It didn't seem right." Sam paused. "On reflection, be thankful. I'd have found Carrie on your bed and probably killed her. I'd now be on a murder charge."

"This is messy, isn't it?" Joey said.

Now Sam was shaking. "Joey, please forgive me. I'm an idiot."

Joey held her hand this time.

"It's okay."

"Are *we* okay?" Sam asked.

Joey placed a light kiss on her forehead. "The greatest gains often come after the biggest hurdles."

"Who said that?"

"Me. Just now," Joey said.

"Do you think we can avoid hurdles like this from now on?"

"I'm game," Joey said.

Sam closed the door behind them and threw her arms around Joey.

❖

Sam found Milo Granger in the admin office at the rear of St. Augustus church.

He was a baldheaded man who wore dark-rimmed glasses. Short and wiry, he was unlike his son, Harry. Sam had only met Harry once. It was during her first year at St. Mary's. He'd been staying with his parents when his marriage broke up. He was tall and had the muscular stature of a rugby player with broad shoulders and a thick neck. But he'd ended up no sportsman. Until medically discharged, he'd been in the army and done several tours in Afghanistan. He'd experienced a series of traumatic events where colleagues in his unit had been killed. He was a survivor, but it had left him with PTSD.

It was why Sam wanted to speak to Milo. She knew he'd tried to stay close to Harry throughout his problems, even when Harry had tried to push everyone, including his parents, away. Sam was looking for any information that would help her understand what Joey was going through. She was desperate.

"Milo, thanks for seeing me."

"I've always got time for you, Sam."

Sam grinned. It was true. If she ever set up a fan club, she was sure Milo would run it. They'd taken to each other from the moment they met...like flies on flypaper. She'd also spent time with him in quiet support on the rare occasion he'd spoken about Harry when things had got bad. He hadn't said much of late. She wasn't sure if that was a good or bad sign.

"Are you okay chatting about Harry and his PTSD?" Sam asked.

"Yes. You know someone who's having problems, too?"

Sam had mentioned this on the phone but kept Joey's name out of it. She'd kept it all sufficiently vague. "Friend of a friend."

"Where do you want me to start?" Milo said.

"I know what PTSD is, the definition. I've read plenty on the Internet, but..."

"You don't know what it really does to them, and how it affects their behavior. How it affects their family and friends?"

"I don't," Sam said. "Anything you can tell me, I'd be grateful."

Milo sat down and beckoned Sam to join him.

"You never knew the old Harry. Ever since he was a kid, he was always into everything. He joined clubs, he organized school events, and he belonged to debating societies. The school made him head boy. He was a real friendly guy who loved socializing. If anyone had a party, you always invited Harry. He was a joker, and a nicer man you'd have to go a long way to meet. I know I'm biased, but I was so proud of him. He joined the army and made sergeant in record time. He cut a real dash in his uniform. Cheryl, his wife, adored him and they had two beautiful children. Then he went to Afghanistan.

"The first time my wife, Helen, and I knew there was a problem was when he was medically discharged. Once he was back home, we quickly found out all wasn't well. He was suffering from terrible nightmares and having flashbacks. He was wracked with anxiety and panic attacks."

It all sounded familiar to Sam.

"Harry was drinking heavily and becoming physically abusive to Cheryl. The kids grew frightened of him. Despite this, he refused to admit he was ill, and he wouldn't talk about it. He was the real tough guy who saw any request for help as weakness."

Joey was refusing to talk too, but thankfully, there was no substance abuse.

"It got bad," Milo continued. "Cheryl threw him out. I don't blame her. She was walking on eggshells. He was unpredictable, and he lost that ability to have any successful interpersonal relationships. He kept pushing us away, becoming more and more isolated. He even distanced himself from the kids…he used to adore them. Cheryl was frightened of him, and the children were stressed and starting to have issues at school. Cheryl tried to help, but he wouldn't have any of it. The mere suggestion of it made him violent."

Joey isn't violent.

SOUL SURVIVOR

"We weren't surprised when Cheryl filed for divorce. Of course, Helen and I took him in. We didn't want our boy on the streets. He was a mess, and becoming worse by the day.

"I'd wake up at night and hear him crying. Sometimes, he would scream. I would go through to him, and—like a child—I would hold his hand, and he would squeeze it. He wouldn't let go till the morning. He suffered from hallucinations…"

Sam went cold.

"…and we already knew he couldn't control his emotions. He was very moody. He became more socially isolated and would lock himself away in his room for days on end. We watched him disconnecting from the world around him. If you *could* get him to talk, he saw nothing but hopelessness about his future. It was terrible, Sam. It was like he wanted to punish himself for living. Harry became more and more self-destructive. It all came to a head one night. It was when things changed."

Sam knew Harry wasn't living with his parents now. "What happened?"

"He hit Helen." Milo sighed. Sam reached out and rested a hand on his shoulder. "He got angry one night because we didn't like his drinking. It made him worse, more unreasonable. Helen told him she wasn't going to stand for it anymore, not in her own home. Harry lashed out."

"Did he mean to hit her?" Sam asked.

"Yes. It was at the top of the stairs. Helen fell backward down them, and I had to call an ambulance. When the police arrived, I told them what happened. They arrested Harry and charged him with assault. That sounds hard, but we were desperate and didn't know what to do. We saw it as a way to get help. And out of bad came good because he did get help and things started to change… for the better."

"Because he hit Helen." Sam didn't know any of this. She suspected no one else did either.

"Yes," Milo said.

"Was she okay?"

"Thank, God, yes. Harry started counseling. A few of his army buddies helped him too. One got him onto a training course where he's learned to fell all sizes of trees. He's now got himself a job working for the forestry commission down in Hampshire. It's a solitary type of job, but he's really taken to it." Milo started laughing. "He lives in a hut in the forest, but it has running water and electricity so not as bad as it sounds. He's grown a beard and has long hair. He looks like a real caveman and nothing like the smart lad he used to be, but he's calmer and happier. I think he's repairing slowly. He's got some control back in his life. He even runs the occasional day course for schoolchildren. They come to the forest, and he shows them around, talking to them about the eco system."

"I'm really glad things are better," Sam said.

"Me, too. I'd love it if he got back with Cheryl, but I don't think that'll ever happen. But he's closer to the kids again."

"Thank you for sharing this with me, Milo."

"I don't know who your *friend of a friend* is, but they need to get the right help. It's not something they can fix by themselves. We've all learned that the hard way."

Milo only confirmed what Sam knew. Joey needed professional help. Her problem was getting Joey to see that.

❖

Joey broke the news to Sam while they were out on a bike ride. It was a couple of weeks after the incident with Carrie; their relationship was good. The recent *misunderstanding* had deepened their bond. Joey's declaration that she loved Sam had helped.

"Sam, I've decided to take my vacation and fly back to Baltimore to see my folks. I know they're missing me. They're worried. The last time I was with them, I was in bits."

Joey's parents were always there for her, full of love and support. She'd kept them at arm's length when she'd returned from Syria. She needed to let them know she was okay...even if she had to fake it. She also wanted to talk to them about the job offer Stallion Productions was proposing. Her mom and dad were good sounding boards. Despite her professional capability, she never felt too old or experienced to ask what they thought. She wanted to talk to Sam about it, too, but now wasn't the right time. Sam was busy and stressed. Joey would talk to her when she returned.

"You're going to be real busy," Joey said. "So I'm going home to spend time with them."

Sam was taking Joey's vacation plans on the chin. Though she looked disappointed, Joey could hear the understanding.

"It's the right thing to do, Joey. My schedule is scary, and you won't see much of me if you stay. Hey, I'm not going to see much of me," Sam jested. "I think it'll do you good to see your parents, and you can thank your father personally for getting my bike rolling again."

Joey scoffed. Her dad would like nothing better than to talk bikes. She wrapped an arm around Sam as they stood by the bike on a hillside looking out over a sweeping, majestic country scene. There were rolling hills before them, full of grazing sheep. The way the sun fell, it was a photographer's dream.

"You are going to come back, aren't you? You're not going to stay?"

Sam's sudden seriousness jolted Joey.

"Hey, what's this all about?" she said.

Occasionally, Sam's concerns for Joey *escaped*. Joey knew how frustrated Sam was. She wanted Joey to get help, but every time she broached the topic, Joey got unreasonable and temperamental, refusing to discuss it. Sam tried hard not to say too much, but Joey could almost hear her thinking.

She leaned into Sam, tightening her arm around her.

"Why would I do that? I love you, you loon." Joey turned to make eye contact. She wanted to chase the frown off Sam's face.

"Sam, when I was hiding from the rebels, I had a lot of time to think. Part of that involved awareness…some of it not too pleasant. If I died out there, few people would really miss me."

Sam tried to interrupt. Joey stopped her.

"No, you listen. Sure, work colleagues would declare how tragic it was to lose such a consummate professional and wonderful associate. They would probably broadcast a special on TV showing how I'd become what I was, and talk about the highlights of my career…the awards I've been honored with. It's the general accepted thing to do. But really, only a few friends would genuinely miss me—"

"I can't believe—"

"—and my parents. They'd be devastated."

Joey had lain in the cramped confines of that cabinet and thought of the death of her team.

"Sam, all my friends who died, they were honorable men with loving families. I promised myself that if I got out of there, I'd be a better person. I would change. I would live my life honorably, too. I'd never again treat relationships superficially as I once did. I promised myself that if I survived, I would live my personal life to a better moral code." She paused deliberately so Sam would really hear what she said next.

"Now I've met *you*, Sam. I'm in love with you. You're everything to me. So…" she gave her a quick kiss on her cheek, "you bet your ass I'm coming back, kiddo."

When Joey flew home, Sam couldn't take her to the airport because of work. A neighbor of Elsa's did.

As the plane taxied out on to the runway, Joey felt as if her heart was made of lead. She hated leaving Sam. She was already counting the days till she came back.

CHAPTER ELEVEN

Joey was gone, and Sam immersed herself in work.
It wasn't difficult to do. She rose early and went to bed late. Despite her crazy schedule, Sam couldn't shift the thoughts of how she never had enough time for Joey. Her own anxieties rose once more.

She sensed time ticking away, and with it her life. Her calling to serve God was no longer strong enough to paper over growing cracks. Sam again grew frightened as she realized she had no life of her own beyond the boundaries of the church. Joey's arrival had brought her hope, but now that seemed threatened by the very vocation that was strangling her.

Louise's sage words haunted her. *Love and life.* Joey had reawakened desires and dreams in Sam. Was this her last chance for happiness? Did Joey feel the same as she did, that this might be for the long term? She'd told Sam she loved her. Sam didn't doubt her. So what was Sam going to do? Her day job was interfering way too much.

The day after Joey flew home, Sam conducted the early morning service at St. Mary's. Straight after, she drove to the bishop's office at the Old Palace in Worcester. It was Neil's official residence and where he normally worked. Sam needed to see him.

When she got to his office, she was greeted warmly by his secretary. Ann Brown was a woman Sam considered a friend. Over the years, and different bishops, they'd interacted a lot. Familiarity had turned to friendship.

"Sorry, Sam, but he's in a meeting on culture and heritage. After that, he's straight into a business lunch and another meeting for international development. I wish you'd phoned. I could have saved you a journey."

Sam didn't care. "What about tomorrow?"

"He's off down to Lambeth Palace to see the archbishop. The rest of the week doesn't look good either."

Something on Sam's face made Ann frown.

"But I can always interrupt if it's an emergency."

With a heavy heart, Sam acknowledged that her personal life wasn't exactly an emergency. "No, Ann. It can wait. It'll have to."

"Are you sure?"

"Yes." Sam tried to smile, but her lips weren't playing.

"I'll let Bishop Neil know you were here."

"No, don't do that, Ann. It'll only worry him. I can catch him later."

Sam drove back to St. Mary's.

She was still there early evening when Neil strode down the aisle toward her. He wore his concern like a cloak. Sam wondered what Ann had said.

"What's wrong?"

He wasted no time in getting to the point. He knew something was up. She'd never turned up at his office before, unannounced and troubled.

Suddenly, Sam had no words. She felt like a load of stitching coming loose. All she could do was shake her head.

He guided her to a pew, and they sat down.

"Talk to me, Sam." When Neil gave anyone his attention, it was intense, sincere, and genuine. Sam felt that now, his voice with its deep tone instantly soothing her.

"I'm struggling, Neil."

He studied her face as if an answer lay there.

Sam didn't know how or where to start. Neil made a best guess.

"Would it help if I said I might have found some extra manpower? There's a recently ordained priest who has shown interest in the parish. And I've an eye on another with more experience. I've called for their reports so I can make an assessment. I can't get either of them until after Christmas, but if you can struggle on until then."

Neil's guess was wrong. Not so long ago, he'd have been spot-on, but now Sam knew this was more. She could see he recognized that almost before he finished talking.

"It isn't that, Neil."

He shifted awkwardly. "Are you losing your faith? It's something we all go through, but often it comes back stronger than before."

"I can't imagine you suffering that," Sam said.

"I did. When Charlie died."

Charlie was Neil and Miriam's youngest child. He'd died eight years ago after a boating accident.

"What changed?" Sam asked, grateful for the temporary respite.

"Miriam." His smile was haunted. "She made me talk and not bury my grief. We grew closer. My faith came back…in time."

"I never knew." Sam recalled the tragedy, and how it nearly destroyed him. She hadn't known it had tested his faith.

"Not something either of us could talk about."

She understood.

"Is that what this is all about, Sam? Losing your faith?"

She managed a smile and put him out of his misery.

"No. My faith is as strong as the day I entered the church. God is part of me. He's in every breath I take. I feel him in my very fingertips."

"Then what is it?"

"I thought I knew this morning, but now I don't. I just don't feel right doing this anymore…being a vicar."

He ran a hand across his face. "But you're a wonderful vicar. You do know that, don't you? Everybody loves you, especially your congregation. You were born for this."

"Maybe, but that's part of it. I chunter on and do everything I'm supposed to, but it isn't enough anymore. In the past few years, I've had this increasing feeling deep inside that I'm missing out on life. When I'm not darting around like a blue-ass fly, it comes over me, and it's growing in strength. It's such a heavy feeling, Neil. I try to tell myself it's selfish, that it'll pass. But it won't be dismissed. I can't talk my way out of it and convince myself to see things differently."

"You're overworking. You need a break."

"If only it were that simple, but it isn't. It started way before all of this." She pointed to the roof repairs. "Where's my life, Neil? Where does Reverend Samantha Savage stop, and Sam start?"

Neil was at a loss to answer.

"What does this mean?" he asked.

"I don't know. I only know I'm unhappy."

Neil eyeballed her, his compassion evident. "We can't have that, Sam. Is there anything I can do to help?"

"I wish I knew. You must think I sound ridiculous. It's like loving wood, and wanting to work with wood, but not wanting to be a carpenter. I know I'm not making sense."

Neil had resorted to biting a fingernail. It was a habit he had when things got beyond him. It only made her feel worse.

"In all the years I've known you," he said, "I've never considered you ridiculous or selfish. Far from it, you've been reliable, a staunch supporter, and the voice of reason when needed. You've also put up with all these manpower shortages, church repairs, and continued on with little complaining. What's pushed you over the edge?"

Joey.

Sam couldn't tell him that. She wanted to be with Joey, but ecclesiastical matters always got in the way. It shouldn't have to be like this. She shrugged.

"Why did you want to see me, Sam?"

"It all seems so stupid now." Sam was embarrassed. Earlier, with Ann, she'd been frightened.

"What?"

"I had some silly idea in my head, but it's gone now."

"Like?"

"I wanted to drop everything and run."

"But you don't now?"

"No. I'm calmer." Sam wasn't sure she was. "And I guess I just needed a friend to talk to." She smiled and was grateful when he smiled back.

"Let me do some thinking," Neil said.

"What can you do?"

"I don't know, but let me think. Mind if I tell Miriam?"

"Of course not."

The two of them were like Siamese twins and the closest friends she had.

"It's a pity you don't have someone special in your life," he said.

Neil's passing comment was spoken with the right intent, but his words struck hard. It was exactly what was gnawing away at Sam. She wanted something more…*someone* in her life. Again, Louise's voice filled her head.

Leave a little space for life and love.

Mindful she'd dumped her anxieties on Neil, she changed the subject.

"Why are you off to Lambeth tomorrow?"

"You were right," Neil said evenly. "The archbishop does want me on his team. I've been called to talk to him tomorrow to discuss the whens and hows of my moving down to London."

Though she'd guessed this was going to happen, the news still shocked her. Her friends would be leaving. Her sense of isolation grew.

"When?" she asked.

"Don't worry. It won't be until after Christmas. Miriam refuses to budge till the festive season is over, and I have commitments I insist I see through…one of which is to get your church problems sorted." He stared at her. "And I will."

When Neil left, Sam wasn't sure she felt better, but she was glad she'd shared her problems.

The simple act of talking to Neil brought some clarity.

Neil had unconsciously voiced it. He thought it a pity no one was in her life.

But how could there be? She was a vicar and vicars didn't have same-sex partners. Some had crossed that barrier, but it always brought controversy. She now realized that she was willing to face that if it meant having Joey by her side, but she worried how the sensational press on both sides of the Atlantic would affect Joey's fragile psyche. And if they did become a twosome, Sam would want marriage. She believed in that. Would Joey?

Sam stopped herself. It was ridiculous thinking of this without knowing what Joey wanted.

Sam didn't want to think anymore. She was tired and emotional. Instead, she locked up the church and headed home.

Chapter Twelve

There's no place like home.

Joey smiled as she lay in bed at her parents' place in Baltimore. It wasn't her childhood home, and she'd never lived here, but it felt good. There was still familiarity in the surroundings—the smells, furniture, photographs, all the things she'd grown up with. There was still the same stamp of love in the house.

Her mom and dad met her at the airport, and from the moment she saw their excited, smiling faces and fell into their warm embrace, she knew she'd made the right decision to come home.

They had changed. They looked older, and yet it hadn't been so long since she'd last seen them. Joey realized she hadn't taken much notice of anything since her return from Balshir. Now she noticed how her father, Len, no longer walked straight and tall. There was a curve to his stance, and the familiar spring in his step was gone. She'd been unaware of that during their recent Skype calls about motorbike problems. Ann, her mother, was ten years younger than her father. She still had beautifully golden coiffured hair, and was immaculately dressed in the latest fashion that showed off her slim, agile figure. But there were lines on her face that hadn't been there before—or maybe they had, but Joey hadn't noticed.

But they were beyond happy to have her home.

She was happy too.

When the excitement of her return, and the superficial chitchat gave way to deeper talks; it was clear they were worried about her. Her mother droned on about her not having put any of the weight back on that she'd lost in Syria. Actually, she had, but she knew she wasn't back to what she'd been before. It also didn't take them long to realize she wasn't sleeping and that the nightmares she'd suffered before she went to England were still there.

She balanced their concerns by telling them about her new job and the possibility of an extension, or even a more permanent contract. They were disappointed that she might stay overseas, but then they'd always accepted she was no homebody. Both thought Stallion Productions was a better option, especially given the continued U.S. media interest in her. The press had raised its ugly head the moment she entered the airport terminal. Some trigger-happy photographer had spied her, and her photograph had appeared in the national press the next day much to her father's anger.

"Like dogs with a bloody bone," her dad moaned. "Why they can't leave you alone? I don't know."

"I'll eventually bore them, and they'll lose interest," Joey said.

"No, they won't, my love. You're always going to interest them, especially the tabloid press. You're media fodder...the internationally renowned journalist who got caught up in tragedy and who broke down on national television. Shit sells."

"Stop this talk. Your daughter doesn't need reminding of any of this." Joey's mother was in protection mode.

"It's okay, Mom. I can handle it as long as I don't put myself in the firing line again."

"Do you want to?" her father asked.

"Return to what I did before? No, Dad. I'm through with that."

"Does Stallion Productions offer you what you need?" He knew her drive. She would never settle for anything less than she wanted, or needed to give.

"Yes. And if I decide I want more, they'll let me spread my wings. The BBC has already made muted noises. But right now I'm happy with the arrangements."

"If you're happy, then we are. Just don't suffer in silence." Her father disappeared into the sitting room, leaving Joey alone with her mother.

The moment she knew he was out of earshot, her mom turned to her.

"And this *Sam*?"

"What about her?"

"She's a vicar?"

"Yes."

"And you've got the hots for her."

"Mother!"

"I'm just calling it like it is. I've never known you to speak about the same woman for more than two days, and the fact that this one is a minister of the church, gives me hope she has more in mind than a quick lay."

"Jeez, Mom."

"Well?"

How could Joey forget that her mother was nothing if not tenacious when she thought something was going on? Joey grinned. This was why she loved her parents. They knew exactly who she was and adored her without reservation. After a few hissy fits, they had come to accept that she was a lesbian and only wanted her to be happy. Her mother was a wise old bird.

"Yes, Mother, Sam is a vicar…and yes, I *love* her." A lump rose inside Joey. Being home was wonderful. It would be perfect if Sam were here with her. "And I think she loves me, but it's early. I don't want to rush this."

"My God, my daughter is taking things slowly."

"Yes, well. None of us are getting any younger."

"She must be an incredible woman…and a vicar. Are you turning religious?"

"No."

Her mother positively beamed. "What a fascinating combination. Your father is going to love this…a vicar in love with his daughter, and who owns a BBR motorbike."

"BSA, Mom."

"Whatever." Her mom's flippant response highlighted her total disinterest in anything remotely two-wheeled. Joey sometimes wondered how her parents ever got along. Motorbikes were her father's obsession. At least she and Sam shared this. She couldn't imagine her mom getting down and dirty with a bike engine. Not with her polished nails.

"Don't say anything to Dad yet. Let's wait and see how this all pans out. I don't want to jinx anything. Besides, if things do move along, we'll face some interesting hurdles."

She watched the machinations cross her mother's face. She was probably thinking of the same issues Joey did. How did one mess with the taboos of the church, even if external appearance suggested it was growing more liberal?

Her mother started to put thoughts into words. Joey wasn't ready for this.

"Don't start, Mom."

"But—"

"No!"

"I haven't said anything."

"You were thinking it."

Her mother sensibly chose to leave the subject alone.

A week passed, most of which Joey spent in a semi-reclusive state, not wanting to be tailed by the press. She bonded with her parents and caught up with a few people she considered trusted friends. She answered all their questions and they too were shocked by her changes in habit. So she was no longer the night owl who partied? Was there someone *special* in the wings? Was her new behavior a sign she was ready to settle down?

Her mother kept giving her odd stares when she thought she couldn't see. Joey figured she thought she was either truly in love, or events in the Middle East were turning her into a reclusive hermit.

Maybe it was a test when her father made a sudden announcement one morning at breakfast.

"Time to socialize," he said. "Your mother and I have been invited to Sandy and Carol Ellingham's wedding anniversary party tomorrow night, and they've extended the invite to you. Would you like to come? You'll know quite a few of the guests."

Sandy was her father's ex-partner in their law firm. They'd both retired about the same time, and remained friends. She saw no reason to decline.

When the evening came, the party turned out to be fun. There were a lot of guests, a few Joey recognized, but many she didn't. Thankfully, none of them took much notice of her. It was either because they never watched television and were blissfully unaware of the celebrity in their midst, or more likely, they were being polite. Either way, it allowed her to relax and mingle.

She was just looking for her next target of conversation when a familiar voice spoke from behind her.

"Josephine Barry, I'd know that cute ass anywhere."

She turned to see Sherry Tyler, a petite woman she'd worked with years ago in radio before Joey got her big break on television. Sherry was much the same except her long dark brown hair was now cut in a bob and had turned strikingly gray. Once Sherry had looked impish, but now she appeared rather distinguished.

"Sherry Tyler?"

Joey hugged her close. She hadn't seen her for almost twenty years. The two of them had started out as journalists working for a local radio station. When Joey had moved to another media, Sherry had stayed true to radio. It seemed a long time ago.

"The one and only," Sherry said as they broke away from each other, "except I'm now Sherry Dexter, with a husband and four children."

"Four?"

"John was married before, and came with two kids. We added a couple."

"Are you still working?" Joey couldn't imagine Sherry being a stay-at-home mom, even with four kids. The two of them had been equally ambitious.

"I sure am. I'm still in radio."

"Here?"

"No, I live in Baltimore, but work out of DC. I'm with NPR. I'm senior producer for news and public affairs. It keeps me busy."

Sherry's eyes twinkled, and Joey laughed. Her fondest memories of Sherry were her inability to cope with boredom. World War Three could have been raging and Sherry would be complaining of ennui. Joey was impressed. She was a huge fan of National Public Radio, a media organization that served as a national syndicate to a network of over 900 public radio stations, producing and distributing news and cultural programming. Sherry had done well.

"What about you?" Sherry asked.

"You really want to know?"

"I do. I'm aware you've taken a sojourn from RSB. Personally, I think you waited too long. They've treated you badly."

Sherry was being kind and Joey appreciated it. "I'm currently over in England. I'm contracted to a company that produces political documentaries for the BBC."

"And when the contract runs out?"

"I haven't made any decisions yet."

"Planning to go back to RSB?"

Joey grinned. "As I said, I haven't made any decisions yet."

"You're still closer than a tick on a hound." Sherry shook her head good-naturedly. She took Joey's arm, and they moved to a quieter part of the room. "Listen, Joey. Serious question. Would you ever consider returning to radio?"

Joey hadn't thought about it. "Why?"

"Because NPR needs people like you. You're informed; you've got a great reputation. You've got a huge following...still.

Your roots were in radio, you've produced and made programs, it would be coming back to where you belong. There are rapid changes in audience trends out there that we're having to adapt to…trends you understand. You could be part of that."

"I have a job."

Sherry ignored her. "Over twenty-six million people listen to us every week, Joey. When your contract runs out, think about it?"

She could see Sherry was earnest.

"Your bumping into me…was it by chance?"

"Totally planned, my dear. When I saw that ridiculous news article last week about you flying home, I started plotting. Sandy's party was entirely fortuitous. It was a sign."

"I'm not interested at the moment."

Sherry passed her a business card. "But you'll keep an open mind, yes? The offer's there if you change it."

"Sure." Joey placed the card in her pocket.

She continued talking to Sherry for the rest of the evening, her old friend didn't hold back in telling her all about her loving husband and the kids.

Joey listened, but her mind was preoccupied. Every waking moment she thought of Sam, always wondering what she was doing at that particular time. Joey imagined her at St. Mary's giving a sermon, or listening to choir practice. She visualized her at home, in the kitchen, talking with Gloria. Perhaps on Saturday Sam was out on her motorbike, and on Sunday was heading for lunch with Neil and Miriam. These silly little thoughts cushioned Joey and brought her strange comfort.

At night, it was different. Sometimes she wondered if she was right for Sam. She wondered when her mental state would improve. It was getting worse, and now it affected her during her waking hours. The nightclub had been a nasty example of its tenacious grip. She hadn't been in control. Joey worried that she might hurt Sam, not physically, but she'd been verbally brutal lately when Sam kept pushing that she needed help. Would this get worse?

Always Joey's thoughts returned to Syria. She'd already hurt others there. Because of her insistence on going for a great story, there were now families without dads. Kurt, Mitch, and Mo. She thought of all their photographs she'd seen showing happy, smiling family units full of love. She'd destroyed all of that. Everything seemed worse at night, and Joey would panic.

Joey sometimes imagined she was lying next to Sam, that Sam was the pillow she hugged. But then she would fall asleep, and her dreams would morph into a nightmarish concoction where she was trapped, frightened, and suffocating. Sometimes she called out to Sam, but her voice wasn't strong enough, and Sam was walking away. As usual, she woke when she screamed out in the dark.

❖

Time crawled for Sam while Joey was in America.

In Joey's absence, the producer of the WM radio series *Forgotten Worcestershire* contacted her. He asked if she'd do a guest slot at the studio and talk for thirty minutes about any historical church topic she felt comfortable with. He thought she'd laid a few seeds in her initial interview when she'd mentioned topics like the radar survey of the churchyard, or the marauding Welsh coming along the River Severn and attacking the Worcestershire borders in the tenth and eleventh centuries.

Sam decided to do it. It was a subject she loved, and there wouldn't be too much preparation as she already covered much of the material on the bishop's certificate course. Neil would be happy, as it was a means of promoting fundraising, and it was also a way for Sam to kill time till Joey returned. When she turned up at the studio for her guest spot, she'd initially worried she might bump into Carrie. It was a relief to find she was on a different team and worked out of offices located elsewhere.

Her time on the radio passed quickly, and the broadcaster was pleased. He was a gentle spoken, congenial man with a warm wit. Sam could see why his program was popular.

"That was excellent," he said. "You really know your history."

"I've always been interested."

"It shows. Would you be interested in doing more?" he asked.

"You don't even know if the listeners have enjoyed this. Best wait for some feedback." Sam was surprised how keen he was.

"I have sixth sense." He smiled. "They're going to love it."

When she returned to the vicarage, she made a cup of coffee and thought of Joey.

She crossed another day off the wall calendar.

Chapter Thirteen

The automatic doors swung open to reveal a busy airport terminal where people were waiting to meet friends and family off recently arrived flights.

Joey looked for her ride—Auntie Elsa's neighbor, the same man who'd kindly brought her here when she'd flown home. She did a quick scan but couldn't see him.

What she did see was a recognizable face amid the mass. Sam. The minute their eyes connected, Sam broke into a huge grin. In one second, Joey went from being a weary traveler to an excited one.

Sam stepped forward. "I nearly didn't make it. There's a huge pileup on the motorway."

Joey flung her arms tight around her. She closed her eyes and melted into her body as she rested her head on Sam's shoulder and breathed in her scent. She had missed this.

Sam pushed back to look at her. "I hope I'm a happy surprise. I told Elsa I wanted to meet you."

"You're the best surprise."

Sam kissed her, then laughed, "I gave up a pulpit experience for this."

"I'm indebted." Joey pulled Sam close.

They were jostled by irritated passengers.

"Let's get out of here before we start a riot." Sam had her suitcase and was already pulling her along the concourse.

It was midday by the time they got back to Joey's place. Joey noticed that the fridge had been stocked and a vase of fresh flowers rested in the middle of the dining room table. She was touched. No one had ever done this for her. It was the little things that Sam did.

"I thought we'd go for lunch. Unless you're jet lagged," Sam said.

"I'd love to." Joey hadn't eaten on the flight.

"Missed you," Sam said as they waited for their order at a small nearby restaurant.

"Missed you more."

Sam reached across to pat Joey's hand. "Have you had a good time with your family?"

"I have. Mom and Dad loved having me home. I've been spoiled."

"I suppose it's too much to ask if you've changed your mind about counseling," Sam said.

"You're spoiling lunch."

Sam capitulated as Joey shook her head. Instead she produced an envelope.

"I've got something for you."

"What is it?" Joey looked excited.

"Open it and see."

Joey ripped into it and read the contents aloud. "Josephine Barry is invited to a bike ride and private tour of Ludlow Castle this Saturday at ten o'clock. Afterward, she will dine at the Compton Hotel where she is booked into a suite for the night."

When she finished, Joey eyeballed Sam. "Who am I going with?" she said.

Sam was grinning like a lunatic. "I thought we'd make a weekend of it. I've got cover for Sunday services."

Joey stared at the invite again. She was beyond happy.

"So?" Sam said. "Do you accept?"

Joey leaned across the table and grabbed Sam's hand. "Josephine Barry has much pleasure in accepting the kind invitation. Now, I've got something for you too. Close your eyes."

She waited until Sam obeyed before taking a small cardboard box out of a bag and placing it in front of her. "You can open them now."

Sam's eyes widened as she stared at the box. She opened it.

"It's a magneto!" she exclaimed.

"It's a BSA A10 magneto," Joey corrected her.

"This is a genuine part. It must be—"

"Nineteen fifties."

"But it's new, Joey. It's never been used." Sam was in seventh heaven as she took the item from the box and kept turning it in her hands.

"Dad acquired it from some place. He thought you'd like it."

"Thought I'd like it? Do you know how rare these are? It's almost impossible to get these now."

"A good gift, then?"

"Shit, Joey. I couldn't wish for anything better." Then Sam blushed. "Well, I probably could, but this is close. Let me have your dad's email. I want to thank him." Sam placed the magneto back into the box like it was a rare bird's egg. When the delicate task was completed, Sam passed another envelope to Joey.

"Another invite?" Joey was already opening it. There were two tickets inside.

"They're to the West Mercia Police Orchestra Concert—"

"—playing at St. Mary's." Joey grimaced. It seemed a bit too much like church business.

"Seriously, they are wonderful, and the tickets always sell out. I know it's *at the office*, but I promise you, you'll enjoy it. I don't have to do anything, either. The police steward the entire event."

After they finished their meal, Sam saw Joey back to her place before returning to church to conduct a service. When she was done at St. Mary's, she wasted no time in driving back to Joey's to spend the night.

"I thought you'd already be in bed," Sam said as she walked in.

"I wanted to wait for you."

Joey's words flooded Sam with love. Jet lag was beginning to show on Joey's face, yet she had stayed up. As she led Joey by the hand to the bedroom, she wondered if she could be any happier than she was at this moment. Joey was in her life, and she felt complete. The loneliness that had lodged inside her like a weight was gone.

As Joey snuggled up to her she couldn't stop a yawn. "Sorry, Sam."

"I guess this means you don't want me to make mad passionate love to you tonight."

"I do, but I think I might fall asleep on you. I wish I'd slept on the flight."

"No matter, my love. We'll have other opportunities." Sam didn't care; being with Joey was enough.

"Hold me," Joey said as she nestled closer into Sam. Sam obeyed.

"I've missed you," Joey mumbled, already half asleep.

"And I you." Sam kissed her forehead. "Never have two weeks gone so slowly. What were they like for you?"

But she didn't get a response. Joey was asleep.

Sam smiled, closed her eyes, and drifted off holding her most treasured possession.

❖

The weeks came and went. Their relationship grew stronger.

It suddenly seemed the right time for Joey to see what Sam thought about her staying in England longer. She wanted to share and discuss with her the opportunity of new contracts with Stallion Productions. It would give them both a chance to talk about where they saw their relationship heading.

Joey wanted to tell Sam in a special moment. She planned a dinner at her place and invited Sam one afternoon as they walked along the riverbank.

"Wednesday evening, come to my place for dinner. I want to cook for you. I also want to tell you something."

"What?"

"I'm not telling you till dinner."

"Not even a clue?"

"No." She loved Sam's impatience.

"It's not bad news?" Sam had stopped walking.

"No. I'm hoping you'll like it."

"And you're making me wait till Wednesday."

"I think it will be worth it." Joey grinned.

Sam's eyes narrowed in fun. "Then I'll just have to wait."

"You will."

Joey and Sam linked arms and continued walking.

Chapter Fourteen

Joey laid the crisp white cotton cloth onto the dining room table.

She placed the cutlery out and polished the crystal glasses until they shone.

Then she took the napkins and turned them into the shape of swans like she'd seen her mother do. It took her a few dying birds to get it right, but when she did, they looked resplendent as she placed them on the table.

In the middle of the table, she positioned two silver candlesticks she'd borrowed from a neighbor and adorned them with red candles. In between, she put a small posy of roses in a bowl.

Standing back, she mentally ran through everything. The wine was warming to room temperature. She had chosen the right background music to play, and had selected a decent range of liqueurs for aperitif and post dinner. The food was cooking. It was going to plan.

She was going to tell Sam of her intention to accept the offer of a permanent contract with Stallion Productions. She hadn't said anything to them yet because she wanted Sam to be part of the decision. This dinner would reveal if they wanted a life together.

If we want a life together.

The strangest feeling came over her.

Joey started to tremble and sweat, her heartbeat increased. There was an edge of familiarity to it—that anxiety she'd felt out in war zones when her inner sense kicked in warning her of approaching danger. But there was no danger here. Her life wasn't being threatened. She loved Sam, and she knew Sam loved her back. But the feeling persisted and with it, such self-destructive thoughts.

You don't deserve happiness.

Why should you be happy when your friends are dead? Friends you killed.

It was your fault.

Now you're going to ruin Sam's life.

If you love her, is that what you want?

This is wrong. You won't cope.

People already think you're crazy.

They're embarrassed by your behavior.

You're losing control.

Run.

Joey was terrified. The thoughts in her head were uncontrollable and irrational. She put her hands to her head.

Stop.

Where was all this self-destruction coming from? Why was she thinking like this? This wasn't her.

"Why am I trying to hurt myself? I don't want to lose, Sam," she said aloud. "Stop this!"

Breathe.

The feelings began to fade, and Joey tried to rationalize.

You, idiot. It's just commitment issues. Cold feet. I'm scared because I know Sam's going to want to spend her life with me. Joey laughed nervously as she visualized herself running from the marriage alter and down the aisle in an attack of nerves.

Get a grip.

Joey glanced at the time. A few more hours, and Sam would be here.

She'd be fine then. Sam always made her feel better.

❖

Sam was in the vestry when the first call came, one of many in quick succession.

It was from Grace Smith, secretary to the headmaster of the local Holy Trinity Convent School. She rang to say there had been a terrible accident involving a coachload of their pupils returning home from a day out. She didn't know much, but the police were talking of fatalities.

The second call came from the headmaster, Alex Durrant. He was calling from the scene, having immediately driven out to the accident, some ten miles away, when the police had informed him. He was emotional and could barely talk. He said she was needed at A&E where many parents were heading and would need counsel. He cried when he told her some children were dead.

The third call came from Bishop Neil.

"I know Neil; the school's rung. I'm on my way to A&E now."

"It's bad, Sam. I don't know how many casualties, but too many. I'm rounding up some help for you. You'll have other clergy with you soon."

On arrival, she learned the coach had collided on a bend with an articulated lorry. Both drivers were dead, as were at least half a dozen pupils. The emergency services were still extracting children from the metal carnage. It was expected that the death rate would climb.

The A&E was a place of organized chaos amidst professional medical staff that were doing their best. Frantic, sometimes hysterical parents paced the waiting area desperate to know where their child was, and whether they were alive.

Sam did the best she could, but felt inadequate. Nothing could ever prepare her for tragedy on this scale. Two other ministers arrived, and between them, they tried to bring solace and comfort. Some wanted to pray, and Sam found a small room where frightened parents could go. Religious belief became irrelevant. Non-believers prayed too and sought her and the other ministers' succor. There were few who did not welcome their support, and Sam treated them all the same.

The Reverend Nicolas Bentley found it more difficult. This became apparent to Sam when the two of them were alone, taking a quick respite, and a chance to gather their own thoughts. He had been helping to comfort the parents and the unhurt but shocked pupils.

"These people aren't churchgoers." Bentley spoke as if their sudden need for prayer was some shameful, loathsome act. Sam considered his attitude out of proportion and put it down to stress. Everyone was under it tonight. Earlier, she'd spied a young police constable who barely looked out of school himself, throwing up outside. No one was spared. She wondered how the A&E staff coped.

"It's not important, Nicolas. They need us. It's our role."

"I never understand," he said. "Half of them don't know what the inside of a church looks like, and yet, when faced with horror, who do they turn to? They don't come to church, but they all want their children baptized. It's a meaningless ritual for them and more an excuse for some petty social gathering. It's wrong."

Sam held her tongue. Could Neil not have found someone else? This man rubbed her the wrong way. She would never understand him. Sam left him alone before she said something she'd regret. She was in no mood for his intolerant vitriol.

By the time she got back to the vicarage it was gone midnight. Other clergy had turned up at the hospital and taken over. Sam was exhausted and dead on her feet. She barely knew how she'd driven home. She longed for bed, and hopefully sleep, before going back to the hospital the next—later—that same morning.

As she started to drag her weary body upstairs, she noticed the bottle of wine she'd bought to take to dinner at Joey's.

The sudden awareness that the dinner had been tonight hit her. She'd forgotten it, and hadn't even called Joey. Everything had happened so fast. From the moment she'd taken the first call mid morning, she'd had no time to think of anything else. Sam turned around, grabbed her car keys, and left the vicarage for Joey's.

As she parked the car, she could see a fraction of light from Joey's sitting room window.

Sam ran up the stairs to the door and hesitated for a moment before using the key. When she walked in, she found Joey awake and seated in an armchair next to a single source of light, a small lampshade to her side. Sam quietly entered the room and closed the door.

"I thought you'd be asleep," she said.

"I was waiting for you," Joey said.

Sam was reminded of these same words not so long ago. Then the room had been full of love. Now Sam felt only tension.

"I can never sleep. Besides, I knew you'd show."

Joey's voice sounded flat, and there was an odd emptiness on her face, her eyes strange. A splinter of fear ran through Sam.

She glanced behind Joey and at the table set for two. It was a romantic, intimate setting, a table prepared with such care and attention. Handsome candlesticks rested in the middle, and the napkins had been beautifully crafted into the shape of swans. The aroma of good cooking, now cold, still lingered. The love was evident. She knew that this dinner was going to be special, and that Joey was planning to tell her something important. Sam's heart ached as she realized she'd ruined it.

"I'm so sorry, Joey." Her words sounded worthless and inadequate. "There's been a dreadful accident. A coach full of kids—"

"I know, Sam." Joey sounded tired. "I caught it on the local news. I guessed you'd be needed, and when you didn't turn up... You've had a terrible time. Are you okay?"

Despite the genuine concern Sam heard in Joey's voice, she sensed a distance between them. Sam struggled for words. She needed to sit down and moved toward an armchair, but as she did, Joey raised a hand.

"Don't."

Sam disobeyed. She was exhausted; her legs were like Jell-O. She'd been on her feet all day as she'd moved from parent to parent, from bedside to bedside. She planted herself on the arm of the chair, hoping the half measure would placate Joey. Joey didn't want her to stay? Sam figured she knew why.

"This is because I've let you down again," she said. How many times had she canceled their arrangements or turned up late? This was what she'd tried to speak to Neil about…that key issue of her inability to have a life outside of the church. "But I'm a vicar. This is what I do."

"I know, Sam, I know. I'm not criticizing. I'd be disappointed in you if you turned from all those people who need you. You make a huge difference to their lives. You were born for this vocation. You are everything a vicar should be."

Sam heard the subtext. She *heard* what wasn't being said. "But?"

Joey didn't say anything.

"This is about me failing you," Sam said.

"No, it isn't."

"Then what?" Sam wished she wasn't so dog-tired.

Joey closed her eyes and placed her head back to rest on the chair. Seconds later, she looked Sam in the eyes. "It's lots of things."

"Like what, my love?" Sam didn't believe her.

"Sam, I don't know." Joey looked lost. "I just know we have to stop…that I can't do this anymore."

"What?" Sam couldn't hide her shock.

"This isn't working."

"It *is* working."

"I *need* to stop." Joey sounded desperate. It was the first real emotion Sam had heard from her since she'd arrived. She couldn't believe what she was hearing.

"I love you," Sam said.

"I know you do. I love you too."

"Then don't do this."

Joey looked sick. Sam felt the same.

"Please, Sam, don't make this any more difficult than it is."

"This isn't making any sense, Joey. You're just tired, and God knows, I am. Give me a chance to make this right. Let's talk."

But Joey was shaking her head.

"If not now, then later," Sam said. But she was already wondering when. Her life for the imminent future would be full of funerals, grieving parents, and traumatized children. *When* was she going to find the time? Sam had no control over her life, and right now, there was nothing she could do about it. She realized she was shaking. This had turned into the day from hell.

"Please, Sam."

Joey avoided eye contact, and Sam hated that. It was as if she'd already lost her.

"I love you," Sam repeated, hoping it would make a difference. Joey remained silent.

"I need you," Sam pleaded. "Don't do this."

"Please go, Sam. Leave."

Joey's words were knives plunging into her. Sam didn't want this. She would never want this. Joey was the woman she was in love with. She was the one she wanted to spend the rest of her life with.

"I don't want to leave." Sam heard the rawness in her own voice.

"But I want you to," Joey whispered.

"Joey, this isn't right. This can't be what you want." But when Joey turned her face away and remained silent, Sam knew there was nothing more she could say to change her mind—not tonight anyway. She stood.

"You remember, Joey, that I love you. I really wanted to be here with you tonight. There was no other place I wanted to be." Maybe if she kept repeating this, Joey would relent.

"Let me call you later," Sam said as she got to the door.

"No." Joey's response was firm. "Leave me alone, Sam. Please do this for me. This can't work...*we* can't work."

Sam stared back at her one last time before she left, hoping Joey would feel different tomorrow, or in a few days.

The door clicked shut, and the moment it did, Joey dropped her façade of control. She placed her head to her hands and cried.

It was the hardest thing she'd ever done.

But it was the right thing.

Now she understood she was wrong for Sam. Why hadn't she seen it before? Joey was losing more self-control, and she knew she'd drag Sam down into her own personal quagmire. She'd hurt Sam badly tonight, but it was better than the damage she'd do to her if they stayed together.

Sam was wonderful. She gave her life to her beliefs, to the church. She had an important role. People sought her out in their darkest moments. They needed her, and Sam always responded. This day, this night, it was evident. Joey couldn't corrupt that.

And she would.

She was breaking down. She didn't want Sam to see her self-destruct. And that's what she was doing. There were all these frightening thoughts in her head that didn't feel like hers. It was like being controlled by unseen forces.

Sam will look at me like the others have, like I'm crazy.

But it's just the tiredness, the crippling exhaustion I'm living with.

She kept flitting from thought to thought like a moth bouncing around light.

Am I going mad? I must be. I've pushed Sam from my life. But I had to.

Everything was hopeless. *I'm hopeless.*

She couldn't think straight.

She had to break with Sam before it was too late. Sam was tenacious and would stay with her to the end.

End of what?

Joey's thoughts took a curve.

How would the sacred institution of the church handle Sam ending up with a lesbian partner? At best, it would bring Sam's life into the spotlight, and she was a private person behind her clerical role. At worst, narrow-minded bigots would attempt to tarnish Sam's deserved and honorable reputation. It might make some of her flock shy from her. Sam would hate that.

Would Joey be able to protect her? No. When had she ever protected anyone? She had the blood of three friends on her hands.

Her nightmares were her retribution, her constant reminder that she was responsible for their deaths. Why did she deserve someone like Sam? She didn't. This is what Gloria had seen and warned her of.

Joey suddenly understood that she was no vicar's wife.

She was no good for anyone.

She needed to go home.

In the weeks that followed, Sam survived in a continuum of nonexistence.

She functioned as an automaton. Her vocation brought her days that were full of funerals, and the counseling of the bereaved. Sam hid herself from their pain, afraid that it would add to her own. She shut herself off mentally and hated it.

A Catholic minister held a school service to allow staff, pupils, and parents to come together in prayer. Sam was invited along with other church colleagues. It affected her. When she closed her eyes at night, she saw only the haunted faces of them all.

Sam longed to go to Joey, but she tried to give her the distance she had asked for. She hoped the absence would make Joey relent.

Several times, Sam phoned her, but Joey never picked up. Sam left messages, but there was never any response. As time drew on, Sam went to Joey's, but each time Joey refused to open the door. She would only tell her to go away.

Sam again tried a volley of phone messages, and again, none were answered.

One weekend morning, three weeks later, Sam went back to Joey's apartment. This time she was determined to see her. She would use the key—she hadn't so far. Sam went upstairs and rang the bell. There was no answer. Sam tried the key, but it didn't work. Had Joey changed the lock?

She went away but returned later that evening. There were no lights on. She rang the bell, but still there was no response.

Sam went to Elsa's.

"Joey's flown back to the States," Elsa said.

"When's she coming back?"

"She isn't." When Elsa saw the shock on Sam's face, she said, "I didn't know how to tell you."

"When did she leave?"

"Four days ago."

Four days ago. Sam left Elsa's and returned to the vicarage. How could Joey have left without saying anything?

She was gone, and Sam was devastated. She didn't know what to do.

She found herself thinking of Louise. The church had won that day Sam made her decision. Now the church had won again. Resentment rose up in her. She had tried to change, to be there for Joey, but her desired actions were always blighted by ecclesiastical needs. Joey had seen this would never change. She'd had enough and left.

Sam nearly went crazy. She felt trapped.

By day, it seemed everywhere she went held the memory of Joey—places they had been, where they'd talked, where they'd laughed. Even St. Mary's resonated with her, and the Sunday lunches at Neil and Miriam's. Bike rides were unbearable. Joey wasn't with her, up tight and close.

By night, Sam couldn't stop thinking of her. She kept running through everything over and over. She remembered their conversation; she kept trying to work out how the outcome could have been different. But it was always the same. Joey was gone because Sam had failed her. She hadn't given her the time and love she needed. And Sam had never known such loneliness.

Chapter Fifteen

Another month went by.

The devastating ripples of the coach accident occupied most of Sam's time, but slowly, even those abated. The funerals took place, the spiritual counseling eased, and those pupils hospitalized made full recoveries. Even the church roof was going back on and great sheets of plastic within the building were disappearing. All was returning to a semblance of normality.

But not for Sam.

Sam struggled. She found it difficult to be upbeat. Listening to other people's problems was difficult when her own weighed down on her. Since Joey's departure, Sam had continued to send her emails, but it was as if they disappeared into thin air. She didn't know where she'd gone.

One day, in desperation she'd gone to Elsa's to try to obtain an address, but when Elsa wasn't in, she'd driven on to Stallion Productions. They could only confirm that Joey was in the States. They said little else and didn't give her any contact details—it wasn't their policy. It was as if the earth had swallowed Joey up.

Time dragged on and people started talking of Christmas. The church began its preparations toward festive services. The scouts and local schools began rehearsing choral and nativity events. It was the time of year Sam normally enjoyed most, but this year her heart felt empty and barren because Joey wasn't here to share it with her.

One afternoon, Sam was at St. Mary's preparing for the next day's Sunday service when she spied the Reverend Nicolas Bentley steaming down the aisle toward her. His face was red, and his body language oozed agitation. She knew she was in for confrontation. She wondered what topic it would be this time. She took a deep breath and waited.

Before she had time for simple courtesy, he spluttered all over her.

"You're not going to do it, are you?"

"Nicolas, good afternoon. Do what?" Sam felt a tension headache building.

"Give a blessing to those two men. I've heard they've been to see you, and you've agreed."

Bentley referred to Miles Crowther and Peter George, two gay men who were now married by civil law but who had approached him for a church blessing. He'd had options. He could have told them graciously that the Church of England did not yet give authorized services of blessings. Instead he'd taken perverse pleasure in letting them know he did not approve of their lifestyle, and had all but turned them away from his church. Miles and Peter had arrived at St. Mary's upset and asking for clarity. Both were strong believers who only wanted the church's sanctification on their fourteen-year relationship now recognized legally by the law.

It was fact the Church of England did not currently conduct same-sex marriages or authorize services of blessings in church, but there were maverick vicars who did unofficial blessings. Sam saw no reason to deny them this. If it meant she would be reprimanded afterward, she didn't care. She'd told Miles and Peter she would do this. It was clear the word had got back to Nicolas.

"As long as I feel they are serious and understand the importance of what marriage is about, I see no reason to deny them," Sam said. "If their love is real and they want it announced in the face of God, I won't turn them away."

"This is not recognized," he spat. "There is no governing body consent."

He stared back at her in fury. She couldn't understand his opposition, but then, this was why the church was being tardy. It was to give people time to accept the inevitable changes that were coming. She reckoned Nicolas could be given a millennium and still wouldn't change.

He scrunched his face up. "This has all gone too far. This sort of recognition is unacceptable. It really is intolerable. What next?"

Sam tried to remain dispassionate. Even his voice was unpleasant. It was brittle and bereft of compassion. His stance was always the same, his hands tight at his side. If he'd been a child, Sam would call his behavior a tantrum. Dear Lord, everything about him grated on her.

"Perhaps you shouldn't be in the church." Sam was beginning to lose her temper. His conduct with some of the parents was still fresh in her mind.

"I'm one of the few who are trying to protect the sanctity and pureness of the faith," he said.

Sam stared at him, fighting to maintain control. She was shattered, both physically and mentally. Her nerves were frayed, and she felt pushed to the limits. She was under stress, she wasn't sleeping, and the woman she loved had flown back to the U.S. without a word. To ask her to put up one more time with the sanctimonious crap coming out of Nicolas Bentley's mouth was asking too much.

"I expect Bishop Neil will be replaced by a woman," he sneered.

Sam recognized the statement for what it was. It was a cheap attempt to rile her. Nicolas was venting again about women's position in the church. He was not an ardent supporter.

It was the final straw. Sam's composure snapped.

"You know what, Nicolas? You're the most miserable representation of a vicar I've ever come across."

"I beg your pardon?" His shock and indignation echoed around the building. Busy parishioners preparing the church stopped what they were doing and looked over at them.

"You're bigoted, full of your own self-importance, and you wonder why your church is losing parishioners?" She stabbed a finger his way. "If you tried treating them like human beings more, instead of the fire and brimstone approach, they might stay. Why… *why* would anyone want to come to you and share their personal problems? I wouldn't."

"How dare you!"

"Shut up. And don't think I haven't heard about your snide remarks behind my back about why I, a woman, should be the vicar of this large parish. I also didn't like your comments about my unsuitability to be a canon. I don't care a fig what you think about me. What I do care about is your total lack of empathy with another human being. You call yourself a representative of Christ? You do the church a grave injustice. You corrupt its moral integrity."

"You think homosexual marriage represents moral integrity?" His red face looked ready to burst.

"Yes, I do. Couples should never be prevented from marrying unless there are good reasons—and loving someone of the same sex is not one of them, you ridiculous man."

"I have never been so insulted in my life," he huffed. "And don't think I'm going to let you get away with this. The bishop will want to know what you're about to do. I shall be making a complaint. I have witnesses." His gaze shifted to the four people who were standing riveted, their mouths agape, watching the altercation. "You haven't heard the last of this," he puffed before storming out.

Sam watched him leave the church and kept her eye on the door as if expecting him to return. When she calmed enough to look around her, she came eye to eye with an elderly man. He had been placing programs in the pews. Now he stood like a deer in headlights. He said nothing, but managed a weak smile.

To her right was a woman directing flower arranging. She smiled too as she said, "Move the display a little to the left, Maureen." This was done while making full eye contact with Sam.

If Maureen did as she was bid, the flowers were about to fall off the stone shelving.

Sam turned and walked back to the pulpit. A woman stood with a large feather duster. She immediately resumed dusting with vigor. "I'm just cleaning this for you, Reverend. You can never have a too shiny pulpit."

Sam stopped and exhaled. "I'm sorry, everyone. I lost my cool."

The man in the pews spoke first. "I thought you were bloody marvelous. Not that I have any personal issues with Reverend Bentley, but his opinions are somewhat medieval."

"You were like a knight on a steed," one of the flower arrangers said. "All you need is a raised sword glinting in the light."

"You have a cup of tea, Vicar. I'll put the kettle on." It was the woman with the feather duster. "Don't know what we'd do if we lost you."

Sam's performance felt shameful. She'd created a scene. "Sorry. I haven't been sleeping."

"Nobody has, Vicar, not since the accident. It's affected everyone indirectly. Everybody knows someone who's been touched, and you've been at the coal face." One of the women took her hand and led her to a seat. "I'll fetch that tea. You have a few minutes' rest."

Sam cringed. They all thought the accident was the reason for her outburst. It wasn't. It was Joey. How was she going to cope without her?

After the tea, Sam went back to the vicarage.

She was surprised to see Gloria still there. She was normally gone by lunchtime.

"I've defrosted the deep freeze, and I wanted to get everything back in."

Gloria's explanation seemed reasonable, but Sam knew she tended to do this chore in the spring, and always moaned about how much she hated it. She smelled a rat.

"Did it need it?" Sam asked.

"No."

Sam frowned.

"I wanted to see you." Gloria was looking at her like a lab specimen.

"Why?"

"I wanted to make sure you're okay."

Gloria's concern shocked Sam.

"Well, are you?" Gloria repeated.

"I'm tired."

"I'm not asking you about your energy levels. I'm asking if you are okay."

Sam was about to say she was fine, but then everything snapped. Instead she burst into tears. Gloria was suddenly holding her in her arms, and Sam was sobbing.

"There, there," Gloria said. "You cry it all out."

For the second time in the day, guilt fell on Sam as she thought Gloria would think her behavior was to do with the accident. But she'd forgotten how astute Gloria could be.

"This is about Joey, isn't it?"

Sam couldn't answer as she extracted herself from Gloria and wiped her eyes with a tissue.

"You're going to have to do something," Gloria said.

"What?" Sam asked.

"I don't know."

"This isn't helpful, Gloria."

"It's not supposed to be. I'm just telling it like it is."

"I don't know what to do either," Sam confessed.

Gloria pursed her lips. "You could start by going to bed and having a decent night's sleep. I expect everything will look clearer in the morning."

"It hasn't yet." How could Sam sleep when she kept poring over and over what had happened.

"Well, maybe it will *tomorrow*." Gloria's sympathy was running out. It only ever lasted in short bursts.

Sam didn't argue and went upstairs to change. When she came down, Gloria was gone, but there was a pot of tea and some scones on the kitchen table. It brought a smile to her lips as she sat down to it. Maybe she would feel better after a decent night's sleep.

❖

Sam awoke with purpose as the first ray of daylight crept through her curtains.

"Enough," she said as she sprang out of bed.

Gloria's predictions had proved accurate and everything seemed clearer. Sam would conduct the early morning service and then go and see Neil. There was something she had to tell him.

Instead of ringing Neil on his cell phone, she rang Ann, his secretary. This was official business and she would conduct it that way. As she waited for Ann to pick up, she prayed Neil wouldn't be in another string of meetings. She wanted to get this over and done with. The thought of waiting another day or two wasn't something she desired.

Ann ended up making Sam's day. Not only was Neil not in meetings, he was working from home.

She drove over to his house and rang the bell.

The moment Miriam opened the door, her face lit up as it always did. It signified the depth of their friendship, but then her smile faded. She wasn't used to Sam turning up during the week unless to a prearranged meeting.

"What's wrong? Are you all right?"

"Hi, Miriam. I'm fine." Sam tried to put her at ease, but it was difficult with a knotted stomach and a still present tension headache. This was likely to be a day they would all remember. "I need a chat with Neil."

Miriam beckoned her inside. She lowered her voice as though to keep a secret. "He's supposed to be working from home today, but he's only just got up. He's in the shower. Is it urgent?"

Sam managed to smile. "Yes, but it can wait until he's done."

They went through to a room off the kitchen where Miriam had been folding laundry. Sam watched as she carried on with her chores.

"Has this got anything to do with Bentley?" Miriam asked.

"Don't tell me he's spoken to Neil already?"

Her need to see Neil had nothing to do with him. Sam hadn't given him a second thought after he'd left yesterday, but now reminded, she considered how typical of him to complain so quickly.

"He rang at eight o'clock last night and was on the phone for an hour. The man's an ass." Miriam was indignant.

"No arguments from me."

At that moment, Neil appeared. He was casually dressed in a pair of jeans, a crisp white cotton shirt, and slippers. He smelled of fresh soap and aftershave.

"I hear you had a bit of a run-in with Bentley." His deep voice was rich and warm; his eyes twinkled with humor. It was clear he found the whole episode amusing. "He can be a bit of hard work."

"The man's a prat." Sam wasn't in the mood for politeness where Nicolas Bentley was concerned.

"All God's children." Neil could be irritatingly virtuous at times.

"That's not what you said last night," Miriam chirped in. "Get off the fence."

"He's a prat," Sam repeated.

Neil caught Miriam's eye. "Okay, he is a prat, but I won't repeat that in a court of law. He rang last night to complain about your *insulting and demeaning behavior* toward him. He also mentioned that you were planning to give a blessing to a same-sex couple in the church, which, of course, Sam, is a big *no-no*. I told him the issue was between two colleagues, and that I wasn't going to interfere in that unless I have voluminous complaints from others…I haven't yet. With regards to the blessing, I said I'd look into it."

Sam's eyes narrowed.

"Relax," Neil said. "You haven't done anything wrong *yet*, and after the blessing, when I find out, I'll speak to you in a severe tone. When are you doing it?"

"A week on Saturday."

"Come to lunch on the Sunday, and I'll discipline you then. It'll probably take a few minutes before sherry. Okay?"

"Is that it?" Sam couldn't believe her heinous misdemeanor would be so lightly dealt with.

"You aren't the first vicar to do this, and you won't be the last. What do you want me to do, throw you into a pit of fire? Strip you of your dog collar in front of your peers? That's Bentley's style, not mine. It's probably why I'm a bishop, and he isn't."

"Okay," Sam said.

"Glad we've sorted that out. Is this why you want to see me?"

"No."

They locked eyes. Sam knew Neil sensed the importance of why she was here. He was probably remembering their other nonsensical chat not so long ago.

"Are we going to talk about wood and carpentry again?"

"Yes, we are."

"Then we should step into the office?"

"Probably best."

Sam looked at Miriam hoping she wasn't offended. She was already pushing them out of the utility space.

"You two carry on. I've sheets to fold."

Sam followed Neil into the room he used as his office. It always felt like walking into a library. Every wall was shelved and covered with books. There were piles of them all around his desk. To say he was a prolific reader was an understatement. Most of the books were either historical or religious, or both. It was a love they both shared.

"This will be a bugger to pack," Sam said, trying to quell her nerves.

"Don't even go there. Miriam always gets bad tempered when we move. I'm dreading it."

They glanced at one another and laughed. But then Neil became serious.

"Removal advice isn't why you're here. What is it, Sam?"

"I won't beat around the bush, Neil. I want to leave the church."

Neil sat down. Sam did too.

"Define *leave*," he asked.

"It's time for me to leave the church, to leave this role I have in life, and to stop being a vicar." She paused at the enormity of what she was saying. It was the first time she was speaking her intent out loud. "I joined the church because I had a calling. Now something else…something stronger is calling me, and this time… this time, I'm going to answer it."

"It wouldn't have something to do with an American, would it?"

Sam smiled. "You don't miss much, do you?"

"I'm a bishop. What do you expect?"

"You're smart. I always knew you were destined for high position."

He scoffed. "I'm no smarter than you. It's my name, Covey-Smartingdon. It's far more suited to title of Bishop, don't you think?"

"You have a point."

He was smiling, but Sam saw the sadness in his eyes.

"You're upset with me," she said.

"No, I'm not, but can I say something? If I told you that I'll be allowed to choose a team to work with me in my new position at Lambeth? I would like to offer you a place on that team. It would take you away from the front line and give you a chance to breathe again."

It was an unexpected and wonderful job offer, but Sam couldn't see it working.

"Thank you, Neil. I'm honored that you'd consider me. And I know what you've been doing behind the scenes, trying to get me staff, but it isn't what I want."

"This isn't something you're doing in haste? Joey?"

"No. This need to leave has been building in me for some years, way before Joey arrived. She's just brought everything to a head and made me see that I can no longer do this."

He steepled his fingers in contemplation. "Then I think you should leave the church, too."

His brazen agreement shocked her.

"Listen, Sam. People have the wrong idea about the boss. They think he wants to hold on to us, but he knows when to let go, like a good parent. You've served him well. He won't mind if you want a career change. You can be a field agent."

"A field agent?"

"You've said yourself that your faith is as strong as ever. You know that God's work isn't solely reserved for the inside of a church. One hopes a church building acts as a magnet that pulls people to the faith, those who want to worship and those who are in need. But we shouldn't forget our role in getting out into the community and doing his work there. He understands."

"You think?"

"I do. And God always leaves a little space in our heart for other things."

Sam was reminded of how familiar those words were.

"Why has it taken you so long to make this decision?" Neil asked.

"Someone had to show me."

"So where is the lovely American?"

Sam's cell structure imploded. "She's gone."

"Gone where?"

"Back to America...to Baltimore." Elsa had told her.

"That's not good," Neil said.

"No, it isn't," Sam said.

"Why did she leave?"

"Because everything else came first."

"I see." Neil continued to study her. "I'll need a little time," he finally announced.

"Time?"

"I'll need to find a replacement. It will be temporary, but I'd like you to be around to give them a proper handover."

It dawned on her the enormity of the task she'd just landed him with.

"Leave it with me, Sam. Let me sort a few things before you do anything."

"Anything?"

"You've a flight to arrange, and time is of the essence."

His support was like a panacea. An invisible weight had been lifted from her. Sam started believing in achievable options for once.

"Do you want my letter of resignation?" she asked.

"Not yet, Sam. I'll tell you when."

Sam hadn't been sure how Neil would take her news. She was grateful he understood.

"You know, Neil, I hope the archbishop realizes the catch he's getting with you."

"He may not feel that way when he hears the changes I'd like to see in the Church of England."

Sam disagreed. "Why do you think he's chosen you? It's because of your viewpoints. I think the two of you will bump along quite well. He's a man of change too. Lambeth is going to be wonderful."

"Tell that to Miriam." Neil stood. "Which reminds me, do you mind if I ask her in? She knows you've been worried about all of this. I spoke to her about our last little chat. She'll be out there in the laundry room pacing like a caged lion." He went to the door and called her.

"Miriam is a lucky lady."

Neil snorted. "I assure you the light doesn't shine out of my orifice. And I'm the lucky one having Miriam. I couldn't do this job without her." He paused. "It's why I think you're imploding. *You* need someone in your life too. It's your time."

"Was. I think my time just went past tense."

"Do you love Joey?"

"With every breath in my body."

"Does she love you?"

"Yes, but I've messed up."

"Bollocks!" Miriam announced her arrival as she entered with a tea tray. "Listen, Sam, hasn't being an emissary for God taught you anything about love?" She placed the tray on Neil's desk before turning to her. "Love isn't something that gets switched off like a lightbulb. Love lasts. If it's real, time can't tarnish it. Time can't fade it, bend it, alter it, corrupt it, stain it, or break it. It's impenetrable. It's like gold…it's better than gold."

Miriam stopped and was looking at Sam and Neil who both stared at her. "What?"

"Nothing, dear. You can be quite eloquent at times." Neil was smiling with such love at his wife.

Miriam poured tea. "Well, what's this all about?"

"It's as we thought, dear. Sam is resigning and going after her American."

"What will you do?" Miriam asked.

"I have no idea. I only know I need to go find Joey and sort *us* out."

For a moment when Sam was leaving their house, she experienced a surge of fear. She was leaving the church after what seemed like a lifetime. There would be a pension, but nothing to get too excited about. She was about to become a woman with no prospects, no job, and probably no fixed abode. You couldn't live in a vicarage if you weren't a vicar. She did have her parents' place in Cornwall. When they passed away, she had kept and rented it out. She didn't think she'd ever live there, but it was something to sell when she wanted.

As she drove back to the vicarage, she thought of Louise.

You must live life. Make sure you leave a little in your heart for love.

Sam took a deep breath as she opened her car door and sat inside. "I hope you're looking down on me, Louise. I hope you know I listened."

CHAPTER SIXTEEN

You've reported from all over the world, and I don't think it would be wrong for me to say you're one of the most iconic female American journalists of the last twenty years. But I'd like to know, and I'm sure NPR listeners would too, were there any early indications in your childhood that you were destined for a career in journalism?"

Joey grinned as she leaned closer to the microphone. She was relaxed and enjoying the studio interview. She had agreed to a three-part radio series of light *chats* with her host, Clara, on the *Clara Dale Show.* This was the first.

"I don't remember waking and thinking I'm going to be a journalist when I grow up, but I think the signs were there. I always had a desire to wander, which gave my parents some worrying moments. They'd leave me playing in the yard and then I'd disappear. I used to go snooping. I always wanted to know what was happening over the fence or the other side of the road. I was basically a nosey kid. I wanted to make the unknown known. I look back at my behavior now and I guess it wasn't healthy." She started to laugh. "It certainly drove the neighbors wild. They would find this six- or seven-year-old cutting across their yard. They'd take me home and I'd get the lecture from Mom and Dad. On reflection, I guess I channeled my wanderlust and inquisitive nature fairly well."

"The seeds were there." There was warmth in Clara's voice, and Joey sensed she was being invited to continue as she wanted.

"Yes. That behavior grew into my love for journalism. Foreign news shouldn't be foreign because it happens someplace else. What happens in any part of the world affects us all. We need to know about it, and I've always wanted to be on top of news as it's breaking wherever that might be."

Clara drew a deep breath.

"We've already spoken of some of the countries you've reported from, but how idealistic were you when you went in to these places, for example Iraq, Afghanistan, Syria? What did you think you'd achieve?"

It was a serious question inviting thoughtful response.

Joey hesitated before answering.

"I don't believe in compromise. There's a story to be had in all these places, and I've always been committed to capturing exactly what is happening and recording it with no embellishments. No matter where I've gone, the story isn't just about the militia, the weapons and the offensive. Sure it's about that, but it's also about everyone else out there. It's about how these conflicts, these wars, affect everyday people and their everyday lives, from the children up to the frail and elderly. I've always wanted to achieve the documenting of that, present the bigger, wider picture. It's often painful and tragic, but these are the stories that I feel must be told and to represent the true cost of what is happening. I'm not sure I'd call myself idealistic…just a curious kid who grew up and who wanted to see with her own eyes what was going on and to show others."

"It's also dangerous, and it's been costly for you too."

"Yes, it has."

"Will we see you on the front line again?"

"I can't answer that, Clara. Not yet. And I'm not going to talk about what happened to me and my crew out there. Enough has been written and spoken of it. Everyone will know that the events left their mark on me. I wouldn't be human if they hadn't. But

I'm also getting to that age where my body isn't as forgiving and cooperative as it used to be, and I'm aware that there are many up-and-coming excellent journalists behind me ready to fill my place. Although I haven't made any decisions, maybe the time has come for me to hang up my desert boots and settle into a less physically challenging role as a journalist."

Clara leaned back in her chair. "Maybe we can talk about that in the second part of our interview." She smiled to indicate their time was at an end.

Joey listened to her formally bring it all to a close.

"Thank you for joining us. You've been listening to NPR and the *Clara Dale Show*. My guest today has been Josephine Barry, international journalist, and until recently, chief news correspondent for RSB. I hope you'll join us again where I will be continuing to chat with Josephine about her long and distinguished career. Until then, good-bye, God bless, and be safe."

Several seconds stretched as Clara and her one-man production team took the show off the air. Clara removed her headphones.

"How was that, Joey?" she asked.

"Good. I enjoyed it."

"You'll come back then?" Clara was smiling as she rose from behind the array of technical equipment in front of her.

"Yes."

Sherry Dexter chose that moment to enter the studio. She walked up to Joey and placed a hand on her arm.

"Hey, girlfriend, I've been listening and that was excellent. Clara, nice questions. You guys all set for the next session?"

"Times are all arranged," Clara said.

"Good. Well if you're finished here, Joey, back to my office for coffee?"

Joey thanked Clara and left with Sherry.

Sherry's DC office was utilitarian and basic. It reminded Joey how compartmentalized her old friend could be. The office felt like a room someone had just moved into. Apart from the necessary furniture and computer basics, there were no pretty pictures on the wall, no family photos on the desk. No frills. Nothing. Paperwork sat in neat piles, and the gaps in between were spotless. Joey remembered Sherry had always been the same. While Joey's space was always messy and busy, Sherry's was well ordered and minimalist. She worked hard but kept her personal and professional lives very separate. When she finished work, she didn't hang around. She went home to her *real* life. Joey had never understood how she could do it.

Sherry thrust a coffee into Joey's hands and seated herself at the desk opposite.

"Do you want to listen to the interview before it airs?"

Sherry had contacted her when she returned to the U.S. and somehow talked her into doing a series of three interviews. They would be prerecorded, with an agreement that if Joey wasn't happy with anything, it would be cut. But Clara had made it clear from the start that she wasn't going to put Joey on the spot and draw out all the unpleasantness of her final months with RSB, and worse, what had happened in Balshir. Joey didn't know whether it was because Sherry had drawn a line in the sand or if Clara was just a decent person.

Joey shook her head. "No, I'm happy with it."

"Good. As before, Clara will give you an idea of where the next session is heading. I promise, no nasty invasive questions."

The tight agreement had been the only way Joey would let Sherry lure her into the studio. Joey hadn't thought she'd agree, but she'd relented.

"These kinds of fireside chats are popular with the listeners, and they are very eager to know more about you. They want to know where you've been and what you're up to. You were full-on in the media and then gone. I know I said it before, but I'm reminding you, when these air, it's going to reenergize the media's interest in you. Beware."

Joey didn't need reminding. Journalists were already sniffing around her parents' home and places she once used to frequent. It wouldn't take them long to find out where she was staying.

"I still think you should come and work for us," Sherry said.

"My, but you're persistent."

"I sure am. It's how I get places. I know you've got other opportunities lined up, but remember, the offer is always open."

"I know and don't think I'm not grateful."

Sherry finished her coffee. "This isn't about me being nice to an old buddy; this is business. If I could get you to work for us, it'd be a coup. We'd be getting one hell of a professional on our team." She stood. "Okay, hon, I've gotta run. I'll catch up with you later. You staying in town?"

"Only for the night and then back to Baltimore."

"See you at the weekend? Give me a call. Maybe you could come over for lunch or dinner, whatever. John is itching to meet you. I think he had the hots for you. Of course, that was before he married me. Anyway, call."

When Joey walked out onto North Capitol Street and headed for where she'd left the car, she contemplated how nervous she'd been as she entered the modern building that was NPR's HQ. It had been her first return attempt at *fronting* the news, even if it was only about her. It was a big step after everything that had happened. But everything had gone well, and she knew she'd be more relaxed when she returned for the other sessions.

She also thought about Sherry's persistence of a job offer. She knew it was genuine. If she said yes, the contract would be there in a flash. But while everything else around her was a mess, Joey had no second doubts regarding her future employment. She had accepted the permanent job in the UK with Stallion Productions. She'd negotiated a break before taking up a permanent contract so she could come home and sort out her affairs. When she went back to England, she would be starting a new chapter in her life, and one that would do much to remove the invasive U.S. media. Distance was queen.

She also wondered if it wasn't too late to learn a few tricks off Sherry, in particular, her ability to compartmentalize. If she could pigeonhole her life, she could separate the good from the bad. Her personal life was in tatters, and while walking away from Sam had been painful, she felt it was for the best. She had tried to cope with a relationship while balancing the effects of post-traumatic stress disorder, and it had proved too much for her. Now she believed that being alone suited her best and was perhaps what she deserved. It was her professional life that could reign supreme. She could and would rebuild it. That was her aim. The opportunity to work for Stallion offered her a different direction with stability, challenge, security, and a degree of anonymity. The UK press was not intrusive where she was concerned, and as if she needed any reassurance that she was making the right career move, Sherry's prophetic warning of the probable resurgence of U.S. interest, post her talk show, convinced her.

She'd taken a first step in putting her life back in order and it felt good.

She headed back to the parking lot.

Sam walked into the office building on N. Charles Street in downtown Baltimore.

It had taken her ages to get there from the motel. As if driving on the wrong side of the road wasn't bad enough in a hire car that felt alien and too big, she'd also been hampered by roadwork. What had looked like a straightforward drive had turned into a nightmare. There was now a system of temporary one-way routes. The Satnav in its confusion had all but announced "fuck it," and the hard copy road map she'd eventually turned to had been equally useless. But finally, she'd arrived.

Sam had nearly given herself vertigo as she stared up at the high-rise building. It housed every sort of legal business imaginable, but apparently, there were some apartments inside, one of which Joey was using.

Feeling tired, Sam walked across the vast expanse of marble flooring and up to the reception desk where a smartly dressed woman was busy answering a phone while another rang out. Sam waited patiently. The woman acknowledged her presence with a tip of her head and a smile that was as plastic as a credit card. Sam sensed the woman was not having a good day either.

"Can I help you?" the receptionist asked when she'd dealt with the phones.

"I'm looking for Josephine Barry."

"Do you have an appointment?"

"No, she won't be expecting me," Sam answered.

A man in an expensive suit and smelling of cologne appeared at her side. The receptionist acknowledged him. "Mr. Gruber, please go ahead. Hampton and Blunt are expecting you. Take elevator four and press for floor ten."

The man disappeared.

"I'm not showing a Josephine Barry on my list," she said, returning her attention to Sam. "If you could tell me what company she works for?"

Sam hesitated. "I don't think she works here, at least I'm not sure. I believe she lives in an apartment in this building."

The insincere smile was back.

"And you are?"

The phones were ringing again. The receptionist wasn't happy, and Sam was presented with an impatient stare.

"I'm a friend of hers. I can see you're busy…if you can just point me in the direction, I can make my own way there."

The receptionist eyed her suspiciously. "One moment," she said as she dealt efficiently with the calls. When she refocused on Sam, Sam sensed her hesitation.

"Does she live here?" Sam asked.

"I wouldn't know."

The answer was deliberately vague. Confused, Sam was just wondering what to do next when she saw the receptionist raise her hand to get the attention of a man and woman exiting one of the elevators. They acknowledged her with a smile and started toward the desk.

Sam studied them.

The woman was attractive and appeared to be in her mid to late sixties. She was shorter than the man, rather petite, and she came across as trim and fit. She was elegantly dressed. Her bobbed hair was immaculate and her makeup flawless. He seemed older and though dressed well, he was more relaxed in appearance. Sam sensed they were a couple. There was affection between them. They looked happy, and as he walked alongside the woman, he rested a hand casually on her shoulder.

As they approached the desk, the receptionist said, "Sir, this person says she's looking for Josephine Barry."

Sam didn't miss the look of understanding that passed between them. Neither did she miss the sharp, intense stare the woman gave her.

"Oh yes, and you are?" the man said. He stood taller than Sam and looked down on her as he spoke.

"I'm a friend of hers." Sam was feeling uncomfortable.

"A friend," he repeated.

Sam was shrewd enough to know she was being assessed.

"Yes, and I believe she's staying here, I just—"

"And you know that how?"

"A friend told me." Sam thought of a conversation she'd had with Elsa.

"A friend?" Though he was polite, it was like being cross-examined. She was certainly in the right venue.

"Yes. I've sort of lost contact with Miss Barry, and I'm trying to reestablish that. All I want to know is if she lives in this building and if so, how I can contact her."

"Don't you have her cell or an email address? Aren't you on Facebook or something?" he said.

With the exception of Facebook, which Sam loathed and avoided, she had all the others. But she hadn't told Joey she was over here. She wanted to surprise her, to see her face-to-face. Sam had also thought that if she gave Joey the heads-up that she was here, Joey might choose not to see her and bolt. Sam didn't want to risk being turned away before she even had a chance. She wasn't sure how Joey would handle her presence. This was information Sam was not about to impart to perfect strangers.

She shook her head. "Lost those too."

"How unfortunate." The statement was far from genuine as the elegant woman spoke.

"I didn't catch your name," the man said. He was looking at her in the same suspicious way as the receptionist still was.

Sam sighed.

"Look, my name is Samantha Savage, and I've just flown over here from England. I met Jo—"

"You're the vicar!" the woman exclaimed, her face breaking out into a huge smile.

"The motorbiker?" the man added, his eyes wide.

"You have me at a disadvantage…"

"Why didn't you tell us who you are in the first place?" he said, his voice full of warmth. "We thought you were press snooping around. We're Joey's parents. I'm Len and this is my wife, Ann."

Sam should have guessed. Now as she studied them, there was a family likeness to Joey. And despite having lived in America for years, Ann still had an undeniable English accent.

The dark made light, handshaking ensued.

"It's okay, Sandy," Len said to the receptionist. "This lady is a friend of my daughter's. We'll take it from here."

Sandy looked relieved and returned to her busy duties.

The three of them moved away from the desk.

"So, how's the bike?" Len said.

Ann looked dumbfounded at her husband. "You're not seriously going to start talking about bikes. We've only just met."

Len couldn't see what he was doing wrong. "Darling, I helped Samantha and Joey fix a carb problem. By the way, Samantha, I'm real glad you liked the magneto I sent over."

"It's beautiful. I haven't attached it yet, but I'm going to when the weather is better and I have more time." Sam's day was improving.

"You won't be disappointed," Len said. "It's an original, none of this replicated trash."

"Will you two stop this!" Ann was appalled.

Len shrugged. "So, Samantha, what brings you here? You on vacation?"

It wasn't an easy question for Sam to answer. She had no idea how much information Joey's parents knew regarding their daughter's love life.

Ann raised a hand.

"Darling, you go to the car, and I'll join you in a minute."

"Why?"

Her face was serene as she cast a slow smile. The warning leveled was crystal clear. "Because I'm asking you to, that's why."

"But we've only just met," Len said.

Ann didn't respond. Only her eyes bored into him.

Len looked from her to Sam and back to his wife again.

"This is going to be one of those woman to woman moments, isn't it? I'm not wanted because I'm a man."

Silence pervaded.

"Okay." He yielded without further deliberation.

Sam remembered that Ann was Elsa's younger sister, the one who'd met the handsome American and run off across the pond. It amused her that such a diminutive figure packed such a punch. Although she could see some family resemblance, she was the antithesis of Elsa who was rather meek and mild.

Len moved off toward the exit muttering away. "But I really don't understand why. We've only just met. Men can be sensitive too, you know."

Sam glanced back to find Ann watching her.

"Don't worry, Samantha. He'll be fine. I don't think he knows what sort of relationship you've been having with Joey."

"You do?"

"Yes. And I know you're having a few teething problems… which I have no doubt is why you're here."

Sam put a hand to her head. "This is surreal. You're her mother."

"And you're a vicar," Ann added dryly. "Okay. Joey is here. She's staying in the apartment my husband had when he was a practicing attorney in this building. He often worked late and would stay over. When he retired, we decided to hang on to the place; it's small but entirely functional. We use it if we come downtown to a concert or an opera. Joey's using it right now."

"Can I go see her?"

"I don't think she wants to see you." Ann wasn't being awkward, just truthful.

"I want to change that."

"Good luck. She's stubborn like her father." Ann reached down into her handbag. "You'll need this." She handed Sam a small blue tag. "You take elevator five, go to floor ten. Get out and then take the elevator to your right. Swipe the tag and select the residence floor. You'll see it on the board. She's in apartment two. Ring the doorbell."

"She's in?"

"We just left her."

Sam took the tag.

"When did you fly in?" Ann asked.

"A few days ago."

"Where are you staying?"

"A Motel 6 near the intersection of Interstates 70 and 695."

Ann frowned. "Is it okay?"

"Yes. It's modern, clean, and simple. I can park the hire car out front."

Ann reached into her handbag again and this time passed a card to Sam. It had her contact details on it.

"Any problems, Samantha, call me."

"Call me Sam. And I hope there won't be *any problems*."

"Sam, you're dealing with my daughter, God bless her."

Sam was already heading for the elevator as Ann left.

❖

Joey opened the apartment door. She was shocked to find Sam standing on the other side.

"Sam?"

"Surprise," Sam said.

Her enthusiastic introduction was wrapped in a smile. It lit her face, but Joey could see the nervousness behind the mask. Her own nerves were now jangling away.

"What are you doing here?" Joey asked.

It was a stupid question. Sam's face held love, warmth, and expectancy all in one. What was to doubt?

Sam cocked her head to one side and feigned nonchalance. "I think the motorbike needs a service. It's sounding rough. I thought you might like to help."

If Sam was using humor to counter the shock of their reintroduction, it wasn't helping. Joey's heart was thumping in her chest. She wasn't expecting Sam to cross the Atlantic and turn up on her doormat. She placed a hand on the door to steady herself.

"How did you find me?"

"Elsa."

"Elsa," Joey repeated. Her mother's sister was not known for her ability to hold confidences.

Sam was looking at her wide-eyed. "I guess I'm the last person you expected to see when you opened the door."

"You're not wrong."

"I didn't call ahead in case you ran out on me again."

Joey didn't know what to say. Sam filled the void.

"I heard your chat on NPR."

"How do you know about that?"

"Elsa," Sam said. "I went to the DC studio the day before yesterday as it aired. I was hoping to see you, but I discovered it was prerecorded. I ended up going round the exhibit in the museum there. It was pretty interesting. I learned all about the history of NPR and how it got started. The displays are interactive you know."

Joey's heart lurched. Sam was trying to hide her uneasiness by talking of inconsequential matters. "Yes, I know."

"I hear you're doing some more chats."

"Yeah."

"You thinking of working for them?"

How could Sam know anything about that? She hadn't mentioned anything to her when she'd returned to England the last time.

"Elsa," they answered in unison.

Joey was going to have to have a chat with Auntie Elsa.

"I've been offered a job." Joey felt deceitful even though she wasn't lying.

They were still standing in the doorway, and Joey knew she should invite Sam in, but she held back. If she allowed Sam across the threshold her resolve would cave in, and she couldn't let that happen. She hadn't gone through all the misery of the last few months for nothing. She was determined to keep things simple from now on…and that meant no Sam. No anybody. It was the only way she could cope.

Sam was fidgeting. She awkwardly stuck her hands in her jacket pockets. The hurt was evident as she looked up at Joey.

"You left without telling me. Why did you run out? Even a letter would have been better than nothing, Joey."

Joey wavered. "I didn't know what to say, Sam. I thought everything had been said. I still think it has. Nothing has changed. I thought it was kinder to just leave."

Sam was shocked. She started to shake her head, and when she spoke, her voice cracked.

"This isn't right, you being here and me being over there. There's something between us, and we can't deny it. Neither can we turn it off like a tap. Joey, nothing is the same without you. I get up, I go to church, and I do what I've always done. I go through the baptisms, the weddings, the funerals, but I just exist. I'm not living. It's not the same without you. And it's all because you're not with me—"

"You'll get used to it," Joey interrupted.

"No. I won't because you're not *here*." Sam placed a hand to her own heart. "There's a big gap *here* since you've gone, and it hurts. I'm not right when you're not around. Every single thing I do…I'm missing you. I wake up missing you. I go to bed missing you. I used to enjoy my bike rides, but I don't now because you're not there behind me, holding me tight."

Sam wasn't finished. "You once asked me what made me happy. I didn't answer then, maybe because I didn't know the answer…but I do now. *You* make me happy. And I think I can make you happy too if you'll just give me the chance. When you left you took my happiness with you…and I want it back."

Sam reached out and grabbed Joey's hand. Joey let it stay there for a second too long before pulling back. Her body would betray her unless she resisted. She saw the disappointment in Sam's face, but the rejection didn't deter her.

"I love you, Josephine Barry. I'll keep telling you that until it sinks in. I don't want you to have any doubts. You fill that empty space in my heart. You make the living worthwhile. And I want to make you feel the same way. I know I can. You matter so much to me. I love you."

Joey was wretched. Sam was bearing everything. She wanted to take her in her arms, hold her close, and never let her go. But she daren't.

Run. You destroy everything. You'll destroy Sam.

"I know that, Sam."

"But?"

"Weren't you listening? I can't do this anymore. I don't want this."

Joey wanted to close the door and hide.

"Listen, Joey. If you think the church is more important to me than you…if you think you're competing with God, you're wrong."

This wasn't what Joey was thinking. She'd never thought this.

"Things have changed," Sam said quietly.

"Changed?"

"God has put you on the top of my list. It means I've got a new job. Well, not exactly…yet…but I will have when I've found it."

"You're talking in riddles."

"I've handed in my notice," Sam declared.

"You've done what? You can't hand your notice in. You're a vicar."

"I can, and I have. I've had a chat with God. I'm still going to be on his team, I'm just going to be freelance from now on." Sam looked pleased with herself. "I've quit, Joey. I've told Neil. I'm not the vicar of St. Mary's anymore…well, I won't be soon. The paperwork has to go through. I'm on vacation at the moment."

"But you're a vicar," Joey repeated. This download of information still didn't make sense.

"The Pope resigned. So can I."

"What does Neil say?"

"He said it's okay. God wants me as a field agent."

Joey was dumbstruck.

"You're not saying very much," Sam said.

"I don't know what to say."

"Joey, I once told you how I chose God over love many years ago. It was right then, but it isn't now. My priorities have shifted. *You* are my priority now."

"What's a field agent?" What Sam was doing was all her fault.

"God's work is everywhere, not just within the confines of a church. He needs people out there, and that's what I'm going to do."

"Do? What?"

"I have no idea, he hasn't told me yet."

"Neil?"

"God." Sam smiled. "But I'm sure he will."

Joey's anxiety escalated. Sam's declaration wasn't helping. Joey's sanity was in jeopardy, and she was gripped with fear. For a long time she convinced herself that she didn't have PTSD. It was a peg they hung her on to explain *her issues*. What had happened to her was simple.

She'd been blown up, attacked, and almost starved to death.

She was responsible for the death of her friends, and she had survived.

Of course she had issues.

She just needed time to pull herself together…on her terms. If everyone left her alone, she would win.

But the craziness that would creep over her frightened her because it came when she least expected it. It buried itself in her psyche. It made her think and do things that made no sense. It scared her that, more and more, she was becoming less and less who she was—who she used to be.

If she could remove the emotion from her life and function at base level, she'd win. She *would* win. She was tenacious and wouldn't give up. What she didn't need were inner struggles, and Sam was all of those. She had to close down. That was *her* coping strategy, not what any stupid counselor advised.

Sam was making it worse. She was telling her that she was walking away from the church *to be with her*. Sam was already falling into Joey's mess of a life. Hadn't Joey predicted this would happen?

"This can't work, Sam. Go home."

"I can't do that, Joey."

"Yes, you can."

"No. I came out to find you, and now that I have, I'm not leaving."

"There's nothing for you here."

It was as if Sam didn't hear what Joey was saying. She was standing rigid like an unmovable force.

"I'm not leaving here without you," Sam said.

"And what if my life, my job, is here?" Joey threw at her, building on the earlier deceit.

"What's Baltimore like?"

"What do you mean?"

"Many lost souls?"

"Souls?"

"If this is where you're going to stay, then I guess I'm going to have to get to know Baltimore. I'll just have to be a field agent in Maryland."

"You don't know what you're talking about."

"I think I do."

"No, no, no," Joey said.

"Yes, yes, yes."

"Please go home. This can't work."

"Are you going to let me in?"

"I don't want you here." Joey hated the lies that fell from her mouth.

"Fine," Sam said. "I didn't think this was going to be easy. Well, if you don't want me here with you, you'll have to get used to me being in Baltimore because I'm not leaving."

Joey was getting angry. "Why won't you leave me alone?"

"Because you love me too. I just have to find a way to make you face up to that, and to scale this brick wall you're putting between us."

"And what if I don't love you?" Joey spat back.

Sam paused and studied her, a momentary look of shock on her face. But it didn't last long. "Nice try, Barry. Not going to work. Now you go back into your sanctuary and hide."

"What are you going to do?"

"I'm not going to tell you."

Sam gave her the strangest look, as if she could see into the center of her. Maybe she could. Maybe this was what this was all about. Sam turned and disappeared around the corner and back toward the elevator.

Joey leaned hard into the doorjamb.

"Damn it, damn it, damn it," she said before stepping back into the apartment and closing the door.

What if I do have PTSD?

❖

"What are you going to do?"

Joey's question kept ringing in Sam's head as she drove back to the motel.

Sam hadn't answered it because she had no idea. She only knew she hadn't packed up her vocation and flown all the way over here to go belly up at the first hurdle. Her resolve was as strong as ever. She wasn't going to lose Joey without a fight.

Sam was distraught. She'd removed what she thought were the hurdles and presented Joey with a fait accompli. It had changed nothing. That failure posed a dilemma.

Did Joey love her or not?

It was the crucial question. If she didn't, Sam might as well hop on the next flight home and go tell Neil she wanted her pulpit back. But Sam trusted her instincts. In her years of ministering, her empathic antennae seldom let her down. She knew Joey loved her, and she'd seen a fleeting glint of it in her eyes as she'd opened the door before putting the barriers up.

Also, when Sam had declared her undying love for Joey, it was what Joey hadn't said that gave Sam hope. She hadn't told Sam she didn't love her.

So, if Joey did still love Sam, then what the shit was the block?

Post traumatic stress disorder.

Milo's words filled her head.

"The PTSD took Harry over...he got worse...he pushed everyone away who mattered to him, the ones he loved, even his children. He wanted to hurt himself, a punishment for living."

Sam's enemy was a mental disorder warping Joey's mind. A disorder Joey was refusing to acknowledge. Until she did, Sam was powerless.

"God, please help me. Show me how I can help her," she prayed as she drove into the parking lot of the motel and switched off the engine.

Stepping from the car, two minor observations hit her. First, the temperature had plummeted, and she was cold. Second, there was a smattering of small snowflakes falling, and already the ground looked like it had been covered in white powder.

"What?" Sam sighed. "Come on, boss. Like I don't have enough problems to contend with. Now I have snow?" She gazed up at the sky and the falling flakes. "You'd better not stick," she growled.

The following morning when she looked out of her motel window, she knew the snowflakes had ignored her.

❖

Joey drove to her parents' place just north of Guilford.

It had taken her longer than usual. Snow had fallen heavy overnight, and although it wasn't snowing now, the roads were chaos.

She'd almost abandoned the trip, but she had a bone to pick with her mother and it wouldn't wait. It was also something she wanted to do in person. Her mother had a habit of putting the phone down when she was being chastised for her behavior.

Right now, they were standing in the dining room face-to-face, eyeball-to-eyeball, and to say the moment was tense was an understatement. Unlike her father, Joey was a match for her mother. Her mother knew it and wasn't happy.

"You drove here to tell me this?"

"You bet. I want to make sure you understand what I'm saying."

"You're being melodramatic, Josephine. You shouldn't have driven in this weather."

"You're afraid of what I'm going to say."

"Don't be silly."

Joey watched her mother fingering her pearl necklace, always a sign that she was jittery.

"I'm angry, Mom. You let Sam up to the apartment. You gave her your fob for pity's sake."

"Of course I did. She's flown all the way over here to see you."

"I didn't ask her to."

Her mother was staring at her as if she was a petulant child. It made her angrier.

"She's come to see you. Of course I'm going to let her up."

"You're interfering," Joey said.

"Only because I have to."

"You're supposed to be on my side."

"I am on your side. You're just not seeing it."

The room went quiet.

"So?" her mother asked.

"So?" Joey echoed.

"What's happening between you and Sam?"

"Nothing's happening between me and Sam."

"You talked?"

"It was hard not to when she was standing in the doorway."

"You did let her in?"

Joey almost laughed. Her mother could register shock better than an award-winning actor.

"I did not. In fact, I asked her to leave."

"Why in the name of Christmas would you do that? This is the woman you told me you loved when you were last here. That's the only time I have ever heard you use that particular four-letter word."

Her mother clearly thought she was an imbecile.

Joey was not going to be drawn into the complications of why she was doing what she was. "I told her to go back to the UK."

Her mother placed her head in her hands and moaned. "And?"

"You're interfering, Mom. This has nothing to do with you."

"Has Sam gone?"

Joey's frustration grew. "She won't."

"She won't?" Her mother lifted her face.

"She says she's going to hang around."

The coy smile on her mother's face irritated Joey.

"Stop it, Mom. This isn't a game. Sam's resigned."

"Resigned?"

"She's handed in her notice."

"She can't. She's a vicar."

"I said that, but she said *if the Pope can.*"

Joey's revelation shocked her mother whose eyes widened as the truth sank in. "She's giving all that up...for you?"

"That's why I've told her to go back."

Her mother's demeanor changed. She grew softer as she placed a hand on Joey's shoulder. "Darling, she must love you very much. And you're turning her away."

"But I don't love her, Mom," Joey lied. If she could convince her mother of that, she'd see reason. She might even convince Sam. But the ploy wasn't working.

"Don't be silly. You're talking to your mother."

One look at her mom told Joey she was wasting her breath.

Did every desolate, miserable emotion show on her face? A face her mother had always been able to read?

A familiar lump returned to Joey's throat. It was hard to deny the obvious, but she wasn't going to talk to her mother about this anymore. She raised a hand to stop further discussion.

"This isn't the only reason I came over." Joey watched her mom arch an eyebrow. "I came to tell you I'm flying out to Albuquerque early tomorrow. I'll be gone a couple of days. I need to see an old colleague and run some thoughts past him for a project I'm doing for Stallion."

"I thought you were between contracts and that this is downtime?"

"I am, but I said I'd put a little polish on a documentary they're working on. It's no big deal."

"When did you agree to this?"

"I spoke with them yesterday."

"Ah. You're running from Sam."

"I am not running."

"I think you are. You could phone this *colleague*."

"I prefer face-to-face discussion."

"As long as it isn't with Sam."

Joey held back. Her mother was infuriating when she was like this, the font of all wisdom. She didn't understand. If she understood half of what she was going through, she'd know to back off. But Joey couldn't tell her that; it would only worry her.

"I'm not running, Mom…I've just made a decision."

"You are running, darling. You've found something to occupy your mind and take you away from the real issues that need attention."

"Nothing needs sorting. I've asked her to leave."

"And as we've already established, she isn't."

Joey felt like she was being cornered. It made her feel worse.

"Have you seen Sam since?" her mom asked.

"I don't know where she's staying."

"You didn't ask?"

"She didn't tell me."

"My God, my daughter is a moron. So you've left the poor woman in a motel on her own in a strange city where she knows no one."

Joey watched her mom staring up at the ceiling in frustration and tutting away. Joey couldn't tell her this was on her conscience too.

"Have you told her you're going back to the UK?"

"No," Joey said.

"Why not?"

"Because I don't see the point of it."

Her mother was looking at her with such disappointment. "You're not going to tell her."

Again, Joey didn't answer. She wanted support from her mother, not the third degree.

"Joey, I don't know what's going on in that head of yours. Whatever is going on between you and your vicar, not telling her you'll be working back in the UK is deceitful. I've brought you up better than this."

"Mother, I'm not a child. I'm a grown woman who—"

"—is making so many mistakes right now. Darling, I love you. I want the best for you. I always have and so has your father, but this is all wrong. You and I know this isn't Sam's fault. I'm sorry to talk of this because I know it's painful for you, but you haven't been the same since Balshir. Please, darling, don't let it destroy your future…your happiness. You have to get help." She paused. "If I thought you really didn't love Sam, I'd be fighting in your corner. But I know you do…I have a mother's intuition. What you are doing isn't the right way—"

"Please stop. I don't want to talk about this anymore. Butt out of my personal life."

Joey saw only sadness in her mother's eyes as she restrained herself.

"You will be back for your recording at NPR?" her mother asked.

"Yes, I'll be back in plenty of time. Don't worry."

"But I do worry, darling. I'm your mother. It's what mothers do."

It was mid afternoon and darkness was already falling when Sam heard the knock on her motel door. She rushed to it half hoping it would be Joey. She'd already called twice at the apartment only to be told by Sandy that Joey was out, and then away for a few days. The only highlight of those visits was that Sandy was a whole lot more genial.

Sam looked through the security peephole in the door and saw Joey's mother. She was dressed warmly in a camel coat with a heavy scarf wrapped around her neck. An ominous weight rested somewhere in the pit of Sam's stomach as she opened the door. Why would Ann be here if not to bring news? She was probably acting as Joey's emissary and about to ask her to go home too.

"Hello, Sam, I hope you don't mind me disturbing you?" Ann was friendly enough, and her smile didn't seem to be in keeping with Sam's foreboding.

"Of course not." Sam ushered her into the small room and closed the door to keep the heat in.

She caught Ann glancing around the room, taking stock of it. She didn't seem too impressed.

Sam grinned. "It's okay, Ann. It's warm, it's safe, and the bed's comfortable."

The smile on Ann's face was strained, and she looked tired. It was clear she was uncomfortable, and she didn't waste time explaining why.

"This is all wrong, Sam. You should not be staying in a seedy motel room while you're here. You should be with Joey, but since she can't bring herself to be hospitable at this precise moment... well, Len and I would love for you to come and stay with us."

The invite shocked Sam. It wasn't what she'd expected. It was a generous offer, but she didn't think it reasonable to inflict herself on Joey's folks. She didn't know how long she'd be in Baltimore, or how emotional everything might get. She'd already raced through a box of tissues. She politely started to decline.

"There's no need—"

"There's every need." Ann was insistent. "If what Joey told me is true, I can't imagine you have any plans to leave soon, and this place will burn a sizable hole in your pocket. Forgive me, but I've never met a vicar yet with throwaway wealth. Please, Len and I are used to having guests over. You won't be an inconvenience. It would be a real pleasure."

It was Sam's turn to feel uncomfortable.

"Len...does he know who I am, I mean *really* know who I am besides a motorbike loving member of the cloth?"

"You mean does he know you're in love with his daughter and that's why you're over here?"

"Yes, that's a pretty good start."

Ann played with the soft leather gloves she was now holding in her hands.

"He knows."

"And how does he feel about that? How do *you* feel about that?"

Ann seated herself on the foot of the bed. "Joey came out very young and we've had a lot of time to get used to her sexual orientation. Frankly, it's become part of who she is and we're very proud of her. It's a non-issue for us both. What is important is that whoever she chooses to settle with, she makes the right decision. When she came home last time, she told me about you. She told me she was in love with you. Sam, I have never seen my daughter so serious about anyone."

"She's not too happy about it at the moment."

"No, she isn't, but if I didn't think she was still in love with you I wouldn't be doing this." Ann studied the room again. "You don't really want to stay here?"

As roadside accommodations went, this was okay, but it was an awful place to be when you were low, depressed, lovesick, and by yourself. There was little charm to the room, and Sam couldn't deny she was lonely and just a little desperate.

"Do you always get involved in your daughter's love life?" Sam asked.

"This is a first."

"This isn't going to endear you to Joey."

"I know."

"But you're doing it."

"I am, and probably for the same reasons you've told her you aren't leaving."

Sam smiled. She liked Ann very much. Joey was lucky to have such wonderful parents. Sam's had been wonderful too, but both had passed away years ago. She would always miss them.

"You do know she's asked me to leave…to go back to the UK."

"I know that too," Ann said.

Sam had always sensed that Joey was close to her parents and that there was a mutual respect between them. The depth of discussion she was having with Ann only confirmed it. It worried Sam that she might drive a wedge between mother and daughter.

"I don't want to cause problems between you both."

"Accepted. But she knows where I stand on this issue."

"Does she know you're here?"

"Inviting you to come be our guest? No, she does not."

"Oh, the fur's going to fly." Sam shook her head as she exhaled heavily.

"I take it you've decided to accept my invitation."

"If you and Len are really sure about this—"

"We are."

"You're very brave."

"We have a vicar on our side." Ann's dry humor was back.

"Then I accept your kind hospitality unreservedly."

Sam was starting to think about one more night in the motel and then driving out to wherever the Barrys lived. Ann was thinking differently.

"Pack your belongings, Sam. Len is waiting for us outside." Ann stood.

"Now?"

"You want to spend an evening alone with this room, explaining to it why you're walking out?"

Ann had a unique style. It was warmly familiar. Joey had inherited some of it too.

Sam shrugged. "You're right. Room, we're through." She grabbed her suitcase and started throwing the little she'd brought with her into it.

A thought occurred to Sam. "What about my rental car?"

"Leave it. We can sort it out tomorrow. Len or I will bring you over so you can drive it back to us in the light or you can return it. We can sort some wheels out for you." Ann was smiling and looked relaxed for the first time.

As they walked across to where Len waited, Ann turned to Sam.

"Would you like to join me for Sunday service at church tomorrow?"

Sam started to laugh. "Yes. I think we may need to garner all the support we can get."

CHAPTER SEVENTEEN

Joey stepped into the DC hotel room off DuPont Circle. She shut the door, flung her coat and shoes off, and dropped onto the bed.

She hated deceiving her mother. She'd told her a pack of lies about flying out to Albuquerque to see an old contact. What she was really doing was escaping Baltimore for a few days so she could breathe. Everything was getting too fraught and claustrophobic. Sam wasn't doing what Joey asked. She'd bedded down in town and was sticking close. Worse, her parents appeared to be siding with Sam.

Joey's head was swimming. Logic told her she was doing the right thing in simplifying her life, but her damned heart wasn't. In low, defenseless moments, she actually felt happy that Sam had flown out and was close by. It was as if a part of her wanted Sam to take control, sort out the mess in her head, and make everything right. Rationality would surge back and confirm it was a hopeless task. Why bother.

She rose from the bed and crossed to the window that looked out on the hectic flurry of the area below. Joey liked this part of Washington. There were plenty of little restaurants, some of which she knew well. She'd become a regular customer to some when she'd worked here on and off over the years. She still knew the owners. They wouldn't hesitate to tuck her away in some shadowy corner and protect her anonymity. So far, the media hadn't been intrusive. It was like the dragon that slept. Maybe it would stay that way. Maybe she was old news. Sherry's prophetic warning might come to nothing.

Her plan was to stay in the hotel until the next NPR recording. Then she'd go back to Baltimore and continue sorting her affairs out in preparation for the move. There was nothing too complicated to attend to. She'd decided not to sell her townhouse just off Inner Harbor. She'd bought the three-bedroom place years ago. It had needed work, but she'd fallen in love with it. For the past few years, she'd been renting it furnished to friends. They would be moving out soon, and she'd put everything into the hands of a local Realtor. She had some pieces of furniture she wanted to move across to England. The rest she'd put into storage or sell.

Joey turned back into the room and looked at the laptop and paperwork she'd brought with her. She hadn't entirely lied to her mother. She had agreed to do some editing work on a project Stallion was working on. It was a straightforward piece and would occupy her mind.

She decided to have a shower first and then settle down to it.

"I think I'll show Sam around the garden, Ann. Maybe walk down to my man shed."

Len gave Sam a guarded look across the dining room table as they finished breakfast. It was a clear coded message meant for just the two of them.

Sam wasn't sure what he was up to, but she knew he was up to something. Whatever it was, Ann seemed oblivious.

"That's a lovely idea, darling. Make the most of this dry spell. They're talking about a bad weather front coming in. More snow. God, I hate the stuff."

Len and Sam dressed for the cold and headed down the sweeping lawn to the bottom of the garden where a large metal shed was.

"I thought you were going to show me the garden," Sam smiled as Len purposely swept her past everything in a determination to get to the shed as quickly as possible.

"Sure," he said without dropping pace. "To your right, rose bed. To your left, Azaleas when they bloom. Over in the corner, the herb garden."

"Nice."

When they arrived at the shed, Len entered a code into a large security padlock that held a thick chain. He then opened two equally large padlocks via keys that held the door firm at the top and the bottom. He pulled open a substantial steel door. Inside there was an inner door which he used another key to open.

"Some man shed, Len. Little over-the-top with security?"

"Yeah, well I don't want anyone snooping inside."

"You get many burglaries around here?"

"Not had one yet. I was thinking more of keeping Ann out."

"Any particular reason?"

"Yep."

He flicked a light on. It illuminated a large space full of the type of equipment you expected to see in a gardening shed. There was a sit-on mower, a regular mower, some hedge cutters, and leaf blowers. The equipment was expensive but nothing overly impressive and certainly not worthy of Fort Knox. To the side was a workbench where Len obviously spent time. It was covered in wrenches, drills, nuts and bolts, cans of oil, steel cutters, saws, and more. Sam considered it normal for what might be needed for repair and maintenance.

But Len was still moving forward.

He led her past it all and toward the back of the shed and up to an area where a large dark green piece of tarp was thrown. He stood awhile waiting as if to ensure he had Sam's full attention before pulling the covering off like a magician revealing a bunny.

Surprise filled Sam.

She couldn't stop her eyes from widening and her jaw from dropping.

She was looking at three motorcycles. And not just any motorcycles. They were classics.

There was a Harley-Davidson VLD, what looked like a late 60s Kawasaki WZ, and an immaculate and beautiful BSA A10 Golden Flash just like the model she had, only in better condition.

"Ta-dah! What do you think?" He stood there beaming at her.

"Hang on a minute while I choke." Sam felt like she'd been transported to motorbike heaven. To see three vintage classics in one shed...she pinched herself.

"My wife thinks I've only got one now," he said with pride.

"I thought you'd got rid of the BSA." Hadn't Joey told her this?

"Nah. Ann thinks I did, but a man has to have some secrets from the love of his life. It's why I keep the place secure."

Sam scoffed. "Sod the padlocks, you should have movement sensors installed, with laser beam technology. Scorch anyone who comes near." Sam caught Len's look of astonishment. It probably wasn't what he expected to hear from a woman of the cloth. Sam added, "God forbid I should think such a thing."

"Understandable." Len nodded amiably. "The Harley's a real old gal, 1934. I bought the Kawasaki a few years back. It was in a bad state. I've been doing it up slowly...kind of a winter restoration project that's stretching over the seasons. The BSA rides like a dream."

"They're beautiful, Len."

"They sure are. They don't get ridden as much as they ought to now. I'm not as young as I was, and I only take them out in the good weather. I thought you might like to use the BSA while you're here."

"I couldn't do that." Sam was shocked he'd even consider this.

"You'd be doing me a favor. It doesn't get used as much as it should. It could do with a real shakedown. Frankly, she's getting too heavy for me now. All I ask is that you bring her back in one piece and maybe keep her out of the snow."

"It's been snowing, Len," Sam reminded him.

"Yeah, but it won't hang around. Never does. It comes in clumps."

Sam couldn't turn the offer down. "I'll ride her like an angel."

"Let's fire her up."

They pulled the bike out. Len got on and kicked the pedal down. It started straightaway. He hopped off and let Sam sit on it to get a feel. It was like being home. Sam felt homesick for her own bike.

They stopped the engine.

"We'll take her up to the house. Get her locked up in the garage."

Len started to wheel the bike toward the door but stopped.

Sam knew something was on his mind.

He looked at Sam with intent.

"So what are your intentions regarding my daughter?"

For a second time, Sam nearly choked. Then she caught Len smiling.

"Relax, Sam. Your pedigree's showing. Anyone who owns a classic has to be all right."

Sam gave a nervous shrug. "Of course."

"And I guess you being a vicar…"

Len's priorities would have amused Sam if she wasn't so tense. *Once a biker, always…*

"This isn't an easy topic for me, Len, but I can tell you I love Joey. My intentions? I suppose if we can work things out, I want to make her happy. I want us to be together."

"Good enough." He was as plain speaking as Ann, but Sam could tell he wasn't finished.

His next question took the wind out of her sails.

"You think Joey's going to be okay?"

She wasn't sure how to answer. She needed to talk plain too.

"I see what you see, Len. I don't know what to do."

"Why won't she let anyone help her?" Len's calm persona couldn't hide his desperation.

Sam eyed him. She hadn't expected such a serious conversation in a shed surrounded by classic motorcycles.

"I'm no professional, Len, but I have my suspicions."

He tipped his chin forward, the silent invitation to speak candidly.

"I think this is all part of a self-punishment regime. She won't accept help in case it starts to make her feel better. She doesn't think she deserves to feel that."

"That's damn stupid."

"Yes, it is, but I guess you and I weren't out there. It's part of her survivor guilt."

"Part of?"

"Just a feeling that there's something else going on in her mind besides the PTSD. Something else happened out there, but she won't talk about it. I may be wrong, but it's what I sense."

Len studied her like he was summing up a client. She wondered what was on his mind.

"Ann and I feel the same. It's just a feeling too. But if we're right and it could be unlocked, we might get the old Joey back. Get her to stand straight again."

He tapped her on the back. His way of showing the topic was finished.

"You really are resigning from being a vicar?"

Sam laughed. "I'm still ordained, Len. I chose to be a vicar... it was the job I wanted after my ordination. All I'm doing is changing job, *which*, I'll be honest, I haven't worked out yet. But I still remain ordained. If I ever wanted, I could be a vicar again sometime."

"I see."

Sam wasn't sure he did.

They maneuvered the bike out of the shed. Len rode it slowly back up the pathway toward the house and into the garage. Sam ran behind.

As Len alighted from the bike, Ann appeared.

Len stood tall. "I was about to come and explain—"

"You think I didn't know? That sound down in the shed every time you fire it up."

"You've known all this time?"

"I've always known you'd never got rid of the SRB."

"BSA," Len and Sam corrected her in unison.

"Whatever. And I know you've got others in there too. Why all the secrecy I don't know." Ann looked at Sam. "Honestly, Sam, you'd think I was the wicked witch not letting my husband have a hobby." She walked back into the house.

Len turned to Sam and narrowed his eyes. "I swear, if I live to be two hundred…"

When Joey arrived at the NPR building, Sherry was waiting for her.

It struck her as unusual. Sherry was a busy woman and not the type to meet and greet. Her modus operandi was usually seeing people after events, making sure everyone was happy. She let her team get on with their jobs and was fairly hands-off.

Sherry walked alongside Joey to the studio where Clara Dale was waiting to do the second recording.

"I don't want to alarm you, but there's been a man here asking for you. He's been into NPR several times. He won't say who he is, but he looks Middle Eastern and has the accent. He's quite insistent. Reception says they've seen him hanging around outside."

"Is he here now?"

"No, hon. I've had a good look. But I saw him a few days ago. Reception called me. He's a tall, thin guy with a heavy dark beard. He's not press. I can smell them at twenty paces."

"But you're worried."

"Not sure worry is the right word, but he's anxious to see you, and I can't imagine we've seen the last of him. You got any idea who he might be?"

"None. Should we call the police?"

"You're thinking about that stalker," Sherry said.

"Hard not to. He was a persistent little bastard. I don't want any more of those."

Joey thought back ten years. It had made the front page news. She'd been stalked by a crazy guy when she was working out of California. He had followed her all over the place, turning up where she least expected him. He'd had a habit of getting into apparently secure buildings and leaving her single roses on her desk. It all became intolerable when a colleague working for a different network suffered a similar problem that had resulted in her being sexually assaulted. The police had acted fast after that and arrested Joey's admirer. She hadn't been bothered since, but there was always the possibility.

"He could be anyone, I guess. A fan after an autograph?" Sherry shrugged. "We'll wait. If he turns up again, we'll call the cops."

Her response didn't inspire Joey with confidence, mainly because she didn't really think he was a stalker or a fan. There was a nasty feeling in the pit of her stomach. Before Balshir, she'd done a documentary that had revealed the funding mechanisms of the insurgent regime. Certain avenues of cash had been terminated after that. It hadn't made her popular and she received threats. Could someone be seeking revenge for the documentary?

Sherry was staring at her. Joey sensed she knew what was going through her mind.

"Stop thinking what you're thinking, girlfriend." Sherry tapped her arm in reassurance. "You're home, and you're safe."

"You can't blame me."

"I can't. I'd be nervous too. Anyway, security knows and will act appropriately if he comes back. I've got a car that'll take you where you need to go when you finish."

Joey smiled. "About six hundred yards to where I'm parked."

Sherry smiled back. "We'll drive you around the block then. Kill any scent."

Joey accepted the offer as she walked into Clara's studio.

It was little over an hour later when Joey walked back into reception.

The man at the desk politely advised her that someone would be out front soon with transport.

Joey waited.

She looked out the large glass windows checking the street for the mystery man. He wasn't there. But someone else was that she knew. Sam.

As Sam walked into the foyer, she caught the display of emotions that ran across Joey's face as their eyes met. Her unexpected appearance was rewarded with a brief smile, and again for a split second, Joey looked happy to see her. But then the smile turned into a scowl.

"What are you doing here?" Joey asked.

"I'm here to see you. It seems to be the only place I can get to meet you face-to-face. You keep avoiding me in Baltimore." Sam smiled at her gently, hoping her presence would melt Joey's heart, but the tactic didn't work.

"You look good," Sam said. She couldn't help herself. She was in love with Joey and missing her. All she wanted to do was to grab and hug all the air out of her. Couldn't Joey feel that?

"How did you know I'd be here? And please don't tell me Auntie Elsa."

Sam's initial excitement started to grow heavy. She'd hoped after their first meeting that Joey might be rethinking things. It didn't look like it.

Sam shook her head. "Your mother."

"Are you two socializing now or what?"

"I'm staying with your parents. They rescued me from the motel."

The minute she spoke, Sam realized she'd said the wrong thing. It hadn't occurred to her that Joey didn't know about her new living arrangements. She'd given it little thought.

Joey leaned into her and lowered her voice. "You're making my life very difficult, Sam. Please just go home and leave me alone. I can't do this."

"No."

"Nothing is going to change."

"No, Joey. I'm staying."

"You're wasting your time." Joey raised her voice.

A man at reception called over to her. "Miss Barry, is everything okay?"

Joey straightened. "Press."

The man immediately attracted the attention of a security officer who came over. He stepped in between her and Joey.

"Please leave, ma'am," he said.

"Hang on, I'm not press."

The security officer's gave her the *you either leave now or I throw you out* look.

"Joey, please." Sam appealed to her, but she was already walking out of the building toward a waiting vehicle at the curb. As she tried to follow, the security officer blocked her.

The last sight Sam caught of Joey was the look of total misery on her face as the vehicle drove off.

❖

"She did what?"

Ann's voice was raised to a high pitch. Len's disposition wasn't much different. He was pacing the kitchen as incensed as his wife was.

Sam was seated glumly at the breakfast table, her elbows on it and her face resting in her hands.

"I can't believe Joey did that," Ann said.

"I can't believe they thought I was press. I'm an ordained minister for heaven's sake."

Sam was trying to make light of what had happened at NPR, but nothing was minimizing the ominous state of tension that filled the room.

"What is going on in my daughter's head? Why is she pushing everyone that matters out of her life?"

Len walked over and wrapped an arm around Ann in an attempt to calm her. It didn't work.

"Sam, what can we do? Please tell me," Ann begged.

"I wish I knew." Sam had no answers despite all her prayers.

"You aren't going to go back to England, are you?" Len looked desperate.

"It's okay, Len. I'm not giving up."

Relief flooded his face.

"You're the only one who seems to understand our daughter right now. I don't." Ann's makeup was its usual perfection, but it wasn't hiding the lines and dark shadows under the eyes. Neither had been there when Sam had first arrived, or if they had, they weren't so pronounced. Sam felt guilty. Her presence was aggravating already existing problems and causing Joey to behave badly. The outcome of all of this was affecting Ann. She was worried about Joey, and she didn't look as if she was sleeping. Len was agitated too but hid it better. Sam wouldn't have told them anything of what had happened in DC, but they'd tipped her off about the time and date of the next recording. Naturally, they'd wanted to know what had happened when she returned. It wasn't something she could sidestep.

"This isn't my daughter."

Ann's voice cracked, and Sam didn't know what to say or do.

"Please try and be calm, my dear. This isn't doing you any good." Len pulled his wife into a hug, and she stayed there for a while. When she pushed away from him, she returned to pacing the kitchen floor. She eventually stopped and turned to Sam, resolve on her face.

"Sam, I might as well tell you because Joey isn't going to."

An unpleasant sensation ran through Sam. Something disagreeable was about to be said, something that Sam had a feeling she didn't want to hear.

"Joey has taken the job at Stallion," Ann said.

"What job?"

"They offered her a permanent contract a few months ago. She told us about it when she was last out here. Didn't she tell you?"

"No." Joey had said nothing to her about any job offer with Stallion. Why not? It hurt that Joey hadn't told her.

"Well, she's taken it," Ann added.

"What's she doing over here then?"

"She's in between contracts and here to sort things out," Ann said.

"She's got a townhouse down near the harbor," Len explained. "She's been renting to buddies for a few years on an unofficial basis. She was thinking of selling it, but now she's decided to hang on to it and rent it but through an agent. She also needed to see RSB. She's had to clear everything with them regarding termination of her contract."

Sam could tell Len wasn't enamored with them.

"They couldn't drop her contract quick enough when she went to pieces in front of the public on a live broadcast. Nothing has pleased me more to know she's free of the bastards."

Ann reacted uncomfortably to his language, but Len dismissed her.

"No, Ann, I speak as I find. They are bastards. If they'd protected and given her time…helped her instead of setting her up for a fall, a lot of this could have been avoided. All they're interested in is their profit margin and increasing viewing numbers. They're a bunch of fuckers." He looked to Sam. "Sorry."

"She hasn't told me any of this," Sam said. A nasty taste rose in her mouth. Why hadn't Joey told her when she returned to England before Christmas, and why the shit hadn't she told her now? She felt betrayed. Worse, she felt betrayed by someone she was in love with and who she thought loved her. A chill settled in her.

"I'm not standing for this," Ann said. "I'm going to get her over here and we're going to sit down over dinner in a civilized fashion and talk things through. I will not let her get away with this

behavior even if she is unwell. She needs to know we love her."
Ann looked at Sam. "All of us."

Sam could see Ann was barely holding it together.

"My daughter is going to live in England, and I'll be damned
if she's going back there with this between us all."

Len didn't look like this was a good idea. Sam wasn't sure
either, but she kept her counsel.

"I'll phone her tomorrow and make the arrangements," Ann
said. "I'm not in a good mood right now." She walked out of the
kitchen.

"This is my fault, Len. I'm sorry." Sam waited until Ann was
out of earshot.

"No, it isn't. It's no one's fault except the rebels and what they
did. They've messed with my daughter's mind and now she's got
PTSD. There are a lot of families out there having to cope with
this. We're not unique. We'll get through. I don't know how, but
we will." He moved to leave the room too but stopped. "I think I'm
going down to the shed to work on the Kawasaki. Want to help?"

Sam rose from the breakfast table. The polite response would
have been to say yes, but she needed time alone. She was hurting.
Joey had kept news from her, and not just recently. This wasn't
good.

"Would you be upset if I declined? I could do with a bit of
time to think."

Len understood. "Sure."

"I might take the bike out for a spin."

The roads were clear of snow and dry for the moment. It
probably wasn't going to stay like that for long. Snow was expected
later in the day. It was her last chance.

"Dress up warm, Sam. There's a cutting wind out there."

"I will."

"And keep her out of snow."

"I'll do that too." Sam smiled.

❖

Joey left the recording studio.

When the NPR courtesy vehicle reunited her with her car, she drove straight home to the Baltimore apartment.

She usually liked driving. She'd get out onto the interstate, put the pedal to the metal, and chill out, maybe listen to the radio. But this journey didn't have its usual calming effect. She was upset, and it seemed every minute her emotions altered between anger, shame, and distress. She was angry because Sam had turned up at NPR. She was ashamed because of how she'd treated Sam. She was devastated because she'd left her there.

She kept seeing Sam's face as the courtesy vehicle drove off from the front of the building. She'd looked wounded, lost, and vulnerable. Joey couldn't believe she was acting this way toward the woman she loved more than her own life. But it was for Sam's own good, and the sooner she went home to England the better. But damn it, Sam was showing no sign of doing that.

Joey blamed her mother.

She was making everything worse by encouraging Sam to stay. But for her, Sam might have gone by now. Maybe.

Joey was still smoldering with anger the next day when her mother called her. Ann didn't waste time in getting straight to the point. She did at least have the decency to tread gingerly.

"Darling, please listen. I know you think I'm interfering. I've never done it before and I'm trying not to now, but sometimes you can't ignore what's going on. I know what happened between you and Sam yesterday in DC. Sam is being very stiff upper lip about it all, but I can tell she's hurting. I know this is not what you intended to do, but…"

Ann paused and Joey stiffened. Instinct told her that her mother was about to tell her something she wouldn't like.

"I want you to come over to dinner tomorrow. It'll just be your father, you and me, *and* Sam. We can sit down like civilized human beings, have something to eat, and then you and Sam can have a chat…a real chat. You can try to sort everything out. You can't expect her to understand when you won't even talk to her. Telling her to go home isn't enough. She's in love with you. You've got to stop hiding."

Joey was right; this wasn't what she wanted to hear, and it made her angry. Her mother was nervous. Joey heard the telltale little cough she had when her mouth got dry. She knew her mother was trying to help, but she wasn't, and Joey needed to tell her a few hard truths.

"If you didn't meddle, none of this would have happened. Sam would have gone—"

"No, darling, she wouldn't," her mother interrupted. "She's not one to be pushed away, not without reason. It's no good blaming me for Sam's persistence."

"You told Sam about the NPR appointment. Of course I blame you. And how dare you invite her to stay with you—"

"Your father and I have every right to invite who we like into our house—"

"Don't drag Dad into this. He just does what you want."

Joey heard the sharp intake of breath on the other end of the line. Her mother went quiet.

"Mom, your interfering is making everything worse."

"Darling, please—"

"Don't *darling* me. You're doing the wrong thing. You don't understand."

"Then come to dinner and make me understand. Enlighten us all."

"There's no way I'm coming over tomorrow. I've said all I'm going to say to Sam."

"Please, darling."

"Stop this meddling. I'm not in the mood. I want you to stop." Joey heard herself shout. There was venom in it.

The line went quiet again.

"Are you listening to me, Mother? Are you hearing what I'm saying?"

"I'm finishing this, Joey. You're not listening *to me*, and I don't feel well."

"Yes, put the phone down on me. You always do this when you know you're in the wrong."

"Please...come to dinner."

"No."

The phone line went dead.

Joey cursed. This was so typical of her mom. Whenever they argued, albeit infrequently, it always ended up with neither of them giving in. Her father said it was because they were too alike—hardnosed, inflexible, and uncompromising. They would walk away from each other for a while, cool down, and realize what they were arguing about was unimportant. They would then demonstrate their unfaltering love in quiet little ways. It drove her father crazy.

But this was different. This was because what they were arguing about *was* important. It upset Joey. It was true that her mother never interfered in her life. But she was doing it now, and she was siding with Sam. Even her father was. Why would they do that?

Joey shivered. She had shouted at her mom. In all their spats, she never did that. But she had today, and her angry words had sounded mean and vicious.

Are Mom and Dad doing this because I really am ill?

Joey dropped onto the couch. Staying away from Sam was supposed to be helping.

Why wasn't it then?

Chapter Eighteen

It was late afternoon and getting dusk as Sam rode back up the driveway of Ann and Len's home.

She was tired and getting cold, but the bike ride had improved her disposition. The expectation of snow hadn't yet delivered, and with the exception of a coffee stop at a roadside café, she'd ridden for hours around the different Baltimore districts and then way out into the farthermost parts of the city before turning back.

As she got parallel to the house, the bike's lights lit up the side entrance to it. Something made her stop.

A side door that led off the kitchen and onto the driveway was wide open, and it struck Sam as odd. It was cold and getting colder. Ann was a hothouse flower. She wasn't the type to let cold air into the house.

Sam stopped the engine and had just stepped away from the bike when Len came to the door as white as it was possible to be without being dead. She knew instantly that something was wrong.

"I'm waiting for the ambulance. Ann's not well…she's in the kitchen."

Sam rushed inside and saw Ann sitting on the floor, semi propped up against the cupboards. Len was flustered as he went over to her. He knelt at her side and kept brushing Ann's usually immaculate hair off her face.

"I came up from the shed and found her unconscious on the floor. She's come around but can't stand."

Ann gazed up at Len. "It's all right, dear. I'll be fine." She was trying to reassure but failing. Her voice was weak, and Sam saw how she struggled to breathe. She was sweating and pale.

"She suffers from angina," Len said.

Sam knew a few people back home who had the heart disorder. They sometimes suffered attacks, would take their prescription, and often the pain went away shortly after. Maybe it would now.

"What about her medication, Len?"

Len revealed a small spray in his pocket. "I put some under her tongue as soon as she came around. It usually calms any attacks, but it hasn't worked, and she's never passed out before. That's why I've called the ambulance."

Sam would have done the same. Right now she could only think how uncomfortable Ann looked. "Would it help if we moved you, Ann? Got you to a chair?"

Ann looked grateful. "Yes…I'm cold here…but I can't stand."

Len and Sam carefully raised her up and onto a chair at the kitchen table.

"Better?" Sam asked.

Ann didn't answer, only managing to nod. The minimal movement had exhausted her.

"Len, can you find her a blanket or something? Let's get her warmer."

He disappeared.

Sam took Ann's hands in hers and rubbed them. They were frozen. "What happened, Ann?"

"I was on the phone. I'd been talking to Joey," she said. "We argued."

A part of Sam went cold. She could imagine what they'd argued over.

"I wanted her to come to dinner—"

"I thought you were going to call her tomorrow when you felt calmer." Len was back with a throw and was wrapping it around Ann's shoulders and back. Ann's news annoyed him. Sam didn't know if it was to do with Ann making the call or Joey's behavior.

Sam wished she'd kept her mouth shut and not told them what had happened in DC. She could have lied and said she'd arrived late and missed Joey. All this upset could have been avoided. Sam cursed.

"I couldn't wait, Len. I was unhappy. I knew I wouldn't sleep tonight, and I thought I could make things better." Ann stopped talking as she groaned and held her chest. "Oh, Len..."

"Shush, honey. Don't talk anymore. Later." He stoked her forehead again.

Sam and Len shared a look. His face spoke volumes. He was in control, but there was no hiding how distraught he was.

Sam heard a vehicle approaching. It was the ambulance.

Len went with Ann, and Sam followed after she'd secured the house.

Joey entered the hospital and ran along the corridors to where she knew her father was.

His phone call had shocked and frightened her. Her mother had been taken to the hospital *in an ambulance.* How could this have happened? If she worried about either of her parents, it was always her dad. He was older and had slowed down over the last few years. He'd also dropped some weight. But her mom? She was fit and healthy. Joey couldn't recall the last time she'd been ill. Now all Joey could think about was their stupid argument on the phone earlier.

When she entered the waiting room, she saw her father and Sam. He was pacing the room. Sam was sitting quietly.

Joey went straight up to her dad and they warmly embraced.

"How's Mom? Is she okay?"

"The doctors are with her. We're waiting to see how she is."

Joey glanced at Sam. She was part of the "we," but it didn't upset her. She was glad Sam was here. It felt right. It made Joey feel safer and somehow protected. She wanted to let Sam see that, but Sam wasn't looking at her. Joey turned back to her father. "Why didn't you tell me Mom has angina?"

"We didn't want to worry you. You have enough to cope with."

"How long has she had it?"

"It started a few years ago."

"You should have told me, Dad."

He shrugged. "She's been on medication, and until now, she's been fine."

A doctor walked into the room.

He raised his hands in anticipation. "It's okay, Mr. Barry. The attack has passed, and she's stable now. We've increased her medication, and she's much calmer and more comfortable."

Her father deflated like a balloon, and Joey clung onto his arm. She wasn't sure who was supporting who.

"What brought it on so bad?" her father asked.

"We'll run some tests and see what they indicate. Is Mrs. Barry under any stress?"

Joey closed her eyes. She'd done nothing but put her mother under stress ever since she'd got back from the Middle East. Her behavior lately had been atrocious too.

"Some," her father answered diplomatically.

"You need to try to reduce that if you can," the doctor said.

"We can," Joey said. Her father gave her a weak smile.

"What happens now?" he asked.

"We'll keep her in for a while. Medication and rest. The tests will show us what we're dealing with."

"Like what?" Joey asked.

"Well, she's been stable till now. It looks like something is aggravating the condition."

"Like?" Joey wanted answers. Though her father feigned patience, she knew he wanted those answers too.

The doctor seemed used to "twenty questions." He smiled sympathetically.

"That's what the tests will show us, but her unstable condition could be poor blood flow."

"You mean like blocked or narrowed arteries," Joey stated.

"I'm sure Mrs. Barry's doctor will have spoken to her about this," the doctor calmly said. "Without those results, we could be looking at anything from increased medication to surgery."

"Surgery?" Joey asked.

"Can we hold back? Let's just say as soon as we know what we're dealing with, we can look at all the options. Second-guessing at this stage isn't going to do anyone any good."

"Back off, Tiger." Her father put his arm around Joey's shoulder in support. "Can I see Ann?"

The doctor nodded. "I don't see why not, but just you for this evening. I don't want her getting overly tired. She can see others tomorrow. I'll send a nurse to tell you when she's ready."

The doctor left.

Joey waited until he was out of earshot. "Dad, this is my fault. Mom and I argued on the phone a few hours ago. I'm the one who has put her under all this stress. She told me she didn't feel well, and I didn't believe her. I thought she was being her usual theatrical self. If only I'd come over when she put the phone down."

Her father put a finger to her lips. "Joey, I know you had an argument, but this isn't your fault. Your mother has a coronary heart condition. You didn't give her that."

"But—"

"But nothing. She *does* put the phone down on us when she doesn't want to hear." He forced a smile as he pulled her into his arms and held her tight.

"It doesn't stop me from being sorry. Tell Mom that when you see her. Tell her I'm ready to sit down to dinner and be civilized." She stopped and pulled back from him. "And tell her I love her."

He ran a hand down her face. "I will. Now I want the two of you to go home. There's no point us all hanging around here. It's late. I'm going to stay with your mother. I'll let you know if anything changes. Go home."

"You sure?" Joey said.

"I'm sure."

"I can stay if you want, Len," Sam said.

He smiled. "I'm hoping we won't need you just yet, Vicar. Now get my daughter home."

Joey watched Sam stand and stretch. Until now, she'd been so quiet that Joey had almost forgotten she was present. Again, she didn't miss that Sam was avoiding eye contact and Joey could sense her anger. She deserved it.

As they walked back along the corridors that led out into the cold night air, Joey broke the silence that hunkered down between them like the Great Wall of China.

"Thank you for being here. It means everything."

It was surely the shock of her mother's collapse that jolted Joey enough to see sense. A thick mist was thinning and allowing the first rational thought she'd had in a long time. She suddenly knew what was right. There was no voice in her head telling her to push Sam away, telling her how hopeless things were. She had to let Sam know how much she needed her, how much she wanted that closeness back they had once shared. But as she looked at Sam, she wondered if that was possible. Sam's face was unreadable, and her body language shouted distance. Joey trembled. Had she pushed Sam away one time too many? Did Sam believe the lies she'd thrown at her?

"I couldn't leave your father to cope with that." Sam's response was flat, her voice devoid of its usual warmth.

"No, Sam. You being here means everything *to me*."

"How did you get here?" Sam ignored Joey's declaration.

"A cab."

"I'd better get you home. I've got your dad's bike nearby."

"He lent you one?"

"Yes, the BSA."

Her father never lent anyone one of his prize possessions. It said much about Sam.

"Are you okay with that?" Sam interrupted her thoughts. "You can call a cab if you want."

"No. It's fine."

Joey felt like she was slowly dying as Sam's distance grew. They'd become polar opposites, and it was Joey's fault. Had she destroyed it all?

When they got to the bike, Sam handed her the only helmet. Joey thought of Maryland's mandatory helmet law. Sam was thinking of it too.

"You wear it, and pray we don't run into the cops. If we do, you're paying the fine." Sam straddled the bike and kicked it into life.

Joey hopped on too, and as she wrapped her arms around Sam, she felt her stiffen.

They arrived back at the apartment without being pulled over, and Joey directed Sam down to the secure underground parking.

Sam stood resolute by the bike silently daring Joey to turn her away. Joey didn't.

"It's been a long night," Joey said as they entered the apartment and she threw keys onto a table. She walked through the small lobby and into the sitting room. Sam followed like a shadow.

"Do you want coffee, something to eat?" Joey hid her uneasiness behind politeness. It didn't help as she reached a hand out to touch Sam's arm, and Sam stepped back. She didn't answer Joey as she slipped her heavy jacket and gloves off.

How many times had Sam waited with relatives at a hospital, or been at the bedside of someone with not much time left? Any familiarity didn't make her feel better. She felt sick because none of this might have happened if she'd declined Ann and Len's invitation to stay at their home. Her clashes with Joey had only fueled Ann's stress.

Her sickness had turned to quiet anger when Joey entered the hospital waiting room.

It was still with her now despite Ann's stable condition.

She eyeballed Joey who was standing in the middle of the room, and she could no longer contain herself. There were truths that needed airing.

"Do you have any idea what you've been putting your parents through? You can't do this to them at their age. They've been worried sick about you...as have I."

"I never meant for this to happen, Sam. I didn't know Mom was ill."

"That's no excuse. What the shit do you think you're doing?"

Joey stood facing her, white-faced and still. The usual signs of defense were gone. It was just as well because anything she did now might only make Sam worse.

"This has got to stop, Joey. Stop hiding your head in the sand. You've got PTSD and all the nastiness that goes with it. It's getting worse and nothing is going to stop it until you get help. But you don't want that, do you?"

"What do you mean?"

"I may be a provincial vicar in a county parish, but credit me with some intellect." Sam was ready to deal the cards she'd always hesitated to for fear of upsetting Joey. But the proverbial gloves were off.

"I know exactly what you're doing, Josephine Barry. You're trying to punish yourself, push away anyone who cares for you, your family...me. Is this what all this is about, some perverse desire to make yourself suffer because *you* of all of them survived? And you weren't meant to?"

"What are you talking about?"

"Only you know the answer to that." Sam took a deep breath. "There's something you're not saying, something that happened out there. Your guilt over being the only one that made it back is way too excessive. You blame yourself, and only yourself, for what happened. You and the team knew what you were up against. It's what you did...always did. You went into the front line, into the danger zone to get the story. You said that in your radio chats."

Joey's eyes widened.

Sam nodded. "Yes, I've listened to the last one...the one where you got me thrown out of the building. I can't believe you did that. My God, but you're running."

"I'm sorry for doing—"

Sam put a hand up to stop her. "This is not the time for apologies, and that's not what this is all about. I listened to that second interview over and over praying I'd hear something that will give me a clue into what's going on in that crazy mind of yours.

"You hold yourself responsible, and as a consequence you're no longer allowed to be happy. You need to suffer. Of course you've refused counseling. Heaven's forbid it worked, the nightmares diminished, and you started to feel better. You're not allowed that.

"That and your illness is why you walked out on me in England without a word. It's why you keep closing the door in my face, avoiding me. You think you can make me angry and disillusioned, that I'll up and leave you. Well, guess what, I'm not leaving, because I love you. It's why I've come all the way over here to show you that. And I *know* you love me too, and if I have to win this battle going on in your head, so be it."

Sam watched as the pain raced across Joey's face before it turned to understanding and then acceptance. Joey all but fell back into the seat behind her. There was a moment of silence before Joey spoke.

"I hate what I've done to Mom. You're right. I've been so busy thinking only of me. I never meant for any of this to happen...not just Mom. I thought if I pushed you away, I could salvage *me*, hold on to the little sanity I have left...cope. But all I've done is transfer the hurt to all of you, and at such a cost. I've been a fool."

"Why push me away, and don't give me the crap about my pastoral workload."

Joey returned a wan smile.

"It's never been that, Sam. I never said it was. The truth is I don't want you to see me disintegrate. I don't want you to look at me like the others have who've walked away. I'm scared to be with you because I don't want to lose what you feel for me." Joey gave a half laugh. "Ironic, isn't it. And I will lose you because I'm not getting any better. My control's slipping...I think I'm going mad. But I thought if I could contain my life, push away and box the emotion, I could function on the most basic level and still work. Work could be my life."

"No love allowed…"

"No. It's safer this way."

"There's no such thing as safe love. If you love someone you let your armor down. You give them the power to love you, to protect you when you need it, to nourish you…maybe even hurt you. That's why when love goes wrong it hurts because you both get hit in the underbelly. Ask anyone going through a divorce." Sam swallowed. She couldn't believe they were suddenly communicating. Why did it have to take Ann's health to achieve this?

"But ask yourself this, Joey. Do you want to continue through life avoiding love because of what happened to you out there? Let me tell you, I've tried to run from my past. I thought I could live without love, and it's almost eaten me alive."

Joey looked broken as she wrapped her arms around herself.

"Sam, this is about me and my messy life, and now messing up yours. I'm going to destroy you if you latch on to me. I'm corrupting you. You've already walked away from the church—"

"Yes, from church but not God. There's a difference."

"You would still be there if it wasn't for me."

"I'm not sure. I've been facing my own demons. Don't you understand that I had no life until you came into it? You've reached somewhere deep inside me and made me feel alive."

"Tell me what to do Sam. I don't know anymore."

As Joey looked up at her, something inside Sam softened. Her mantle of confrontation dissolved. Joey was vulnerable and exposed, and Sam's fighting talk was over.

"Sometimes to move forward, we have to go back. We have to return to the basics to rebuild the foundations. We have to ask questions and move forward based on the answers."

"I don't even know what the questions are."

"Maybe I do," Sam said. "The first one is crucial, and it demands a truthful answer. Do you love me, Joey?"

"You don't underst—"

"Do you love me?" Sam repeated. "And look me in the eyes when you answer."

Joey was struggling, but Sam wasn't taking prisoners.

"Confession time, Joey."

"How can I answer that?"

"With the truth. Do you love me?"

Sam heard the quietest, "Yes."

"Louder, I'm not getting that," Sam said.

"Yes."

"I can't hear."

"I said yes." Joey raised her voice.

Sam stepped forward and opened her arms. Joey stood and entered them.

"Okay, there's no need to shout," Sam whispered into her neck.

Joey held her closely, as if she was scared to let go. Sam felt something deep inside her, something right, recharging. How she'd waited—and prayed—for this moment. Her *boss* had delivered.

"Don't let me go," Joey said.

Sam realized this embrace was everything to Joey too. She hoped it was reviving her, giving her hope.

"I have another question," Sam whispered. "Why didn't you tell me about the Stallion contract?"

Joey's arms tightened around her. "I was going to tell you that night of the dinner, but—"

"The accident."

"I wanted it to be a surprise."

"And I ruined it."

"It was no one's fault. That was an awful day for many."

Sam ran a hand through Joey's hair. It was like silk.

"I guess my parents told you I've accepted the job back in England."

"Do I have to confirm that?" Sam said.

Joey laughed a little. "They really love you." There was the minutest pause. "Me too. You're amazing, Sam. You're the only person, besides my parents, who hasn't run a mile as soon as you've discovered my problems."

"Problems can be sorted." She felt Joey shrug.

"I think mine may take time."

"Another question," Sam said. "Do you want to get better?"

Joey grew heavier in her arms.

"Yes. I'm so tired of feeling like this. Please stay with me, Sam. Help me."

"I'm not going anywhere."

They remained locked together. Sam closed her eyes.

When she opened them, she found she was looking at the reflection of her and Joey in the apartment window. They looked good, like they belonged together. Sam gazed beyond their image and grew aware that something was falling outside.

"What's that?" she said.

Joey loosened her grip and looked. "It's snow, Sam."

"I *know* it's snow."

But it was falling fast and heavy. The promised storm had arrived. She thought of the bike. It didn't like snow, and Len had asked her to avoid it. It occurred to Sam that the *boss* was working overtime. She grinned. "I guess this means I'm staying the night."

"I guess it does. Are you all right with that?"

"I am. I'm staying."

Joey started to say something more but Sam took no chances.

"I've come all the way from England to be with you. I'm not spending another night at your parents. Delightful though they are, they aren't who I want to be with."

"Okay." Joey didn't put up a fight and pulled Sam back into her arms.

"This might not work," Joey said.

"The nightmares are worse?"

"They're no better," Joey said.

"And they won't be until you talk…until you tell me what happened out there."

Joey pushed back, holding Sam's arms gently. "I know."

It was an important first step. Sam knew it. So did Joey. The shock of her mother's ill health had triggered a change in her.

"Do you think mom will be okay?"

"She's in the right place. The doctor said she's stable."

"I must see her, Sam. I have to tell her I love her…that I'm sorry."

"You will tomorrow if we're not snowed in."

They walked over to the window and looked at the falling snow that was settling thick and fast on the ground below.

"I'm going to have to talk with the boss about this weather." Sam's attempt to lighten the moment earned her a chaste kiss on the cheek. Its sweetness filled her soul with happiness.

"Let's have that coffee now. Second thoughts, have you got anything stronger?" Sam said. It had been a hell of a day for both of them.

Joey flicked her hair back behind an ear and looked around. "I think Dad keeps some alcohol here somewhere."

As Joey removed her jacket and threw it over the couch, something hard hit the ground and rolled. It was a small shiny metal object that Joey picked up and held as if it was precious.

"What's that?" Sam asked.

Joey held her hand out so Sam could see it.

"It looks like a bolt—"

"It's my lucky bolt," Joey said. "It's the one you gave me. I keep it on me."

It was the way Joey was looking at her, as if the world had melted away and they were the only living entities left. Sam couldn't breathe as she closed the gap between them and reached her hands out to cup Joey's face. The touch sent electric shocks through her body.

"I don't really want a drink," Sam said.

"Me neither."

"Let's go to bed."

"Are you tired?" Joey asked.

"Not in the slightest."

Joey smiled at Sam as she led her to the bedroom.

Their eyes never left each other as they undressed. Joey pulled Sam to her as they fell into bed, pushing her body tight up against hers.

There was no foreplay. They were suddenly beyond that, and Sam felt her own hunger rising inside, its power stronger than she'd ever experienced. She was barely breathing as her hands roamed Joey's body needing to feel every part of her. Every touch of Joey's skin sent an explosion of sensation through Sam.

Joey's arousal was strong too.

"Touch me, Sam."

When she did, Joey moaned.

Sam felt her grow hot and clammy, she felt her trembling. She smelled Joey's sex. There was an urgency to their lovemaking; a starvation desperate for sustenance. It had been too long for both of them.

Sam moved over Joey and slipped her hand between Joey's legs. She found an abundance of wetness. She began to pump.

Joey rocked beneath her.

"Deeper," Joey groaned.

Sam pushed harder, faster, as she felt her own need grow.

Joey came first, her body tense and stretching as she climaxed.

Sam was losing her control as she felt Joey's knee rise between her legs. It seemed like it was barely there a second, rubbing against her. Sam came. She arched her back and cried out.

The room went quiet and all movement ceased. They wrapped themselves in each other's arms.

"That was quick." Joey broke the stillness.

"I'd have come just looking at you," Sam panted.

"Well, it's sure going to save a lot of time."

"I prefer the old method. I'm a traditionalist."

"Me, too."

"I'm alive again," Sam sighed.

"I've been dating a corpse?"

Sam laughed. "You know what I mean." All her doubts—and she had had them since she'd flown to Baltimore—disappeared. Joey loved her. There would be obstacles. Joey had issues, but Sam's faith was strong, and she knew the power of love. Together they would find a way through.

"Will you say a prayer for mom?"

Sam heard the worry in Joey's voice. Their lovemaking had not chased all the fears away.

"I'm way ahead of you, my love. I've been FedExing the boss," Sam said.

"Thanks, Sam. I can't lose her, not like this."

"My child, you're not turning to God are—?"

"Can it."

Sam grinned. "Just asking."

Sometime after they had slept, they found a stash of whiskey.

They poured themselves a glass, returned to bed, and cuddled up watching the snow fall.

It was Nirvana for Joey.

Sam lay at her back scrunched up close with her head nestled to hers as they watched a blizzard ebb and flow with the gusts of wind.

"The snow's lovely." Joey found it mesmerizing. She always had.

"It's beautiful," Sam said. "Beautiful like you."

"You're going to be a romantic, aren't you?"

"I guess I am," Sam said.

Joey adored Sam's love talk. It made her feel like she was the only woman in the world for Sam. She now knew she was.

"Forgive me for pushing you away. I'm sorry I've scared you," Joey whispered.

Sam draped an arm over her and hugged her closer. "It's in the past now."

"Yes, but I'm sorry."

They didn't speak for a while. Joey eventually broke the silence.

"You want to know what happened out there. What I haven't spoken about?"

"Whatever is haunting you, it needs to be brought out into the open. You have to release it. If you can talk about it, I think you'll diminish its power over you."

"A trouble shared..." Joey said.

"In a way, yes, but I don't want to make light of it. You have to share what's going on inside you with someone. That someone doesn't have to be me, and I won't be offended if you chose not to. But find someone. I'm not sure you can move forward if you don't."

"I tried a counselor before."

"Did you tell them everything? Were you able to do that then?"

"No." Joey hadn't. She couldn't.

Now she made a conscious decision. If she was going to change the pattern of her life, she'd take the first steps here with someone she loved and trusted.

Joey opened her mind and let the memories of that last journey into the Middle East flood back. She shut her eyes for a moment. It was a place she'd learned to deliberately avoid thinking of. In the early days, when she'd been rescued and when the counselor had probed, remembering only brought her pain. Then she'd played the events over and over in her head. They only increased her nightmares and made the flashbacks worse. She'd tried to block it all. She felt Sam squeeze her hand reassuringly.

"I never told anyone," she started. "When we got there, everyone was telling us not to go out to Balshir. They said it was a powder keg about to blow, that the insurgents were close, too close. Sometimes you would get armed assistance to accompany you, but even the militia had given up on the area, choosing to place their forces elsewhere. Nobody wanted to go in. But I didn't listen and we went anyway."

"Was that so unusual?" Sam asked.

"No. I was a journalist wanting to get frontline breaking news. We would go where others wouldn't to get those stories. That's what news is about. It's not about sitting comfortably or hiding behind fences and walls. News is about showing people back home what is happening in these volatile regions. It's dangerous. So we took the decision to go in anyway."

"*We* took the decision. Define *we*," Sam asked.

"The team—Kurt, Max, and our interpreter, Mo. And me of course."

"Were they your usual team?"

"Yes, we'd covered a lot of war zones together. We were like family."

"So they knew the dangers."

"Yes."

"You said you all took the decision to go in."

"We did."

"You didn't force that decision?"

"No."

"So what was different this time?" Sam asked.

"Abu Rashid Ibrahim." A chill went down Joey's spine. She wrapped Sam's arm around her tighter. This was what she couldn't face.

"He was one of the interpreters in the region. We'd never worked with him, but he was a regular, well known and respected. A good man. The night before we left camp to go to Balshir, he came to see me. He told me not to go, that the area was too dangerous. *Never* had an interpreter done that. But when I showed no signs of listening, he *begged* me, Sam. I ignored his warnings. If I'd listened to him, the team...my friends, would still be alive."

"Did you tell the team?"

"Of course. Kurt was with me when Abu was there. We all discussed it but decided to go in anyway. We'd done a lot of planning."

"No one held back."

"No. Kurt was the most insistent of all of us. We all ignored the warnings."

"How can their deaths be your fault, Joey, when you all, to a man, decided to go in anyway?"

"You don't understand. I was the one who should have put the brakes on. It was me wanting to go in to get the story. The whole idea was mine."

"Yes, but they could have said no at any time...and didn't. They were grown professional men."

"Sam, I had this incredible international reputation for going after and getting the great stories. From the very beginning of my career, it seemed I had the golden touch. Little incidental stories broke into huge ones, and they brought me to prominence. I never planned that; it just happened. I've won an impressive array of awards and honorary degrees for being this indomitable journalist who goes right to the edge, regardless of danger, and gets the story. The team trusted my judgment. I'd never let them down before. They trusted my reputation. They'd have followed me to Satan's gate if I'd asked them.

"I was so arrogant, so self-confident. I thought I was invincible and smart. I did all the checks, took all the precautions. I thought I'd weighed everything up and down to the finest detail of which route we'd drive in, where the safest place was to stay. But this time I blew it, and I got them murdered."

"Did your own interpreter warn you?"

"No, because he believed in me too." Her sigh echoed in the room. "Oh, Sam."

Sam stroked her forehead, comforting her.

"I miss them, Sam. And I never got to say good-bye."

The snow continued to fall. Joey's heart ached, but she was glad Sam knew. She'd never told anyone about Abu's warning. It wouldn't have helped, or at least she hadn't thought it would back then.

"I think you should try counseling again," Sam said.

"Maybe. I don't know." Joey didn't push the idea away like she had in the past.

"Think about it?" Sam asked.

"Okay, I promise." She would. "I'm cold."

Sam left the bed and found a blanket. She threw it over the bed and then drew up close behind Joey again and wrapped her in her arms.

"Better?"

"Better, Sam."

"Now go to sleep, darling."

Joey didn't answer. Sam hoped there would be no nightmares this night, but her prayers weren't answered.

It was about three in the morning.

Something woke Sam, but when she reached out for Joey, she wasn't there.

She found her in the bathroom behind a closed door.

Joey was kneeling on the floor gasping for breath and sobbing. The scene terrified Sam. For a split second she thought Joey was having a heart attack. But Joey looked up at her and Sam saw the fear in her face. Sam knew Joey was having a stress attack. She'd seen one of these before back in England.

"What are you doing here?" Sam reached down to her.

"I didn't want to wake you."

It was cold and Sam dragged Joey back to bed. She wrapped her in blankets to stop her shivering.

"Nightmare?" Sam didn't know why she asked. She already knew the answer.

Joey sobbed until she could sob no more.

Sam waited until Joey grew calmer.

"Tell me," she said as Joey sat up and Sam got close in behind her, supporting her weight as she leaned on the backboard.

"It's always the same. I'm in this dark place. I'm hiding and crouched low. I know there's something on the other side of what I'm behind. I don't see it at first, but I know I'm afraid. Everything is dull, and there's no sound. I'm alone. Then I see a wall. Halfway up it, something starts to push through. I see this shape materializing. It's wispy black smoke, but it gets thicker and then it starts to fall to the ground. It's menacing, and I can't move. All I can do is watch it. As it falls, it takes form. It gets thicker and blacker. It becomes an arm with long tentacle fingers like molasses that turn and snake toward me. The fingers keep rising and pushing toward me, and I'm trying to push back...stay away.

"Then I must scream out and wake. I'm sorry I've woken you too."

Sam wrapped her arms and legs around Joey, and she kissed her neck.

"You hid inside a cupboard."

"The cabinet under the sink. I guess that's where I am in the nightmare. I know I feel trapped and can't move. I couldn't then; the heat was suffocating."

"How long were you in it?"

"I can't remember. I got sick. I drank contaminated water, and I had a head injury. All I recall is being completely alone and that I didn't want to die out there where no one would ever know what happened to me...or find me."

Joey shivered. Sam hugged her closer.

"Promise me, Joey. Promise me that when you are in that dark space when the nightmares come, that you'll share them with me. I might not know what to say. I might not know what to do. But I'll be here for you. You won't ever be alone."

Seconds passed before Sam heard Joey reply, "I promise. But I was the only one who survived, Sam."

Sam moved to face her. She wiped the hair from Joey's face. "And I'm so glad you survived. I wouldn't have you here in my life if you'd died too. You've given me a life I thought I could never have. I have a chance to love and be loved. I thought that was beyond me."

Joey smiled.

"I love you, Reverend Samantha Savage."

"And I love you, Josephine Barry."

Joey eventually fell asleep in Sam's arms.

CHAPTER NINETEEN

S am stared out the sitting room window.
The snow was no longer falling, but it lay deep and treacherous. Nothing moved. The army of city workers wasn't visible, and she expected they'd stayed at home, unable to get to their places of work. She could see only a few daring, arguably mad, souls braving the wintery elements below. Rather them than her, she thought.

They had slept late, and she was grateful that Joey had finally managed to sleep restfully.

"I really need to see Mom," Joey said as she handed Sam a coffee and joined her at the window.

As if by divine providence, a snow truck plowed its way down the street below.

"I don't fancy our chances getting back to the hospital just yet," Sam said. "We might this afternoon after the roads have been cleared and if it doesn't snow again."

Joey looked resigned to the fact. "I'll phone Dad and get an update." She grabbed her cell and dialed. She waited as it rang and was about to disconnect when her father answered.

"Hi, Dad, it's me. How's Mom?"

Sam could hear Len talking but couldn't make out what he was saying. Whatever he said, it made Joey brighter.

"That's great, Dad. Sam and I are at the apartment, but we're snowed in too. We'll try to join you later this afternoon. The plows are out so as long as it doesn't snow again." She paused as Len talked. "I don't know if the MTA is running, but I'll check. We won't drive in this, don't worry."

"Tell him his bike's safe." Sam grinned.

"Sam says to tell you the bike's safe."

Sam heard Len laugh.

"Tell Mom I love her and not to worry. I'll see her as soon as I can get in."

There was more incomprehensible chatter from Len.

"Love you too, Dad. Take care."

Joey set the phone down. "Mom had a good night, and he's been with her. He got snowed in at the hospital so he slept in her room in a chair. He wasn't going to leave her anyway. They want to keep Mom in for another day or two, to run the tests, but they're pleased she's responded well to the medication."

"That's great."

"I hope we'll be able to get in this afternoon. You'll come with me?"

"Of course." Sam knew Joey wouldn't be happy until she saw Ann.

"I can't believe Mom has a heart condition. I've always been more worried about Dad."

"Why? He seems a sturdy enough chap."

"He's ten years older than Mom, and over the last few years he's aged."

"Still looks healthy to me." Nothing Sam had seen had ever worried her regarding Len...or Ann. On reflection, maybe her reassurance wasn't worth much.

"I guess. It's just come as a surprise that's all." Joey paused. "I think we should get out."

Sam raised her eyebrows. "Out? Out where?" There was a mound of snow outside. Had Joey lost her mind?

"We'll go for a walk. It'll be fun."

Joey *had* lost her mind.

"Fun?" Sam said.

"Don't tell me you're put off by a little ol' snowstorm."

"People die in this."

Joey ignored her.

"Come on, dress up warm, Sam. We'll just go around the block, maybe see if the Metro is up and running."

Sam wasn't sure why she caved in so easily. It was either because she knew Joey needed to take her mind off her mother, or what they'd spoken of last night…or maybe Sam was just in love and couldn't refuse her. Whatever the reason, Sam kitted up, zipped and buttoned everything that could be zipped and buttoned, and walked out into the perishing arctic conditions.

An hour later, as she high stepped snow heaps, she reminded herself that a Brit's idea of a block wasn't the same as an American's. It was longer…a lot longer. They passed a Metro station that was closed, but when they got back home, the radio said there was limited service. Joey looked into it on the Internet.

"We'll be able to get to the hospital later today, Sam. We just have to walk a few blocks to get to the nearest functioning subway."

Oh joy. The thought of going back out there didn't fill Sam with enthusiasm, but if it got Joey to Ann, so be it.

"You don't like snow, do you?" Joey said

"I love snow. I'm just not the South Pole sort of woman."

"No, you're the English vicar sort."

Sam shrugged. "I'm not even that at the moment." It reminded her she wanted to ask Joey something. "Are you still coming back to Stallion?"

"Of course I am."

"Are we going…" Sam wasn't sure how to voice it.

"You want to know if we're going to live together."

"Yes."

"I think we should."

Every organ inside Sam's body smiled.

"Does it bother you my being an ordained minister?" Sam asked.

Joey stepped back to look at her, her face serious. "Of course it doesn't bother me. I don't have a great profound philosophy on life. I'm not a religious woman, but I'm not an atheist. My mother believes in God, as do you. That makes me pause. I wonder how two such intelligent, wonderful people who I love and respect can see something I can't. But I can't, and that's all there is to it. I'll stick with being agnostic, deeply spiritual and someone who is nice to children, animals and bikers. Will that do?"

Sam nodded. "My prospects are also a little questionable at the moment. I've no job, and probably no home. Vicarages are for vicars. I handed my notice in."

"Then you'll have to find work, and the sooner we get somewhere to live the better. What will happen to Gloria?" Joey asked.

Sam frowned as she thought about her housekeeper. Leaving her wouldn't be easy, and Gloria was no spring chicken. Would she want to "break in" another vicar? The thought of Gloria giving up the job and being alone bothered her. "New vicar," she answered.

It pleased Sam that Joey didn't look happy regarding Gloria's change of fortune either.

Joey spent over an hour with her mother.

Sam stayed with Len in the waiting room. There was a one-visitor policy so as not to overtax Ann.

"I don't hear screaming," Len said, looking toward Ann's room.

"No. A good sign, yes?"

"Not bad." Len glanced at his watch. "In fact I'd say it was downright encouraging."

Sam sipped the liquid the vending machine called coffee. It wasn't good, but it was wet. Len had declined her offer to buy him one. She knew why now.

"You spent the night with my daughter." Len wasn't asking a question.

Sam choked.

"I meant," he added, "that you stayed over at the apartment because of the snow."

Sam relaxed. "The blizzard came in fast. I couldn't get back to your place."

"Would you have had to?"

This was turning into a meaningful conversation, one of those "man-to-man" chats. Sam felt inadequate. Normally, she asked the probing, confessional type questions.

"Len, you're not going to ask me my intentions again, are you?"

His tired face broke into a grin. "Nope."

"To answer your question, Joey asked me up to the apartment."

"You're on better terms."

She put her coffee down and faced him. "We had a good chat." *And a few other things.* "I think it's safe to say we're on better terms."

"Good terms as in long-term?"

"Could be."

How Sam hoped it was the truth. It looked like Len hoped so too. There was a smile on his face and a look of contentment.

"You're a bit of a miracle worker, you know. I guess it's being a vicar and all."

"I don't think my clerical background has anything to do with it. The time was just right, and I think Ann's attack has shocked Joey back to her senses."

He played with the strap on his watch. He was a good parent. He still worried about his adult daughter despite all her life experience.

"What happens now?" he asked.

"One step at a time."

"But you're optimistic."

"I'm optimistic." Her answer seemed to satisfy.

The door opened and Joey stepped out. She was smiling.

"All good? No blood?" Len said.

"We're good. Mom and I have had a great chat. I've put it right."

Len stood and gave her a kiss on the cheek.

"And she's asking for you, Dad."

A soft look settled on his face.

"We're going to head back," Joey said, "but call me if anything happens...if you need me. Keep me up-to-date." She gave him a hug. He kissed her cheek again.

"Don't worry. I will."

They watched him walk into the room before they turned to leave.

"Everything okay?" Sam asked.

"Yes. I won't put Mom under any more stress. I'm done with that."

They started back for the Metro.

About half an hour later, Joey's cell rang.

Sam watched as her face turned from delight at hearing from someone she knew and liked, to concern.

"That was Sherry Dexter," Joey said. "She's an old friend of mine. We used to work in radio together years ago. She now works for NPR in DC. She's the one who cajoled me into doing the talks on Clara Dale's show."

"Problems?"

"Not sure. Last time I was there, Sherry told me there's been a man looking for me. Quite persistent. He's been in to reception a couple of times, but never leaves his name. He's stopped going in now but hangs around the building a lot. The staff say he's Middle Eastern and that his accent could be Syrian or from that region. Sherry's seen him too. She's worried in case he's not too friendly."

"What's happened?"

"He turned up again yesterday morning before the storm hit. This time Sherry called the police, but by the time they arrived, he'd disappeared again. She had decided not to tell me but changed her mind."

"No idea who he might be?" Sam asked.

"None. He could be anyone. He could be an avid follower who just wants to meet me, get my autograph." Joey scoffed and made light of it. "They're out there, and I've had plenty of them over the years. When your face is well known, these things happen."

"But you don't believe that."

"Sherry doesn't believe it. She's worried in case he wants to do me harm. It's no secret that I'm not popular with everybody out there. The militant Islamists don't share my viewpoints. There are those who've named me and who'd like retribution. I'm not alone. Any investigative journalist who shines a light on corruption and evil isn't going to be popular. It comes with the job."

Joey must have seen the concern on her face. "It's okay, Sam. This is probably nothing to worry about, but I won't take any chances."

"You'd better not." Sam could only think that the sooner she got Joey back to England, the better.

Three days later, the snow was almost gone, and Joey's Mom was home.

Sam and Joey had visited her daily at the hospital, but now they were at Len and Ann's for lunch.

Len had cooked, and Sam was impressed with his culinary expertise. He'd prepared rosemary and lemon roast chicken served with salad.

"Some of Ann's abilities have worn off on me," he said as they sat down to the light lunch at the kitchen table.

"I should have done this," Ann said.

"Remember what the doctors said; you have to take it easy," Joey said.

Sam glanced around the table, and everyone looked happier than they had for some time.

Ann wasn't quite out of the woods. Tests had revealed an arterial blockage and there was talk of angioplasty, but the diagnosis was good. The operation was scheduled before Joey was due to return to the UK. Sam was grateful. It took the pressure off Joey. She didn't need more stress.

Later, as they rode the Metro back to the apartment, Joey asked if Sam wanted to accompany her up to DC to do the final studio recording of her talks with Clara.

Sam started to laugh.

"If I say yes, I won't get thrown out of the building again, will I?"

"Not this time."

"In that case, I accept the invitation."

A thought occurred to Sam. "You're not worried about this sinister chap hanging around NPR, are you?"

"I'm asking you because I want *you* there." Joey squeezed Sam's hand.

"I know that. But the question is still relevant. Are you worried?"

"Not worried but aware that if Sherry is concerned, maybe I should be. Maybe he'll turn up when I'm there and he'll ask me for my autograph."

"Maybe." Sam made light of it too for Joey's sake. But she was glad she was going with her. She'd be watching out like a hawk.

"Now you're worried."

"No, I'm not. I'm just thinking."

"What?"

"Can you cook like your parents?"

Joey grinned. "Yes."

"Good. Things are looking up." Sam planted a chaste kiss on Joey's lips.

CHAPTER TWENTY

When they arrived at NPR, Joey invited Sam to join her in the studio.

"Come with me? You can sit at the back, listen in but no heckling."

Sam declined.

"No, I'm going to sit here in the lobby and keep an eye out for Mr. Sinister."

"He's not here now. He probably won't show." Joey recognized Sam's attempt to make light of it all, but she knew she was concerned. As they'd walked there from the parking lot, Sam had scanned every alley, every side route. "This is your chance to see me in action."

"My presence will only ruin your concentration. Besides, there's a sunbeam over on that chair with my name on it. I'm going to sit there and warm up."

"Are you sure?" Joey said.

"I am."

The idea that someone might be stalking her, albeit not very well, was disturbing, but Joey felt safe with Sam here and was actually enjoying the day. This would be the last part of her series on Clara's show, and Joey was beginning to get excited with thoughts of going back to England to start her new life.

As she walked through the door that led to the studio, she glanced back to see Sam settling in her sunbeam.

It was an hour and a half later when Joey returned to the lobby. After the recording, Clara hadn't wanted to stop talking, and then Sherry had intercepted her on the way down to ask her over for dinner at the weekend.

"Bring your vicar. I want to see the woman who's won your heart."

Sam's face brightened the minute Joey entered the foyer, and she stood to join her. Joey was in a state of happiness and about to tell Sam about the dinner invitation when she saw the smile disappear from her face. Sam was looking over Joey's shoulder into the street and whatever she'd seen had alarmed her.

Joey followed her line of sight. At first she saw nothing but regular people going about their business. But then she spotted a bearded man of Arabic appearance crossing the road. He was coming toward her and fast. Her heart started slamming in her chest and she heard Sam whisper, "Dear God."

The man at reception saw him too. "I'll get help," he said.

Joey stared at the man and became aware that something about him seemed familiar. "Wait. I know him."

He entered the building then paused for a second before they hugged each other like old friends.

When Joey stepped back from the embrace, she looked at Sam. "It's all right," she said. "This is Abu Rashid Ibrahim, one of the Syrian interpreters."

She watched Sam's panic give way to understanding. They had spoken of him not long ago. This was the man who had warned Joey not to go to Balshir.

Several men pushed through the door Joey had earlier disappeared through. It wasn't clear if they were security or office staff. They rushed forward and surrounded Ibrahim.

"It's all right," Joey said. "I know him. He's a friend. He means me no harm." She looked at him, smiling. "You don't do you?"

He was standing mute and wide-eyed.

"They think you're a fundamentalist out to get me," Joey said.

"Never," Abu stated.

It took Joey a while to convince everyone that he wasn't a threat. It was only when Sherry appeared and told everyone to stand down that the men disappeared.

She saw Sherry and Sam catch each other's eyes and share similar understanding. They were both on edge and trying to safeguard her. Joey eased the tension by doing brief introductions. It seemed to return the moment to a level of normality.

Sherry eventually left but not before voicing her displeasure at Abu's surprise appearance. She turned to Sam. "I look forward to meeting you properly and under more relaxed surroundings this weekend."

"I didn't mean to frighten you, Joey," Abu said.

The smile on Joey's face was forced. His reappearance after all this time *was* disturbing. It was bringing memories back, and they weren't good. "It's okay," she said. "They didn't understand and were only trying to protect me."

Though the commotion had died down, he remained tense, and Joey wasn't sure why.

"What are you doing over here?"

"I applied for political asylum. I am one of the few lucky ones to be given it."

"And your family?" Joey asked.

"My wife and child also."

Joey turned to Sam. "Abu has worked with the military and international humanity organizations for years acting as interpreter."

"Everything became untenable and too dangerous," he said. "Attempts were made on my life and my family. We had to leave. Your government has been very generous."

"I'm glad," Joey said. "It's a bad time to be an interpreter out there."

He gave a single serious nod. "I have been most fortunate."

"You've also been very persistent," Sam said.

"You've been seen here many times—" Joey said.

"I had to see you, to tell you something, Joey," he interrupted. "It's very important."

At that moment, a large truck rattled past them making it difficult to speak without raising their voices.

"There is a park about a block and a half away," he said. "Can we go there and talk?"

Sam kept her counsel but wasn't keen. She could only believe Joey when she said she and Abu were friends, but if they wandered off, and anything went wrong, they no longer had the protection of NPR. She knew the area of green he was referring to. It was off New York Avenue. It was where she'd walked to calm down after being thrown out of the building the last time she was here. If Joey and Abu were going there, so was she.

"I know it, Joey. It won't take us long," Sam said.

Her personal invitation to join them appeared to worry Abu. He stopped. It was clear he didn't want her to join them.

"What I have to tell you, Joey, you may find sensitive."

Sam stuck like mud to Joey's side. She was rewarded with an arm wrapping itself around her shoulder.

"Abu, this is Sam…Samantha Savage. There is nothing you can say to me that I wouldn't want her to know. I'd place my life in her hands and know it was safe. There is no one I want more at my side than her."

Joey looked at her, and the love Sam saw snatched the air from her lungs.

Abu eyed her respectfully.

They walked in silence until they came to the park. Abu wasted no time.

"When I heard you were doing these radio talks, I knew I had to see you. I wanted to tell you I am sorry for what happened to your team…and to you. I am here to ask your forgiveness," he said.

"For what?" Joey was taken aback.

"For what happened to you in Balshir."

"Why? You're the one who warned me. You begged me not to go, but I didn't listen. You have nothing to be forgiven for."

His eyes grew sad. "I did not tell you all I should have."

"You were very clear, Abu. You spoke of how dangerous it was...the area, the people."

He shook his head. "You do not understand. There was more I should have said. If I had, you would never have gone." He seemed reconciled to what he had to say. "You were betrayed."

Sam heard Joey's intake of breath.

Abu continued. "The evening before you departed camp, Mohammad came to see me."

"Mo." Joey straightened.

Abu nodded. "He was crazy, mad. I could see on his face that he carried some terrible burden. At first I did not think he would share it, but I made him tell me. He told me the rebels had his family and that they would be butchered, his girls raped, if he did not tell them where you were to be. They wanted the blood of Westerners to feed their propaganda machine. They wanted *your* blood." Abu lowered his head in shame. "I was torn. If I betrayed him, my old friend, he would lose everything, his family, his work. If I said nothing, then you and your team were placed in danger. I did try to stop you, but my reasons were not strong enough...and you left."

Joey was expressionless as his words sank in. She didn't move. Sam couldn't either. She felt like she was witness to a murder. She could only worry how Joey was taking this revelation.

"His family?" Joey asked.

"Butchered. All dead. They killed them anyway." He opened his hands in a fatalistic gesture.

"They killed him too," Joey said. "I saw his head on a spike."

Only now did Abu's resolve falter. His eyes grew moist.

"I should have told you the truth. Mohammad would have lived, as would your team. I carry such guilt and the blood of my friends, but no road I would have taken could spare life."

Sam's heart pounded in her chest.

Joey was first to break the unbearable tension that now hung in the air like dampness.

"Poor Mo," she said. "We sensed something was wrong but didn't know what. He was quiet and withdrawn. Usually, we couldn't shut him up." A small smile graced her lips. "I thought it was something we'd said, but I see what was really wrong. He loved his family. Poor, poor Mo."

The strain showed on her face.

"Knowing this has weighed heavy on me. I pray you can forgive me. I know that its secret cost dearly. I can never make this right, but I wanted you to know. Since I have been here I have heard how you suffer. I carry much guilt," Abu said.

Sam's attention switched between Joey and Abu. Both were remembering events that neither wanted to.

Joey puckered her lips before staring Abu in the eyes.

"There's nothing to forgive," she said. "You didn't betray us. You were trapped. Mo had no choice. The only guilt rests with those that attacked and murdered. This isn't our guilt to carry." She touched his hand. "It's taken a lot for you to tell me this, and I thank you."

"Do not hate Mohammad for what he did."

"I don't hate him, Abu. What would any of us have done in those circumstances? I don't know."

"Then what I wanted to do is done, and I will leave you now. I doubt our paths will cross again. Perhaps I hope they won't. I begin my new life in a new land. I no longer want anything to do with what has passed or be reminded of it. You must do the same. I wish you and all those you love, the fortune of your Gods." He bowed his head. "Take care, my good friend. Find peace."

He was already walking away as Joey said, "And you. Be happy."

Abu didn't look back, and Joey watched him until he disappeared out of sight.

Sam moved closer to her. "Are you okay?"

"I don't know."

"What now?"

"Let's go home, Sam. Take me home."

"Thank you for not asking me questions, Sam. I know you want to talk, but I don't want to just yet. Okay?" Joey said.

"Okay," Sam answered.

It was later that same day, and they were back at the apartment. Their journey home had been quiet. Sam had driven. When they had spoken it was only of incidental, mundane matters. It was all Joey felt capable of. Her head ached as she replayed Abu's words over and over.

She glanced at Sam and loved her for her understanding and ability to remain as good-natured as always. But she saw the concern and knew that Sam was worried for her. What Abu revealed today had shocked them both.

"Shall I make us a drink?" Sam was moving toward the kitchen, but Joey stopped her.

"Would you mind if I went for a walk…alone?"

Sam looked outside. "It's getting dark, and it's cold."

"I know, but I want to think. I just need to be alone to process it all. Make sense of it."

"I can walk with you and not say anything."

"Won't work."

"Then I'll leave you here if you want. I can go see a movie."

Joey smiled. Everything Sam was doing was for her. She was lucky to have her in her life…finally.

"No. It's the fresh air on my face that I want. You stay here."

"Will you be okay?"

Joey rubbed a hand up and down Sam's arm. "I'll be fine. Don't worry. I just want to think, that's all. I promise not to go near any dark alleys or cross any roads without looking."

"You'll take your cell phone?" Sam asked.

"I'll take it."

"You'll call me—"

"Stop worrying, Sam. I'm just going for a little walk, that's all."

"And don't talk to strangers."

Joey grinned as she left the apartment.

It was three hours later when she eventually returned from her walk.

Sam was faking a relaxed look on the sofa trying to read a book. Joey wasn't fooled.

She removed her heavy overcoat, the scarf Sam had wrapped around her before she left, and her gloves. Then she sat next to her, snuggling up close. Sam placed an arm around her shoulder, waiting for her to talk.

Joey kissed her. Sam's face turned soft, and some of the worry she wore disappeared.

"Thank you, Sam, for giving me space. I do appreciate it and I know you're concerned, but I think the walk has done me good. It's been therapeutic." Joey rested her head on Sam's shoulder.

"Since I came back from Balshir, I haven't found any peace. There's been this whole agitated mess inside me that never stops moving. It's like being on some caffeine high without the caffeine. Seeing Abu has been a shock, more so hearing what he said, but it's made me feel *different*. Something inside me has stopped. Sure, the horror of what happened is still there and that will haunt me to the end of my days. It was vile…traumatic. But I feel like a weight has lifted."

Sam just listened and Joey continued.

"I understand the missing part of the puzzle. I always wondered why Mo left the rooms just before the missile hit. It never felt right. I know I thought a lot about that when I was in hiding, but I never connected the dots because I had no reason to. He went to get water despite the fact we had enough until the following morning when we were going to leave anyway. Now it makes sense. It wasn't because we'd upset him. He knew what was going to happen.

"If Mo hadn't done what he did, if he hadn't told the insurgents we'd be there, maybe we'd all be alive today. Kurt, Mitch…they'd still be around. We'd have gotten our stories and we'd be looking for the next one. And I was always the planner. I used to drive the guys crazy. They thought I went in for overkill, but it was always attention to detail with me. I'd plan everything down to the last chocolate bar. But for Mo, we might have made it out." She looked at Sam. "Of course, I'd never have met you."

"Can you forgive Mo? Truthfully?" Sam asked.

"I don't know. I expect some days I will and other days I won't, but I'll try. He was a good man, and he had no choice."

"How does all this make you feel?" Sam asked.

"Better."

Sam tightened her arm around her.

"How does it make *you* feel?" Joey asked Sam.

"Anything that makes you better makes me feel better too."

"You've been worried," Joey said.

"Only because Abu took you back to a place I long for you to leave."

"But it's helped. I really do feel…lighter. Abu gave me a gift today." At that precise moment, her stomach made a rumbling sound.

"Strange," Sam said. "Mine made that same noise just before you came back."

"So, Sam, my wonderful rock…I *feel* better. I also feel hungry. We haven't eaten since breakfast. There's a burger joint around the corner. How about something unhealthy?"

"Dear Lord, yes. My stomach thinks my throat's been cut."

They moved off the sofa. Joey reached out and held Sam's face in her hands.

"Thank you for being there with me today. Thank you for understanding. Thank you for coming over here to find me. And thank you for loving me without reservation even when I tried to push you away. I don't know what I'd do without you in my life. You are my everything. I want you to know that."

Sam turned to kiss Joey's hand. "Thank *you* for loving me. You've saved me."

"We've saved each other." As Joey stood there, she didn't think it was possible to love anyone more than she loved Sam. She had fallen in love with her so easily, and despite the complications that had followed, she couldn't imagine life without her. "I'm in love with a vicar," she whispered.

"A jobless one." Sam grinned.

"You need to talk to Neil and see what's happening."

"Tomorrow. Now can we please go and eat?"

Sam dragged Joey out of the apartment in search of food.

It didn't matter to Sam that she ordered—and ate—the biggest burger, covering it with everything you weren't supposed to if you wanted to avoid a heart attack. Never had a burger tasted so good. It occurred to her as she ate that everything was going right. Her prayers had been answered. She was eating. She was in love and she was loved in return. Joey was opening up. Sam thought life couldn't get much better.

But it did the next morning when they arose.

"It's early," Sam bellyached. She just wanted to stay in bed, but Joey was up with the larks.

"Come on, we've got loads to do."

"We?" Sam didn't think there was anything on her agenda. She was unemployed.

"You need to talk to Bishop Neil and see what's going on, and—"

"What do you mean, *going on*?"

"You said yourself, you've had no confirmation of your resignation, and you haven't been asked to vacate the vicarage yet. Talk to Neil and find out what's going on."

Sam sighed. Joey was right. "Fine."

"I also need you to do me a favor. Can you find me a good counselor in the UK, one who specializes in my sort of trauma?"

Sam couldn't believe what she was hearing. *Thank you, God.*

"I'm ready to talk. I have PTSD, and I don't want it. I'm not going to let Balshir dictate the rest of my life. It's time to let the professionals give me a hand." Joey looked down at Sam. "Now get up."

Sam was already pushing the covers back. "Your parents are going to be so happy."

"I know."

"I'll talk to Neil. He's worked with the military over the years. I'm sure he has good contacts. I'll drop him an email."

"You should call him."

"Too early. England still sleeps."

"Then call him later. In the meantime, you can help me figure out what stuff I have to put into storage and what we want shipped to the UK. Get dressed, Vicar. We have a busy day ahead."

"I've lost it," Neil told Sam over the phone.

"How can you have lost it? I sent it to you in an email."

"Are you sure?"

"Yes. It was an attachment."

"Ah," Neil said. "That's it then. Letters of resignation have to be hard copy."

"Why haven't you chased me for it?"

"No time. I'm starting the new job, and Miriam has been boxing everything at the house that isn't sentient."

Sam sensed Neil wasn't being entirely truthful. She always knew when he was being evasive. She hoped he wasn't planning on cajoling her back to be vicar of St. Mary's. That option was untenable now.

"How are you explaining my absence then?" Sam asked.

"You're taking all your accumulated leave and on a short sabbatical."

"And no one is asking why?" Sam smelled more than a rat now. The rodents were breeding.

"They ask."

"And?"

"I'm evasive," Neil answered. Sam could almost hear him grin.

"You're not expecting me to come back to St. Mary's, Neil."

"Be calm, Sam. Of course not. There's a new vicar who'll be taking over shortly. He's an older man who has left his career as a successful prison psychologist to enter the church."

"He'll fit right in." Sam's dry response earned a chuckle from Neil.

"You'll like him…The Reverend George Hale. He's coming to us from Stratford. He's had a very successful first parish there but wants to be closer to the children's schools. He's got a bigger family than I have…seven children."

"Seven?"

"Several adopted. Good man."

"You'll want me out of the vicarage soon then."

"Yes, but not because of George. The place is too small so the diocese is making alternative arrangements. The church is looking to cut costs so they plan to sell the current vicarage. It's too small and needs modernizing. They consider it no longer fit for purpose and too expensive to bring up to a decent living standard."

"Thanks. You've had me living in a hovel all these years."

"You've never complained," Neil said.

"Where will the new one be?"

"They're thinking the other side of Kidderminster."

It was a considerable distance from the old vicarage. Sam thought of Gloria. She wouldn't be able to continue as housekeeper if they did that.

"When will you be coming back?" Neil asked.

Sam had told Neil that she and Joey were now *an item*. She had also apprised him of Joey's new job and decision to move permanently to England.

"Imminently," Sam said. "We're just waiting for Joey's mother to have her operation and make sure she's okay. Then we'll be on the first flight back."

"Good. I need to see you as soon as possible."

"Any particular reason?"

"Do I have to have a reason to see a dear friend? Miriam is missing you too."

"Why do I think you're up to something?"

"I have no idea, Sam. However I do have a proposal for you."

"A proposal."

"Yes. Something I'm working on."

"With regards to what?"

"Just come and see me as soon as you get back. I'll drop you an email if I hear of any date you have to vacate the vicarage."

Sam knew she'd get nothing more out of Neil. When their phone chat finished, it didn't stop her from wondering what he was up to.

She suspected he wanted to offer her another church position. But Sam was adamant that she didn't want to be a vicar anymore with all the demands that entailed. She wanted to have more time for Joey. Neither did she want to be a vicar for a small country church. While she wanted more personal time, she also wanted a job that would challenge her. Sam hoped Neil wasn't rethinking the idea of offering her a position on his team at Lambeth Palace. She didn't want to be in London and commuting home to Worcestershire. She and Joey would start house hunting as soon as they returned, and they wanted somewhere around the area they were already living. Joey was also fond of Auntie Elsa—despite her inability to keep confidences. She knew she was growing old and wanted to be around.

Sam put her anxiety on hold and glanced at her watch. Joey wouldn't be home yet. She was with the Realtor who was letting her townhouse.

At a loss for something to do, Sam contemplated going for a bike ride but decided to check her emails. She was surprised to find one from the producer of *Forgotten Worcestershire*. It appeared her earlier sortie into the households of WM radio listeners had proved popular and she was being invited to do more, possibly a series of six. Would she like to contact them?

Sam replied immediately. It was something she'd enjoyed doing, and the chance to do more and this time be paid wasn't something she would pass up. It seemed her day was turning into a series of possibilities.

She waited for Joey to return so she could tell her the news.

CHAPTER TWENTY-ONE

Their return to England came at the right time. The American tabloid press had started showing interest in Joey. Photos of her leaving NPR and speculation she might be considering working for them abounded. Sherry Dexter had done nothing to kill that rumor. She loved toying with the types of media that fabricated stories based on lies and innuendo to boost their circulation or Web hits. Some of the rock-bottom press was already discussing why RSB had canceled Joey's contract. They would voice their sympathy for her, but there was always an edge of unpleasantness to their articles. One even went as far as stating RSB had let Joey go because she was having a lesbian relationship with one of the married station producers. There was never any truth to these articles. Joey always seemed to take it in her stride, but Sam and her father didn't.

As soon as Ann had undergone angioplasty and the operation was declared successful, Joey and Sam flew back to England.

The first thing Sam did was put the house her parents had left her up for sale. The second thing on her list was to go and see Neil at home.

"I hope you don't mind, but I've booked you a job interview," Neil said.

Sam stared at him. He habitually surprised her, but this was surpassing his usual method of attack. Based on their last chat,

Sam was sure he was going to ask her to reconsider her resignation as vicar. She still wasn't sure he wouldn't.

He was sitting in what was left of his home office. It was currently nothing more than organized crates with a desk and a few chairs in the middle of the room. Neil had already started working in London, but the family had yet to move and join him.

Sam leaned back in one of the armchairs the movers hadn't yet taken and placed her mug of coffee on a package box.

"You did say you're still looking for gainful employment," he added.

"Am I allowed to ask for what?" Sam loved mysteries, but this was a curious one. She watched Neil lean forward and pick up a sheet of paper. He started to read from it verbatim.

"The Worcestershire Tudor Rose Historic Churches Trust. It supports appeals from churches for building and restoration projects, the repairs of church fabrics, church communities initiatives, religious charities, other charities that preserve the UK heritage, etcetera, etcetera." He stopped reading and looked at her. "The trust office is in Worcester, and they're looking for an ordained minister to replace the Reverend Dominic Bell who will be retiring at the end of the year."

"I know Dominic. I approached the trust for a grant for St. Mary's," Sam said.

"I know. Dominic was very impressed with your application, which is why you were successful. He's also been very impressed with *you*. He likes how you think outside the box and how you've used the media to push fundraising."

"Really?"

"Yes."

"I've always found him a bit dry and humorless. I didn't think he was too keen on me."

Neil chuckled. "He's not an easy man to read. I agree he lacks a certain charm and possesses the warmth of a taxman, but his heart is in the right place. He just doesn't hand over money lightly. As he says, it's hard to come by and shouldn't be squandered frivolously.

I think he sees the trust funds as his own money and doesn't like to part with it without good reason. You should be honored that St. Mary's got that grant."

Neil placed the sheet of paper down. His face was more serious.

"When I mentioned to Dominic that you were looking to go 'field agent' he actually asked if you would be interested in applying for his post. Whoever gets the job they would start fairly soon and work alongside him to pick up the reins when he leaves. I thought this would be right up your aisle. And of course with your treasurer experience…"

"Is that your attempt at dry humor?" Sam had many butterflies about leaving the church, but the post of treasurer wasn't one of them.

"Is it working?" Neil grinned.

"No."

"But are you interested in the job?"

"Yes."

"There's a small team on the trust and the usual amount of requisite paid professionals so I don't think you'd be revisiting your treasurer skills. The job would give you enormous flexibility, Sam. Dominic says he drives his own schedule. He spends as much time as he wants in the office, balancing it with the need to get out and view applications. It's a people job, and you'd be meeting the applicants face-to-face." Neil let the proposal sink in. "What do you think?"

Sam couldn't hide her excitement. "I think I'm very interested."

"Thank the Lord." Neil looked relieved. "I told you God would find you something."

"I haven't got the job yet."

"They want an ordained minister. You fit. They want someone with restoration experience. You fit. They want someone who understands fundraising and who can think outside the box. You fit."

"Oh, Neil…" Sam couldn't believe it. This morning she'd woken up fairly jobless and with just a short radio series on the list. Now she had real *prospects*.

"Well, I'm glad that's sorted. What are you doing tomorrow morning?" Neil asked.

"Er…"

"Excellent. I've got you an appointment with Dominic at the trust office in Worcester tomorrow morning just to make sure the job lights your fire. He's keen to tell you about it, and you can both talk through all the detail. Then you can fill this in."

Neil handed her the job application. "The formal interview is next Friday."

It was all so quick it left Sam speechless. When she overcame her shock, she asked, "Is there anything you haven't done?"

"We still haven't found St. Mary's a treasurer, but…" He gave a reluctant smile. "That's no longer your problem, Sam. It's not mine either now. My replacement, Bishop John Clement, will have that challenge."

"Neil, I was blessed the day you and I became friends. I know I haven't got the job yet—I may not—but *thank you* for all of this. I admit this morning I felt the first surges of panic that I don't have full-time employment, or any irons in the fire that might provide some. I told Joey she might have attached herself to an over-the-hill ordained minister with no job prospects, and that she might be the sole breadwinner."

"What did she say?"

Sam smiled. "She told me to stop whining and that something would come along."

"And it has."

"Yes, thanks to you."

When Sam got back to the vicarage, she was over the moon to find Joey there.

Officially, Joey wasn't staying at the vicarage. They both agreed that it didn't look good to have a vicar *living in sin* at the place. They would play it tactfully until they found a home of their own. Then they could sin all they wanted. Joey had moved back in with Auntie Elsa. However, the self-imposed rules did get bent on occasion, and Joey stayed over at the vicarage more times than she didn't.

Sam swept into the kitchen and gave Joey a huge hug.

"I've missed you, and I've been thinking of you all day. How has the first session gone? Am I allowed to ask?" Sam pulled back to study her. Joey's first counseling session had been today. Sam was praying it went okay. She knew Joey wouldn't chuck it all in again like she had before, but it didn't stop her from worrying.

"It's gone well. It's still early, but I like John. I feel he understands. His military background helps."

Her counselor, John, was an ex lieutenant colonel in the Royal Marines. He had been Special Forces and served all over the world in some of the most hostile places. He too had suffered from post-traumatic stress disorder. It was why he'd eventually left the military and trained as a counselor. He wanted to help others overcome their problems.

Joey laughed. "I still find it surreal. He's built like the side of a mountain and all muscle. I can't believe he's the one I'm going to reveal my inner demons to."

"But you will."

"Yes. I trust him." Joey watched as Sam removed her jacket and hung it up. "He did say that things might get worse before they get better."

Sam turned.

"I just want to forewarn you, Sam. It'll take time and—"

"I know. But we do this together. You're not alone this time."

Sam was always so strong. Joey knew she'd be there for her.

"John said that if you ever need to talk to him…"

"I'll know where to find him." Sam patted Joey's face with affection. "Stop worrying about me. I'm ready, and I have a very good support system."

Sam raised her eyes to the ceiling, to *the boss*. It reminded Joey that she'd come straight to the vicarage from counseling to get Sam's news. She was itching to find out what Neil was so secretive about.

"Well? Don't keep me in suspense." Joey saw a twinkle in Sam's eyes that suggested good news.

"I might just have a job," Sam said. "It's working for a trust that supports appeals for church building restoration projects and church charities. The office is in Worcester. One of the team is an ordained minister who is coming up for retirement. Neil seems to think the job might be mine if I want it. Of course, I have to be interviewed, and I've no idea how many other applicants have applied."

Joey didn't have to ask if Sam was interested. She was smiling like a birthday girl.

"When's the interview?"

"Next Friday, and I'm going to the trust office tomorrow to have a chat about the job."

"That's wonderful news." Joey flung her arms around her. Sam hadn't said much, but Joey knew she was worried about not having proper work. The radio series was something, but it was unlikely to become permanent employment. Sam kept joking about going out onto the streets with a begging bowl, but Joey saw behind her façade. Sam was nervous and desperate for a new role in life, preferably one that improved her bank account.

"Let's celebrate with a cuppa. You're happy with John, and I might have a job." Sam started to fill the kettle with water.

"You've only just missed Gloria."

Sam turned. Joey saw her disappointment. "Is she okay?"

Joey could never hide her feelings.

Sam stopped what she was doing. "What's wrong?"

"I hoped you'd be back before Gloria left. She's been very low today and not her usual talkative self."

Joey signaled Sam to get on with making the tea as she sat at the table. "No, not wrong exactly, but yes. She's just sad, Sam. She hasn't said anything, but I can tell she hates all this change."

"Do you think it's money worries…about losing the job?" Sam had told Joey that the new vicar didn't want a housekeeper, and even if he had, the new place was too far for Gloria to travel. She didn't drive, and the bus routes weren't good. While Gloria wasn't broke, her husband hadn't left her in the land of the Rockefellers, and her state pension wasn't much.

"It's not the job. She's going to miss *you*."

Sam poured the tea, and Joey could see she'd burst Sam's happy bubble. She hadn't wanted to. She felt miserable about Gloria's future too.

"I know," Sam said. "It's crazy, isn't it? She's such an irascible sort, but I love her to bits. She's like family."

"What do you think she'll do?"

"Gloria is the wrong age to break into new employment. I guess she won't do anything."

"Whatever happens, we'll stay in touch with her…have her over for dinner. Maybe she can come and stay over."

"I'd like that," Sam said.

"She's a cantankerous old bird, but I love her too." Despite Joey's assurances, Sam didn't look any happier. She thought of other news that might return Sam's smile.

"Something else happened today. I'm not sure, but I think I might have found us a house."

Sam's eyes widened.

"When I drive to work, I come to a set of traffic lights and I've often seen a house set back on a hill. It's such a pretty place, and with a lovely little garden. Anyway, this morning I was caught up in morning traffic and we'd come to a stop. I happened to look up at the place and it's got a For Sale sign outside. I hope you don't mind, but I gave the Realtor a call. She told me it's empty and that it's been on the market for a few months. The owners have gone abroad and are interested in selling as soon as possible. They're willing to consider a sensible offer. It's in our price range. Do you think we can go see it?"

"I'd love to. Maybe we could take a drive past it after we've had tea. Have a snoop."

Joey started to get excited. There was something about the place calling to her. It was the same when she'd seen the townhouse in Baltimore. No one else had shown any interest in it, but the minute she'd opened the door she knew it would be hers. She hoped Sam would like it enough for them to call the agent back and book a viewing.

After tea, they went to see it.

They drove up the short drive, parked the car, and "snooped."

It was a four-bedroom detached house in a semi-rural setting. A well-tended garden wrapped itself around the property, and there was a balcony and a patio to the rear. There were numerous garden sheds at the bottom of the garden, and a large double garage at the side of the house. Joey noted how Sam's eyes locked on to the garage. She was probably thinking of a place for her motorbike.

They peered in at the ground floor windows and saw rooms that were well proportioned and with good ceiling height. The kitchen was less inviting.

"It looks tired and in need of modernization," Sam said as she pressed her face up at the window.

"And it's small," Joey added.

"Yes, but there are several doors off it. I don't know what's behind them, but we might be able to open the kitchen up and make it a more open plan."

"You like it, don't you," Joey stated.

Sam stepped back. "The place is dated but nothing a lick of paint won't change. If the upstairs is as promising as downstairs..."

"And it's a perfect location for commuting."

"Small, not too big," Sam said.

"Big, not too small," Joey added.

The next day, after Sam returned from her appointment with Dominic Bell, and when Joey finished work, they went around the house with the agent. The day after that, they put in a formal offer subject to the usual checks, which was later accepted.

Three months later, they were standing outside the property with the keys in their hands. They were the new owners.

"Is it me or is everything going well?" Sam leaned into Joey as they looked up at the front of the house. "I have a new job. You enjoy yours. And we are now the proud owners of a house."

"It's almost perfect," Joey said.

"Almost? What more do you want, woman?"

Joey narrowed her eyes. "Something else needs sorting."

"What?"

"You'll see."

Sam and Joey were at the vicarage loading boxes into the back of a hire van.

They had moved into the new house and were in the final throes of taking the precious possessions Sam hadn't trusted to the removal company. Sam's happiness would have been perfect but for the fact this was the last time she'd set foot in the vicarage... and with Gloria as housekeeper.

Gloria was in her usual place in the kitchen. Though she was no longer employed, she'd turned up to help pack things into boxes, and to make copious cups of tea and bacon sandwiches.

For all her bluster and acceptance of the change, Gloria couldn't hide her grief. Sam had caught her sniffling into a handkerchief earlier on. The two of them had developed a bond, albeit an odd one, and Sam suspected that coming to the vicarage nearly every day and taking care of her had become Gloria's life. Stripped of it, Sam worried that Gloria might wither away.

As Sam and Joey were in the back of the van sliding and organizing boxes, Joey stopped and put her hand on Sam's.

"You're upset about Gloria." Joey had earlier caught Sam wiping a few tears of her own.

"I can't stand this. She's breaking my heart. I'm going to miss her, and I'm worried what will happen to her."

"We'll stay in touch, Sam."

"Sure." But Sam knew their good intentions of *staying in touch* would eventually fade. And Gloria was such a proud woman. She'd sense what they were doing. Sam hated all of this.

Joey sat down on a box.

"Sam, do you remember I told you there were a few other things that had to be sorted? Well, I've been busy. I think I've found Gloria a job, but I want your approval before I tell her. You might not like my idea."

"What?" Sam asked.

Joey had waited until today to surprise Sam and Gloria. Sam was staring at her, waiting to hear her news. Joey tried not to let her excitement show.

"Pretty much the same work as she does now and for a couple. The place is nearby too," Joey said.

"Are they nice?"

"I think so."

"Will they pay her as much…like her sense of humor?"

Joey smiled at Sam's protectiveness. "I think they will."

"They know she's not young…that she can't lift heavy things? They'll have to carry the vacuum cleaner up the stairs for her."

"They know."

"Who are they? Where do they live?"

Joey leaned into her and whispered in her ear. "They're us." She waited till she saw the smile on Sam's face before she pulled her from the van. "Come on."

As they walked into the kitchen, Gloria had her back to them and was washing up.

"Gloria, can you stop? We've got a proposal for you," Joey said.

Gloria turned with the brush still in her hand.

Joey linked an arm through Sam's. "It's quite simple. Sam and I both have busy jobs. The new house is fairly large. Neither of us is particularly good at housework. You already know what Sam's housekeeping skills are like."

"Joey's aren't much better," Sam added dryly.

"We've spoken about this, and we've decided we need a housekeeper. Would you be interested in becoming *our* housekeeper? The house is no farther travel for you, and there's a direct bus route…better than here."

Sam looked at her surprised.

"I've checked them," Joey explained.

"Impressive," Sam said under her breath before speaking to Gloria. "The current kitchen is not good, but it's the first room we're going to modernize. We're knocking a few walls down so things will be messy to begin with."

Joey took over. "Now I know you'll probably have other jobs lined up and—"

"What are you paying?" Gloria crossed her arms, the brush held like an assault weapon.

"Same terms as here?" Sam answered.

"So no extra travel involved?" Gloria said.

"None," Sam and Joey answered in union.

"And you're not expecting me to clear up brick rubble?"

"Heaven's forbid, no," Sam said. "Joey can do that."

Gloria stood awhile before she finally said, "I'll take it."

Seconds later, Gloria burst into tears. "I'm so happy."

Joey and Sam stepped forward and indulged in a rare group hug.

Gloria sniffed. "When do I start?"

"Yesterday," Sam said.

"You're a wonderful woman," Sam whispered in Joey's ear as they lay in bed. Not a day went by where she wasn't grateful for the life she now had. Everything could have turned out so differently, but somehow both of them had managed to overcome hurdles and find each other.

Joey pulled Sam's arms tighter around her.

"It was the perfect solution. I was worried Gloria might say no and that she might see our job offer as charity," Joey said.

"One look at the kitchen and she'll know it isn't," Sam said.

They laughed. The kitchen was still in its original state and was horrible. The builders were moving in next week to start knocking down walls. Both could imagine Gloria's bellyaching over dust and rubble.

When their laughter died down, Joey turned to her, her face serious.

Sam wondered what was on her mind.

"Can we talk about the civil ceremony?"

They had fixed a date and the guest list had gone out. Ann and Len were flying over. The marriage arrangements had been put off until Ann was able to travel. They would be arriving in less than a month and were going to stay on for a while after the ceremony so they could do some traveling.

"There's something I want to do while Mom and Dad are here."

"Go on."

"I've done something and I hope I've got this right. I've asked Neil if he would bless our marriage…not in a church because I know he can't do that, but maybe sometime after the civil ceremony. I thought we could have another smaller reception the following week."

"You aren't religious."

"No, I'm not, but I know it's important to you, and Neil is a good friend. I asked him…I told him I'm not a believer."

"What did he say?"

"He's jumped at the suggestion and really wants to do it. We could arrange it while Mom and Dad are here, before they start their travels."

"Where?"

"In our back garden. It'll be beautiful. We can put up a small tent in case it rains." Joey paused. "What do you think?"

Sam shifted and gazed into Joey's face. "I think it's a wonderful idea. Neil will love doing it. I know he's disappointed he can't marry us at St. Mary's."

"It'll mean a lot to Mom too."

"And Len?" Sam asked.

"Dad will be happy if Mom is."

Sam ran a hand across Joey's forehead, pushing her hair back. "I thought I was going to die an old, unloved woman. But you've come into my life and totally changed all that. Have I told you, Josephine Barry, how happy I am and how very much I love you?"

Joey smiled seductively. "A woman can never be told that enough...or shown." She reached a hand up and pulled Sam's face down to hers. She gave her a long passionate kiss. "Show me, Vicar."

About the Author

I. Beacham grew up in the heart of England, a green and pleasant land, mainly because it rains so much. This is probably why she ran away to sea, to search for dry places. Over the years, and during long periods away from home constantly traveling to faraway places, she has balanced the rigidity of her professional life with her need and love to write.

Blessed with a wicked sense of humor (not all agree), she is a lover of all things water, a dreadful jogger and cook, a hopeless romantic who roams antique stores, an addict of old black and white movies, and an adorer of science fiction. In her opinion, a perfect life.

I. Beacham can be contacted at: brit.beacham@yahoo.com

Books Available from Bold Strokes Books

Escape in Time by Robyn Nyx. Working in the past is hell on your future. (978-1-62639-855-9)

Forget-Me-Not by Kris Bryant. Is love worth walking away from the only life you've ever dreamed of? (978-1-62639-865-8)

Highland Fling by Anna Larner. On vacation in the Scottish Highlands, Eve Eddison falls for the enigmatic forestry officer Moira Burns, despite Eve's best friend's campaign to convince her that Moira will break her heart. (978-1-62639-853-5)

Phoenix Rising by Rebecca Harwell. As Storm's Quarry faces invasion from a powerful neighbor, a mysterious newcomer with powers equal to Nadya's challenges everything she believes about herself and her future (978-1-62639-913-6)

Soul Survivor by I. Beacham. Sam and Joey have given up on hope, but when fate brings them together it gives them a chance to change each other's life and make dreams come true. (978-1-62639-882-5)

Strawberry Summer by Melissa Brayden. When Margaret Beringer's first love Courtney Carrington returns to their small town, she must grapple with their troubled past and fight the temptation for a very delicious future. (978-1-62639-867-2)

The Girl on the Edge of Summer by J.M. Redmann. Micky Knight accepts two cases, but neither is the easy investigation it appears. The past is never past—and young girls lead complicated, even dangerous lives. (978-1-62639-687-6)

Unknown Horizons by CJ Birch. The moment Lieutenant Alison Ash steps aboard the Persephone, she knows her life will never be the same. (978-1-62639-938-9)

Divided Nation, United Hearts by Yolanda Wallace. In a nation torn in two by a most uncivil war, can love conquer the divide? (978-1-62639-847-4)

Fury's Bridge by Brey Willows. What if your life depended on someone who didn't believe in your existence? (978-1-62639-841-2)

Lightning Strikes by Cass Sellars. When Parker Duncan and Sydney Hyatt's one-night stand turns to more, both women must fight demons past and present to cling to the relationship neither of them thought she wanted. (978-1-62639-956-3)

Love in Disaster by Charlotte Greene. A professor and a celebrity chef are drawn together by chance, but can their attraction survive a natural disaster? (978-1-62639-885-6)

Secret Hearts by Radclyffe. Can two women from different worlds find common ground while fighting their secret desires? (978-1-62639-932-7)

Sins of Our Fathers by A. Rose Mathieu. Solving gruesome murder cases is only one of Elizabeth Campbell's challenges; another is her growing attraction to the female detective who is hell-bent on keeping her client in prison. (978-1-62639-873-3)

The Sniper's Kiss by Justine Saracen. The power of a kiss: it can swell your heart with splendor, declare abject submission, and sometimes blow your brains out. (978-1-62639-839-9)

Troop 18 by Jessica L. Webb. Charged with uncovering the destructive secret that a troop of RCMP cadets has been hiding,

Andy must put aside her worries about Kate and uncover the conspiracy before it's too late. (978-1-62639-934-1)

Worthy of Trust and Confidence by Kara A. McLeod. FBI Special Agent Ryan O'Connor is about to discover the hard way that when you can only handle one type of answer to a question, it really is better not to ask. (978-1-62639-889-4)

Amounting to Nothing by Karis Walsh. When mounted police officer Billie Mitchell steps in to save beautiful murder witness Merissa Karr, worlds collide on the rough city streets of Tacoma, Washington. (978-1-62639-728-6)

Becoming You by Michelle Grubb. Airlie Porter has a secret. A deep, dark, destructive secret that threatens to engulf her if she can't find the courage to face who she really is and who she really wants to be with. (978-1-62639-811-5)

Birthright by Missouri Vaun. When spies bring news that a swordswoman imprisoned in a neighboring kingdom bears the Royal mark, Princess Kathryn sets out to rescue Aiden, true heir to the Belstaff throne. (978-1-62639-485-8)

Crescent City Confidential by Aurora Rey. When romance and danger are in the air, writer Sam Torres learns the Big Easy is anything but. (978-1-62639-764-4)

Love Down Under by MJ Williamz. Wylie loves Amarina, but if Amarina isn't out, can their relationship last? (978-1-62639-726-2)

Privacy Glass by Missouri Vaun. Things heat up when Nash Wiley commandeers a limo and her best friend for a late drive out to the beach: Champagne on ice, seat belts optional, and privacy glass a must. (978-1-62639-705-7)

The Impasse by Franci McMahon. A horse packing excursion into the Montana Wilderness becomes an adventure of terrifying proportions for Miles and ten women on an outfitter led trip. (978-1-62639-781-1)

The Right Kind of Wrong by PJ Trebelhorn. Bartender Quinn Burke is happy with her life as a playgirl until she realizes she can't fight her feelings any longer for her best friend, bookstore owner Grace Everett. (978-1-62639-771-2)

Wishing on a Dream by Julie Cannon. Can two women change everything for the chance at love? (978-1-62639-762-0)

A Quiet Death by Cari Hunter. When the body of a young Pakistani girl is found out on the moors, the investigation leaves Detective Sanne Jensen facing an ordeal she may not survive. (978-1-62639-815-3)

Buried Heart by Laydin Michaels. When Drew Chambliss meets Cicely Jones, her buried past finds its way to the surface—will they survive its discovery or will their chance at love turn to dust? (978-1-62639-801-6)

Escape: Exodus Book Three by Gun Brooke. Aboard the Exodus ship *Pathfinder*, President Thea Tylio still holds Caya Lindemay, a clairvoyant changer, in protective custody, which has devastating consequences endangering their relationship and the entire Exodus mission. (978-1-62639-635-7)

Genuine Gold by Ann Aptaker. New York, 1952. Outlaw Cantor Gold is thrown back into her honky-tonk Coney Island past, where crime and passion simmer in a neon glare. (978-1-62639-730-9)

Into Thin Air by Jeannie Levig. When her girlfriend disappears, Hannah Lewis discovers her world isn't as orderly as she thought it was. (978-1-62639-722-4)

Night Voice by CF Frizzell. When talk show host Sable finally acknowledges her risqué radio relationship with a mysterious caller, she welcomes a *real* relationship with local tradeswoman Riley Burke. (978-1-62639-813-9)

Raging at the Stars by Lesley Davis. When the unbelievable theories start revealing themselves as truths, can you trust in the ones who have conspired against you from the start? (978-1-62639-720-0)

She Wolf by Sheri Lewis Wohl. When the hunter becomes the hunted, more than love might be lost. (978-1-62639-741-5)

Smothered and Covered by Missouri Vaun. The last person Nash Wiley expects to bump into over a two a.m. breakfast at Waffle House is her college crush, decked out in a curve-hugging law enforcement uniform. (978-1-62639-704-0)

The Butterfly Whisperer by Lisa Moreau. Reunited after ten years, can Jordan and Sophie heal the past and rediscover love or will differing desires keep them apart? (978-1-62639-791-0)

The Devil's Due by Ali Vali. Cain and Emma Casey are awaiting the birth of their third child, but as always in Cain's world, there are new and old enemies to face in post Katrina-ravaged New Orleans. (978-1-62639-591-6)

Widows of the Sun-Moon by Barbara Ann Wright. With immortality now out of their grasp, the gods of Calamity fight amongst themselves, egged on by the mad goddess they thought they'd left behind. (978-1-62639-777-4)

Lightning Source UK Ltd.
Milton Keynes UK
UKOW04f0114130917
309091UK00001B/38/P